THE PICK-POCKET'S RETURN

LINDSEY HUTCHINSON

Boldwood

First published in Great Britain in 2025 by Boldwood Books Ltd.

Copyright © Lindsey Hutchinson, 2025

Cover Design by Head Design Ltd

Cover Images: Shutterstock

The moral right of Lindsey Hutchinson to be identified as the author of this work has been asserted in accordance with the Copyright, Designs and Patents Act 1988.

Every effort has been made to obtain the necessary permissions with reference to copyright material, both illustrative and quoted. We apologise for any omissions in this respect and will be pleased to make the appropriate acknowledgements in any future edition.

A CIP catalogue record for this book is available from the British Library.

Paperback ISBN 978-1-83518-910-8

Large Print ISBN 978-1-83518-909-2

Hardback ISBN 978-1-83518-908-5

Ebook ISBN 978-1-83518-911-5

Kindle ISBN 978-1-83518-912-2

Audio CD ISBN 978-1-83518-903-0

MP3 CD ISBN 978-1-83518-904-7

Digital audio download ISBN 978-1-83518-906-1

This book is printed on certified sustainable paper. Boldwood Books is dedicated to putting sustainability at the heart of our business. For more information please visit https://www.boldwoodbooks.com/about-us/sustainability/

Boldwood Books Ltd, 23 Bowerdean Street, London, SW6 3TN

www.boldwoodbooks.com

For Carolyn Buckley whom I have known for over forty years. One of my staunchest supporters, Carolyn is never afraid to speak her mind. Carolyn, thank you for being my friend.

1

1867

Bertram Jordan, BJ to his friends, was yelling at the top of his lungs. 'Pete, fetch the cattle in and corral them!'

Pete Worthington, the chief drover on the cattle ranch in Fremantle, Australia, saluted and leapt onto his horse. A moment later he was galloping away, his steed's hooves kicking up little clouds of dust in its wake.

BJ, who had arrived at the ranch as a convict and had now worked his way up to the position of overseer, kept his eye on the plume of smoke in the far distance as he, along with every man on the ranch, dug the ground furiously. A wildfire had broken out and was raging across the land at an alarming pace.

Gerald McNally, the ranch's owner and known as Mac, was shoulder to shoulder with his workers as they deepened the trench that surrounded his property, providing a fire-break. It was his fervent hope that if the wind brought the inferno this way, then the trench would stop it reaching his ranch by turning it away in another direction. All businesses and homes in this part of Australia had a trench of some sort to provide a natural fire-break, as well as having plenty of buckets stacked near their water supply.

For days the convicts had been hard at work ensuring the channel would be deep enough to do its job. No one wanted to be burned alive or see the big house, canteen, bunkhouses and showers reduced to ash.

Word had spread quickly about the fires starting sporadically due to the uncommonly hot summer, and everywhere had seen the same rapid response.

Sweat soaked the men's hats and rolled down their dirty faces as they toiled for all they were worth. Cookie, the resident cook-cum-doctor, was kept busy making sure fresh cool water was on hand by filling casks and trundling them around on a horse-drawn cart.

BJ looked up, hearing the rumbling of hundreds of cows being herded towards the corrals. 'Get ready, here they come!' he shouted. Dropping their shovels, the men ran towards the enclosures, ready to close and secure the gates once the shorthorns were inside.

The drovers were experts in their trade, and slowly separated the herd into smaller groups so the waiting men could drive them into the pens. The noise of the cattle and men coughing through the bandanas wound round their faces echoed across the land. Whistles, yips and calls as well as shouts ensured every last cow was eventually brought safely in.

As the last rays of the sun gave the ranch a golden glow, the convicts and drovers alike sat on the ground feeling completely exhausted. Hundreds of pairs of eyes, sore and red from the dust, stared at the horizon and the smoke.

Cookie and his assistants brought out trays of glasses filled with home-made lemonade, which was drunk with grateful thanks. When everyone had refreshments, Cookie turned to Mac. 'Cold supper tonight, Boss.'

With a nod, Mac replied, 'Thanks, Cookie.' After slaking his thirst, Mac stood to address the men. 'Thank you for the incredibly hard work you put in today. Now we just need to pray it was worthwhile.' He saw the nods of agreement before he went on. 'I believe it will be, but just in case, the buggies and carts are standing ready to get us all to safety.'

'What about the cattle, Mac?' someone yelled.

'If we need to, we'll set them free; instinct will take them away from the flames.'

'May I speak, Mac?' John Tobias asked. John, a highly educated Englishman, had been BJ's tutor for many years. He had taught BJ to read, write and do arithmetic as well as how to speak with hardly any trace of his Black Country accent. Mac nodded and John got to his feet. 'All of your records are in a steel box ready to go with us should we need to flee.'

'And our gold?' a voice called from somewhere in the crowd.

'That is in the box as well, my dear fellow,' John replied. A ragged cheer broke out and John flapped his arms, saying, 'Oh, you boys!' Despite the tiredness weighing them down, their laughter rang out. Everyone was quite used to John's effeminate ways and accepted him for the thoroughly nice bloke that he was.

The gold the men referred to had been discovered on Mac's land by BJ four years ago, when pipes were being laid to carry water to the ranch. Mac had promised each man a share of the profits as recompense for digging it out as well as panning the spoils from the pipe laying. Gangs of men working the gold were swapped out every few days so each man would earn his share. The drovers and cooks were also promised a portion of the spoils.

As the workers sat wearily watching the smoke plume rising higher, Cookie and his team were frantically putting together a meal for everyone. Cold pasties of meat and vegetables, lettuce, tomatoes, pickles, bread and butter, and fruit were prepared before Cookie rang the dinner bell – a metal spoon clanging on an old tin kettle.

Dragging themselves to their feet, the men shuffled to the canteen where they collected their food and returned to sit outside once more so they could keep an eye on the fire.

Colin and James, who had been transported at the same time as BJ, sidled up to him. 'Have we done enough to save the place?' Colin asked.

'I hope so,' BJ said in answer. 'We'll know later, I suppose.'

The two young men had originally been sent to a sheep station on their arrival in Fremantle, and, after four years of searching, Mac, on BJ's behalf, had finally discovered their whereabouts. He had managed to bring them to the ranch but at a cost. Then he had gone back for Clem Read, their friend and protector from the station's cruel overseer. Clem was a lifer but when a man called George Newman died of a heart attack, Mac had come up with a solution to Clem's predicament. Clem would swap identities with the deceased George, thereby enabling him to be freed at the same time as BJ, Colin and James. The release date for all four was almost upon them, and each was looking forward to receiving their Certificate of Freedom, providing, of course, that they didn't perish in the wildfire.

Once they had eaten, the men returned their plates and glasses then went back to their spots on the dirt-packed ground to keep a keen lookout on the raging fire which was being fuelled by the wind. Darkness descended but no one moved, instead watching the sky turn orange, enabling them to track the direction of the inferno which was ravaging everything in its path. They knew they had done all they could to help save the ranch, and as the smoky sky rolled into a scarlet hue they began to pray.

Mac, BJ and John sat on the steps of the big house, their eyes also following the fire's course. The cattle were frightened by the smell of the smoke and their calls echoed into the night as they milled around inside their enclosures.

'Well, BJ, this is something you can tell Alice about when you write to her next,' Mac said. BJ blew out his dirty cheeks and nodded.

Alice Green and BJ had met seven years ago when, at thirteen years old, she had run away from her abusive father. BJ had taken her under his wing and, living as brother and sister, they had built a shelter on the heath in Wednesbury in the heart of England's Black Country.

They had survived by scavenging and BJ putting his pick-pocketing skills into action. He had taught her how to pick-pocket too to ensure, if anything happened to him, she would not starve to death. They had been happy together until the fateful day when BJ had been caught trying to burgle a house. Although he had not actually stolen anything, the police had been called and the Justice of the Peace had sentenced him to seven years' penal servitude.

Whilst Colin and James had been sent to the sheep station, BJ was brought to the ranch.

Sitting, his hands and face filthy from digging, BJ thought of Alice and whether he would ever see her again. The whole time he had been in Fremantle he had dreamed of the day he would return to England and Alice. Now as he watched the scarlet glow flicker and roil, looking like the aurora borealis, he feared for his own safety as well as that of the men.

Suddenly John jumped up and pointed. 'It's turning!' he shouted. 'Look there, it's moving east or is it west?'

The men chuckled as they too got to their feet. 'He's right – at least about it moving away,' a fellow said.

Spontaneous applause rang out as every man breathed a sigh of relief.

'We'll be fine as long as the wind doesn't change direction again,' Mac said quietly.

Nobody was willing to go to bed that night and, sitting down once more, they watched the horizon until their eyes stung and watered. There was no bird song to herald the dawn, just the lightening of the sky to a pearly grey. Not one person had slept a wink, each afraid they could be cooked where they sat. Slowly the sun rose, already filled with a fierce heat, but still the workers stayed put. They could see the smoke drifting on the breeze before it dissipated, finally confirming their belief that the wildfire had either moved on or had burned itself out.

Cookie's team prepared a breakfast with gallons of hot coffee, after which Mac addressed the men. 'It looks like we're safe, boys, thanks to you. Therefore might I suggest, once the cattle and horses are seen to, that we all take the day off and get some rest.' A round of applause sounded and slowly the workers ambled away to their respective bunkhouses to catch up on much-needed sleep.

'Cookie,' Mac called as he walked across to the canteen, 'I'd like to thank you and your lads for keeping us fed and watered.' The man smiled as Mac shook his hand before saying, 'It's what I'm paid for.'

'Indeed,' Mac went on, 'but a little bonus in your wage packet wouldn't go amiss, I'm sure.'

'You'd be right about that, Mac. Thanks.'

'Get some rest because that lot will be hungry again before too long,' Mac said, jerking his thumb over his shoulder.

Cookie rolled his eyes. 'A woman's work is never done.'

'You're beginning to sound like John,' Mac teased.

Cookie burst out laughing and Mac joined in from sheer relief that everything had turned out well in the end.

2

Later that day, Pete and the drovers rode out to assess the fire damage at Mac's request. The gold mining and panning was resumed on the new section of land Mac had purchased three years before. He had hoped the gold seam had extended in that direction and time had proven him right. With each new day, the workers' share of the profits grew and the men toiled long hours in the hot sun for a glimpse of the shiny precious metal.

Every couple of months, Rory Cranston, the gold buyer, would come to the ranch to weigh and purchase Mac's treasure. The chit attached to each man's record would then be updated; anyone having earned their Certificate of Freedom and leaving the ranch would be given a share of the money as shown on the chit at that time.

Colin, James and Clem helped to feed the shorthorns in the pens while they awaited Pete's return. He would know if it was safe to take the cows out again, providing there was any pasture left to graze. John sat in the schoolroom reading and BJ was writing to Alice, telling her of their scare with the wildfire.

Mac sat on the rocking chair on the veranda in the shade,

watching for Pete and the drovers to come back too, and it was just before lunch when they at last arrived. Jumping from his horse, Pete joined Mac. 'The pasture is fine. We rode for miles just to check and it seems everyone's fire-breaks worked. You can see where the blaze was and where it burned itself out.'

'That's excellent news, thanks, Pete.'

'We'll grab a bite and a drink, then we'll take the cattle out again.'

Mac nodded his approval before he strolled across to the canteen.

The drovers took their horses to the stables where the grooms fed and watered them before giving them a good brush down.

Everything was back to normal on the ranch, and as Mac took his midday meal his mind returned to BJ. His trusty right-hand man's sentence was coming to an end and BJ would be leaving to go home to England. Mac pushed his half-eaten food away, no longer feeling hungry. He was going to miss BJ; it would be like losing a limb. He had come to love the young man like a son and their parting would cause him great sorrow.

The Certificates of Freedom were all made out for BJ, Colin, James and Clem/George for when they would be needed, and Mac wondered, yet again, whether John would be joining the little coterie when leaving day came.

Striding from the canteen, Mac returned to his office where he could think clearly in the quiet of the room. Sitting at his desk, the ranch owner looked back over the last seven years since BJ had first arrived. A skinny kid with a Black Country accent had been transformed into a muscle-bound young gentleman. He'd had pluck even back then but now he had been refined into a confident businessman. Feeling the sadness begin to bite, Mac jumped up and strode to the schoolroom. It was time to have a talk with BJ, one he had been putting off for so very long.

* * *

Thousands of miles away in England, Alice Green was up to her elbows in flour. She was using a recipe brought in by Jean Pitman, the red-headed baker hired a few years before. Jean hailed from the Northeast and when asked for ideas she had related how stottie cake, which is actually a bread, was a firm favourite. It gained its name from the Geordie word 'stot', meaning to bounce, reflecting the bread's unique texture. Round and flat, it was quartered to make sandwiches. Once it was in the oven, Alice took a break. Washing her hands, she made tea and then carried her cup into the living room. Sitting with her feet up, she glanced around with a smile as she recalled buying the building which housed one of her bakeries from the bank. She had shaken hands on the deal but the board had tried to renege on the price agreed. But eventually, and after taking her accountant, Grayson Atherton, with her, she had been able to secure the acquisition at the price originally shaken upon.

Alice and Sylvia Wilkins, the shop manager, had moved to live in the Union Street building as soon as it was kitted out while Ellen Fergis and Joyce Clements, bakers, had remained in the Russell Street shop which was given over to the sole making of wedding cakes. Mary and Phoebe Wilkins worked at the Church Street branch decorating the cakes, having been taught by Ellen. Sophie Harris, née Wilkins, continued as kitchen manager at Church Street with her sister, Joan, in charge of the shop. The Wilkins girls' mother, Doris, managed the wedding cake side of the business in Church Street also.

Each of the three shops had plenty of serving staff as well as bakers, all working to Alice's time-honoured recipes and instructions.

Alice's thoughts moved to the Wilkins family and how one by one they had come to work for her. Sadly, Paul Wilkins had died three years ago, leaving his wife, Doris, bereft, but her five daughters and Sophie's husband, Jake, had rallied round to support each other.

Since that time, Sylvia Wilkins and Grayson Atherton had begun to walk out together, as had Joan and Philip Sanders, the estate agent who had helped Alice find her shops.

Having been given Doris's blessing, Sylvia and Grayson were planning their wedding, something everyone was excited about. It had been agreed that Jake, Sylvia's brother-in-law, would give her away at the ceremony with Sophie as maid-of-honour and Joan, Mary and Phoebe would be bridesmaids. The happy couple had chosen the design for their cake which was to be white with double rows of dotted swags in pink icing. In the place where the swags joined there would be tiny pink roses, and on the top larger ones in various shades of pink with pale green leaves set delicately between them.

Grayson had no family of his own but he did have a wide circle of friends and colleagues, one of whom was Joan's sweetheart, Philip Sanders, who was to be the best man.

Alice sipped her tea as all these thoughts flashed through her mind, while always lurking at the back was her dear friend, BJ, and how he would soon be home. She wondered, yet again, what he would look like now after seven years had passed, and whether he would indeed be able to secure a passage back to England. With each passing day, Alice's excitement grew at the thought of meeting up with her friend again, although she knew his journey would take months after his release date. She was relying on him telling her when that would be in his correspondence.

Maybe soon she should be considering looking for somewhere for BJ to live when he eventually arrived back in his native land. Finding work would be up to him; all Alice really cared about was that he got back safe and sound.

A yell brought Alice out of her reverie and she jumped to her feet; she was needed in the kitchen.

'I've made the flat-cake,' Jean said as Alice walked through the open doorway.

'Marvellous!' Alice replied as she eyed the flat pastry with its layers of raisins and mixed spice. 'The rice cakes?'

'They're next,' Jean assured her.

'Excellent. I'll get on with the chocolate sponges,' Alice said.

Sylvia's head appeared around the door as she called out, 'We're running low on drop cakes and fruit scones.'

'Thank you,' Alice said before directing one of the other bakers to make another batch of each.

'I wonder if your other shops are this busy,' Jean mused as she checked on the bread dough put to rise.

'I'd like to think so,' Alice replied with a smile.

'Do you realise you have three shops and yet we still can't seem to keep up with demand?'

Alice stopped what she was doing and considered Jean's words. 'Would another baker help?'

'Two might,' Jean returned as she stepped around a colleague to get to the oven.

Alice nodded. 'A further visit to the Servants' Registry is called for then. I'll do that when trade slows just after lunch.'

Jean blew out her cheeks and pushed her titian hair out of her eyes with the back of her hand. 'I'm suffocating in here. I'm gonna prop the back door open.'

'I'll open the windows and doors so we can get a through breeze,' Alice said, dashing away to complete her task. Within minutes, cool air began to flow from room to room, eventually reaching the kitchen, much to everyone's relief.

Around two o'clock, Alice took a cab to the Registry, paid her fee and put in her request for two bakers. The early afternoon trade was not so brisk which gave them all a chance to take a short break with a cup of tea, and when Alice returned to the bakery she decided that after her evening meal she would visit Russell Street then Church Street to see how busy they had been.

Grayson and Sylvia were sorting out a buffet menu for their wedding so Alice thought they might appreciate having some privacy while she was out visiting.

But as she arrived at the Church Street bakery, she got the shock of her life.

3

Alice walked into the Wilkins household to hear yelling and crying.

'Whatever is going on?' she asked, seeing Joan sobbing her heart out.

'That stupid bugger has gone and got herself pregnant!' Doris shouted, pointing at her crying daughter.

Alice's mouth dropped open then she snapped it shut when Joan replied to her mother, 'I d'aint do it on purpose!'

'You shouldn't 'ave been doing it at all!' Doris lambasted.

'Maybe everyone should calm down,' Alice interceded and as the noise level dropped she turned to Joan. 'Are you sure you're pregnant?' Joan nodded, looking thoroughly miserable. 'All right, does Philip know?'

'Yes, I told him last night,' Joan replied.

'And what did he say?' Alice asked.

'We should get wed as soon as possible.'

'Well, that's something at least!' Doris put in.

'That will need organising right away then. Philip must see the vicar and book the service; you will need a gown, we can bake the cake, flowers, food and bridesmaids will have to be sorted out.' Alice had immediately taken charge, more to calm the situation down than anything else.

Doris sat at the table, clearly still fuming, her fingers drumming out a rhythm.

Alice went over to her friend. 'They were destined to wed, this just means it will be sooner than originally thought.'

'Paul will be turning in his grave!' Doris said, before dissolving into tears.

'No, he would have agreed with me, Doris, you know he would,' Alice said gently.

'You're right. He would have forgiven his wenches anything,' Doris sniffed.

'Now you must do the same. Instead of being angry with Joan, you can look forward to becoming a grandmother.' Alice was doing her best to placate Doris by pointing out the positives. 'Just think, you can babysit your new grandchild, and I'm sure Joan would appreciate anything you can knit.'

'I would, Mom,' Joan whispered.

'Ar, well,' Doris conceded, 'that, I can do.'

Alice watched as Doris began to soften.

'You can buy a new hat for the weddin' an' all,' Phoebe said.

'With shoes to match,' Mary added.

Slowly the atmosphere changed from cold fury to warm excitement as the rushed wedding-to-be was discussed. Following hot on its heels came ideas for baby names which brought laughter as Joan dismissed them with a grimace.

By the time Alice stood to leave, the anger and shock had dissipated and been replaced by happy chatter. Hugging Doris, Alice said, 'Sylvia should be told too.'

'Will you do it?' Joan asked. 'I can't face anyone else shouting at me.'

'Of course. Don't worry, Sylvia will understand.' However, as Alice walked home she wondered if her statement would prove true, or whether Sylvia would see Joan as stealing the limelight of her own wedding.

Once indoors, Alice took a deep breath, now she would find out how Sylvia felt about her sister's predicament.

'Everybody all right?' Sylvia called from the kitchen.

'Yes, but I have something to tell you,' Alice replied, taking a seat. She was pleased that Grayson had gone home for this was something she needed to discuss with Sylvia privately.

'What's that?' Sylvia asked as she brought tea through.

'Sylvia...' Alice hesitated while the teacups were placed on the table and her friend sat down. 'Joan is getting married.'

'How wonderful!' Sylvia exclaimed.

'In about three weeks' time,' Alice added.

'What? Oh, no, please don't tell me she's...' The statement hung in the air as Alice nodded. 'Bloody hell! What did Mom say?'

'She was furious in the beginning but she calmed down after the shock wore off.'

'Poor Joan,' Sylvia muttered then in an instant her anger rose. 'Bloody Philip Sanders! Oooh, I could wring his neck! He should know better than to put temptation in our Joan's way.'

'Sylvia, we don't know the circumstances...' Alice began but immediately realised her mistake as Joan's ire grew.

'If he forced her, I'll kill him!' Sylvia was out of her seat and pacing the room.

'No, I meant... maybe their love got away from them both.'

'Oh, right, yes, I see.' Sylvia dropped into the chair, breathing heavily from sheer anger.

Alice sat quietly thinking, *when will you learn to think before you speak, Alice Green?*

'He's gonna marry her then?' Sylvia asked.

Alice nodded. 'It would seem so.'

'Christ, what a mess!' Sylvia whispered. 'The whole town will be gossiping about it. She'll be shunned everywhere she goes, because folk can be really spiteful over things like this.'

'Maybe they won't realise; they might think the wedding was planned ages ago,' Alice suggested.

'Hopefully. I'm guessing she ain't too far gone and she won't show when in her gown.'

'It will be fine, I'm sure,' Alice said.

'You know you'll have to fill her place at the bakery at some point.'

'I suppose I will, but it won't be for a while yet.'

'I tell you what, I'll be glad when she's wed and we can stop worrying.' Alice gave a tight-lipped smile in answer. 'You know what else as well? This has made me like Philip Sanders even less than I did before. I've never trusted him.'

Sylvia's words gave rise to a memory in Alice's mind; the day when she went to pay her rent and she caught Philip kissing a young woman's cheek. Although it was scandalous behaviour, Alice chose not to mention it as it was not her business. A question arose in the wake of the memory – was Philip Sanders a womaniser? Alice recalled the times he had invited her to dinner, all of which she had politely refused.

'I'll pop round and see our Joan tomorrow after work.'

Sylvia's words brought Alice back to the moment. 'I'm sure she'd appreciate your support.'

* * *

Across town, Philip Sanders sat in the study of his spacious house, brandy in one hand and cigar in the other, trying to imagine how his parents would take the news of his impending marriage.

His father would explode and probably refuse to allow the wedding to take place. William Sanders had always maintained that his son should marry into a good family; someone who was on their own social standing at least. He would see Philip's relationship with Joan for what it was – a dalliance with a shop girl. He might even try to buy the young woman off by paying her a huge sum of money to just... go away.

Philip sighed loudly. He knew he should never have offered to wed Joan but in the heat of the moment, and with her in floods of tears, the words were out before he had time to think.

Elise, his mother, would take the news calmly as was her wont. She would request he bring Joan to meet them before deciding on the best course of action.

Philip swallowed his drink, threw his cigar stub into the empty fireplace and left the study. He crossed the hall and climbed the winding staircase, ignoring the portraits of his family hanging on the walls. Passing three bedrooms and the indoor bathroom, Philip threw open the door at the end of the landing. Stepping inside his own bedroom, he slammed the door behind him. The gas lamps had been lit by the maid and Philip stripped off his clothes, dropping them on the floor. Pulling on his nightshirt, he got into bed and once more pondered the question of how to explain to his parents about the mess he'd got himself into.

Elise would understand; hadn't she always indulged her only son? Like when his father had demanded Philip work for a living, Elise had bought him the premises he ran his estate agency from. Hardly more than a hobby really but Philip enjoyed it and the commission boosted his monthly allowance.

Stretching out in the huge bed, Philip realised he would

have to share this, along with the rest of the house, with Joan once they were joined in matrimony. He grimaced and shook his head. He didn't want anyone living with him other than his servants.

'You are such a bloody fool, Philip,' he said aloud, then he turned over to try to sleep.

An hour later, Philip was pacing his room, dreading the coming morning when he had to visit his mother and father to inform them they were going to become grandparents.

4

Having taken only coffee for his breakfast, Philip strode out to the stables. Leaning against the wall, the tip of his riding crop resting on his shoulder, he watched the groom saddle his horse. Climbing up, he nudged the mare with his heels and walked her out onto the street. Keeping a steady pace, Philip was in no hurry to get to where he was going. He traversed the streets before veering off and onto the heath where he put the mare to a trot. Slowing again as streets came into view once more, Philip led the horse towards his parents' home.

'Master Philip,' the stable lad said, knuckling his forehead.

'Johnson,' Philip replied as he dismounted, 'take good care of her.'

'Will do, sir.'

Philip walked across the yard, his crop tucked under his arm, while he took off his leather gloves. Pairing them up, he slapped them across his left palm then stepped into the house. Going straight to the sitting room, he called out, 'Hello, Mother.'

Elise was sitting at her escritoire catching up on her correspondence. Putting down her pen, she turned. 'Darling! How lovely to see you!'

Philip and his mother greeted each other with a hug. Elise then went to pull the rope at the side of the fireplace to summon the maid before sitting in the armchair opposite her son. 'How are you?'

'I'm very well, thank you, Mother. And yourself?'

'I too am well.'

There was a knock on the door before it opened and the maid appeared. 'Coffee, please, Jenny,' Elise requested. The maid bobbed a knee then disappeared, closing the door quietly.

'How are you getting on with your work?' Elise asked.

'Fine, I've sold quite a few properties recently.' Philip laid his gloves, crop and riding hat on the seat beside him then crossed his legs.

'Good. Your father was asking about it only the other day in fact.' Elise watched her son as his eyes roved the room as though he'd never seen it before.

'New drapes, Mother?' At her nod, he added, 'Very nice.'

'I had them changed weeks ago, but you wouldn't know that as you haven't visited for a while.'

Philip nodded with a strained smile. 'I must apologise, but my work has kept me very busy.'

'Your evenings also, I assume, carousing with your friends,' Elise remarked quite pointedly.

Philip lowered his eyes, clearly taking the chastisement to heart. The conversation halted, much to his relief, while the maid brought in the refreshments.

Once they were alone again, Elise poured the coffee and handed her son a cup. Whilst seeing to her own, she asked, 'So are you going to tell me?'

'What?' Philip replied with a question of his own.

'Why you are here? I only seem to see you these days when you need some money or something is amiss.'

'You know me so well,' Philip said with a little laugh which, even to his own ears, sounded forced. 'Mother... I seem to have got myself into a spot of bother.'

Elise sighed. 'What is it this time? Drunken brawling?'

'No, erm, I'm not sure how to put this delicately.'

'Then simply spit it out,' Elise said.

'Right, yes. I'm getting married.'

Elise stared at her son, her mouth hanging open in a most unladylike manner. Then she asked, 'To whom?'

'A lady called Joan Wilkins.' Philip gulped, his drink burning his throat in the process which made him cough.

'I don't think we know any Wilkinses,' Elise said with a frown.

'No, you wouldn't know them,' Philip said quietly.

'Are they from out of town perhaps?' Elise was under the impression the family in question were of high status and well-to-do.

Philip knew this and swallowed hard at having to burst her bubble. 'No, Joan works as a shop manager in a bakery.'

Elise spat out the mouthful of coffee and immediately began to dab her dress with her handkerchief.

It was all Philip could do to contain the grin fighting to grace his countenance.

'A shop girl?'

'Yes, Mother.'

'But why?' Elise was aghast at the thought of her son marrying beneath his social class.

'Because...'

'Do you love her?' Elise interrupted.

'Not really.' Philip had the good grace to lower his head but he heard the sharp intake of breath.

'Philip, is this young woman pregnant?'

'I'm afraid so,' he whispered.

'Oh, my Lord! Your father will have apoplexy when he hears this!'

'I'm sorry, Mother, truly I am.' Philip sniffed and in a heart-beat Elise had laid down her cup and crossed the room to him, holding him in her arms.

'It's all right, my darling, we'll sort this out one way or another. Don't you worry about a thing.' Elise had very much wanted her son to marry well but now the situation had changed dramatically. She had tried to raise him to honour his obligations and this one was no different; Philip would have to marry the girl and face his responsibilities.

With his head buried in her ample bosom, Elise didn't see the smile spread across Philip's face.

Nothing more was said and after an early lunch of roast pork, potatoes and vegetables, Philip settled down with the newspaper and around an hour later he heard his father arrive home. His stomach churned and he began to wish he hadn't eaten so much.

Bursting into the sitting room, William bellowed, 'Philip, my boy, nice to see you!'

'Hello, Father,' Philip managed, then instantly turned his eyes to Elise in a plea for help. Her surreptitious nod brought him a little comfort, but he was still dreading his father's ire.

William kissed his wife's cheek. 'M'dear,' he said before taking his customary stance with his backside to the fire.

'We have some news for you,' Elise said. 'Our son is to be married.'

'Congratulations, m'boy, who is the lucky lady?' William asked.

Elise imparted the information her son had given her that morning, watching the anger build in her husband.

'No, no, no!' William boomed out. 'I forbid it! I will not have you wed to a shop girl and that's that!'

'I promised her, Father,' Philip said meekly.

'I don't care! You will just have to tell her the wedding is off!' Turning to his wife, William went on, 'Drinking and rabble-rousing is one thing but this time, Elise, your son has gone too far!'

'But what about the child?' Philip asked morosely.

'There are ways to deal with that. Pay her a handsome sum to get rid of it.'

'William! That's our grandchild!' Elise said sharply.

'Not mine, not this way! I insist that this matter be put to rest as I have said, and I'll hear no more about it!' William strode from the room, slamming the door behind him.

'Well, that went better than expected,' Philip said, where-upon his mother couldn't help herself and she burst out laughing.

* * *

Back in Church Street, Joan was busy in the shop. Doris wrapped a shawl around her shoulders as she went through to the kitchen, calling out, 'I'm just going to visit Alice, I'll see you later.'

As she walked down the street, Doris considered again what she would discuss with Alice, and whether she was being silly.

Passing the inn at the end of the road, she heard laughter coming from within. *I could do with a gin or two myself*, she thought as she turned into Union Street. Glancing at the drab houses looking like a line of little boxes all shoved together, she felt sorry for those living in them. At least she lived in a big property with her family around her. She didn't stop to look in the shop windows as she usually did; she was in a hurry.

There was something Doris needed to get off her chest and Alice was an excellent listener.

5

Australia was unusually stifling hot, the land was parched, the grass turned yellow, and there was still the threat of wildfires breaking out in the tinder-dry bush.

BJ, John and Mac sat in the cool schoolroom with three glasses and a jug of fresh water.

'It's October next month, BJ, your release time, and I was wondering what your plans are – and yours too, John,' Mac said.

BJ had known this day would come and he had not been looking forward to it. 'Mac, you've been aware from the beginning that it was my intention to go home to England.' BJ saw his boss nod and he went on. 'You've been kindness itself to me since I arrived, and I'll never have enough thanks to give for what you did for Colin, James and Clem. They could very well have been dead had you not brought them here to your ranch when you did, and I know it cost you to do it.'

Mac waved a hand in dismissal but said nothing.

'That's one reason why it will be so difficult for me to have to say goodbye when the time comes.' BJ's emotions were running high and it was all he could do not to cry.

'You will be a very wealthy young man when you get home. Have you thought what you might do if you choose to work?' Mac also was keeping a tight rein on his emotions, but John could not be said to be doing the same as tears rolled down his face.

'I could buy a farm and raise cattle,' BJ said with a wry grin.

'Gentleman farmer, eh? That would suit you well,' Mac said with a small smile of his own. 'And what of you, John?'

'I... would like to see England again before I die, but it will be hard leaving you and the ranch, I've been here so long.'

'Well, how about this? If either of you get fed up with the cold and rain, you will always be welcome back here. And we can write to each other so we'll know what the other is up to.' Mac stood to go back to his office. 'See ya later, fellas.'

'Thanks, Mac, from the bottom of my heart,' BJ said with a catch in his voice.

Mac strode from the room with a wave over his shoulder, glad his back was to his friends so they could not see the tears coursing down his cheeks. Closing the office door, Mac dropped into his chair and, covering his face with his hands, he cried his heart out. The young man he thought of like a son would soon be leaving and Mac realised they might never see each other again.

Back in the schoolroom, John was sniffing too. 'We should ask the others whether they're going home as well.'

'Yes, in a minute,' BJ replied, pulling out his handkerchief and wiping his eyes. 'Today was bad enough, how will it be on the day we leave?'

'Horrendous! I can't even think about it,' John replied, flapping his hands in the air.

After another glass of water to steady themselves, the two set out to find their closest friends.

Clem was helping with the gold sieving and when BJ and John walked over to him, he relinquished his task to another man.

'We've just been talking with Mac about our release date next month,' BJ said, 'and John and I have told him we are going home.'

'Count me in, I want to get back to my daughter.' Clem wiped the sweat from his brow with his neckerchief then tucked it into his pocket.

'Right then, I'll let Mac know.'

Next the two went in search of Colin and James, who they found mending the gate on one of the corrals. Explaining why they were there, BJ was not surprised to hear that both Colin and James were eagerly planning their return to England.

Returning to the big house, John and BJ knocked on the office door and walked in. 'The others have elected to go home too,' BJ said as Mac looked up from his newspaper.

'I guessed they would. In that case, we had better get you kitted out with some decent clothes that you can wear in the cold. We'll also need to book your passages on a ship. We'll have to go into town and get it sorted out pretty soon.'

'All our money is tied up with the gold,' BJ said.

'Don't worry about that, I'll pay for everything and then deduct it from your share.'

'Thanks, Mac,' BJ said quietly. He and John left Mac's office with mixed emotions. Sadness at leaving the ranch which had been their home for years, but with a tinge of excitement at finally being able to secure a cabin on a tall ship which would carry them back to their place of birth.

'You know, if the winds are fair we might arrive in England for Christmas,' John said nostalgically.

'Mac's right then. We'd best get some warm clothes because it will be freezing cold.'

'I can't remember what that's like, not really,' John said with a shake of his head.

'I can; stinging nose, numb fingers and toes, muffler up to your eyeballs, black ice, white snow...'

'Oh, yes! Pristine white silently blanketing the land while we slept.' John raised his arms and fluttered his hands as they lowered to his sides.

'Dirty slush in the thaw...' BJ said with a grin.

Giving him a little nudge, John said, 'Don't spoil the picture.'

'Don't forget the filthy smoke from the chimneys making everybody cough.' BJ couldn't resist teasing his friend.

John grimaced. 'Ah, but then would come the spring when the trees awaken from their slumber and on into summer when we complained about the heat...'

BJ's laugh rang out. 'We had no idea what heat was back then, not like we do now.'

'So very true,' John added with a sigh.

'I suppose we should get over to the canteen and see what Cookie has for our lunch.' With that they wandered out of the house, across the yard and into the building where they joined the queue.

'Thank God it's not hot food!' John whispered.

Piling their plates with boiled potatoes with butter, lettuce, cucumber, tomatoes, ham, cheese, beetroot, crusty bread and butter, they found a place on one of the long benches. Clean glasses and jugs of water and cutlery were already laid out. Liberally sprinkling their food with salt, they joined in the conversation which was taking place around the amount of gold being discovered.

'Ah, now, if you're to be heading home soon, then Mac will have to call in the buyer, so he will.' An Irishman directed his words to BJ.

'I expect so,' BJ replied between bites.

'You'll have enough money to buy yourself a title,' someone else piped up.

'Lord BJ, it doesn't sound quite right,' John answered, causing a ripple of laughter.

'Well, I'm gonna drink the pub dry when I get back on the Emerald Isle,' the Irishman said before emptying his water glass.

'Why does that not surprise me?' BJ said with a grin.

The jovial chit-chat continued throughout lunch and slowly the men drifted back to work. Cookie reset the tables ready for any latecomers then went back to the kitchen to help with washing the dishes.

'I shall miss all this,' BJ said quietly when only he and John remained at the table.

'Me too, it seems like I've been here forever.'

As they left the canteen, they heard the ruckus of men shouting loudly.

'What now?' BJ asked before he and John ran towards the melee.

6

BJ and John pushed their way through the crowd of men to find a foreman and one of the newer convicts rolling around on the ground. Dust from the dry land flew into the air, and the shouts of encouragement from the men surrounding the brawling pair were loud enough to deafen.

BJ shoved his fingers into his mouth and let out a harsh whistle. Almost instantly quiet descended and the fighters let go of each other.

'What the hell is going on?' It was Mac's voice that rang out, although no one had seen him arrive.

'He,' the foreman, Jed Evans, said, pointing at his adversary, 'refused to do his job!'

Mac turned to the man in question, asking, 'Is that correct?'

'It is,' the young fellow replied.

'So how did it come to this?' Mac demanded to know.

'Because he...' the convict stabbed a finger at the other man, 'said it was my turn to clean out the latrine!'

'And...?' Mac asked.

'I did it last week with Paddy!'

'Ah, now, Boxer is correct in that, sir,' the Irishman confirmed.

'Boxer?' Mac turned to BJ for an explanation.

'Peter Shilling – he used to do a bit of boxing, I believe,' BJ supplied the explanation.

Turning back to the foreman, Mac said, 'Firstly, Jed, you shouldn't have picked on a boxer; just look at the state of you. Now then, was there a reason for you to think it was Boxer's turn at the latrine?'

'I didn't know he'd been assigned that duty last week by another foreman,' Jed said, dabbing his bloody lip with his neckerchief.

'For God's sake! Don't you foremen ever talk to each other? Make sure this doesn't happen again because I will *not* have fighting on my ranch!' Mac's eyes scanned the crowd, making sure all were aware of his anger. 'Jed, get off to Cookie and get that lip seen to. Boxer, get back to work and rein in those fists.' Mac strode away as the men dispersed, all muttering how it was a shame the fight had been broken up as they would have liked to see the finish.

BJ and John followed Mac into the house and on into the office.

'Mac, maybe the foremen should have a weekly meeting in the canteen, then the workload itineraries could be shared.' BJ had come up with the idea the moment he discovered the reason for the exchange of blows.

'Good idea, sort it out, please, BJ.'

'What I don't understand is... well, everything has worked well for years and suddenly...' John held out his hands and shrugged his shoulders.

'That's true. I wonder what really sparked it off,' BJ mused.

'I don't know but I'll have no more of it,' Mac assured them.

BJ left the office, saying he would go and see the foremen straight away.

'You know, you might want to consider hiring a new overseer before BJ leaves,' John suggested.

Mac sighed loudly. 'I have thought about it but...'

'I understand. BJ's boots are big ones to fill, but there needs to be one man in overall command – beneath you, of course.'

'I'll think on it, John, thanks.'

John returned to the schoolroom, leaving Mac brooding over how to go about employing someone with a strong enough character to oversee the hundreds of men on the ranch. He would not have another like Boney, the previous overseer, who took delight in making others suffer his cruelty, that was for sure, but clearly John was right – he needed someone.

Pushing back his chair, Mac strode from his office. He was going to have a stroll around to see if anyone in particular stood out; a potential candidate for BJ's job when the time came.

As he walked across the huge open space known as the yard, Mac wondered if it was a good idea to choose a man from those within his workforce. Eventually most of his men would complete their sentence and, with their share of the gold money, would probably wish to return to their homes, thereby leaving him in the position he was in now. Maybe it would be better to advertise in the town, but then again he needed a man he could trust. He would have to spend time training a new bloke, and then keep an eye out to ensure he was doing his job properly; more importantly, without violence.

Standing by one of the corrals, Mac leaned on the log enclosure, watching the men checking for weaknesses and fixing the latch gate. His eyes roamed over the workers but he was not that impressed with any of them. Oh, they worked well enough but there were none who could step into the role of overseer.

Moving on, Mac slowly visited each of the corrals before coming to the gold sifting area. 'How's it going?' he called out.

'Great, Mac,' one fellow said as he walked to join his employer, a metal box in his hands.

Mac glanced into the container and was surprised to see a layer of glittering particles covering the bottom. He nodded. 'Clearly we were right to buy this section of land after all.'

'You betcha!' the man replied.

'It's Jack, isn't it?' Mac asked.

'Yes, Boss, Jack Simpkins.'

'Remind me, Jack, why you are here and how long you have left.' Mac knew the answer but had asked the question anyway. Mac prided himself on knowing every one of the men on his ranch, not only by name but why they were there and their release dates. However, his reason for prompting an answer was to see if the man answered truthfully.

'I'm a lifer, Mac, here for murder.'

The two men stood eyeing each other and when Mac nodded, Jack went on, 'I'm from Birmingham in England. I went to work at the coal pit one day and just as I came up after my shift, the boss was waiting to tell us we were all being made redundant. He was closing down the mine so I went home where I found a burglar who was battering my wife.'

'My God!' Mac gasped with mock surprise.

'Well, I gave him what for. Unfortunately I hit him too hard and too often; by the time the police arrived, he was dead.' Jack spoke in a matter-of-fact way which said he had told this story many times and was resigned to his fate.

'And what of your wife?' Mac asked.

'She died of her injuries in the hospital that same night.'

Mac shook his head sadly. 'I'm sorry to hear that, Jack. Do you have any children?'

'No. No siblings or parents either. I'm the last in the Simpkins family. When I go, the name will die with me.'

'How long have you been here?'

'Ten years.'

'Would you go home to England if you could?'

'Nah, I like it here. There are too many bad memories for me back there. I'm happy to live out my days here on the ranch.'

'Right, thanks, Jack, I'll see you later.' Mac wandered away, thinking he may have found his new overseer.

7

Doris asked for a moment of Alice's time and together they sat in the living room with tea and cake.

'What can I do for you, Doris?'

'You can lend me your ear,' Doris responded.

'What's the matter?' Alice was concerned, particularly as her friend had not touched the cake before her.

'Alice, I'm worried.'

'What about?'

'I have a feeling that Philip Sanders is gonna do a runner.' Alice's mouth opened in surprise. 'I think he's either gonna do a moonlight flit or he'll leave our Joan at the altar looking like an idiot.'

'What brought you to this...?' Alice began.

'I don't know! I just feel it in my gut.'

'Have you spoken to Joan about this?'

Doris shook her head. 'Our Joan is so excited about the wedding, now that we all know about the babby. I can't spoil that with what is just a feeling.'

'Oh, Doris, I see your point, but you know it could all be fine. I'm sure Philip would not be so callous as to...'

'Maybe you're right. I'm just being silly and I should stop fretting.'

'It's not silly, Doris, I'm glad you told me. As for fretting, you will anyway if I know you, so all I can say is try not to. Easier said than done, I know, but I don't want you making yourself ill.' After a moment's hesitation, Alice asked, 'Has anyone else said anything similar?'

'No, why?'

'I just wondered if that was what sparked your feeling.'

'Well, I ain't gonna mention it to the others, it wouldn't be fair to spread my misgivings and it gets back to our Joan.'

Alice nodded but noticed Doris had still not eaten her cake, which was unheard of. As Doris stood to leave, Alice hugged her. 'Very wise. I'm always here if you need me.'

'Ta, cocka, I appreciate that.'

After Doris had left Alice took a moment to ponder their conversation and again she recalled the day she saw Philip kissing the cheek of a woman in his office.

With a sigh, Alice knew Doris was right to worry. *He tried his best to court me at one time.* The thought floated through her mind and suddenly her heart was heavy, and her stomach felt like it was carrying a lead weight. *I pray our concerns prove fruitless.* However, as she returned to her work, Alice couldn't shake off the despair which wrapped itself around her.

'Everything all right?' Sylvia called out.

'Yes, fine.' Alice felt wretched at telling the little white lie but she didn't want to worry Sylvia, or discuss Doris's visit here amongst the staff.

The kitchen was working flat out to ensure the shop was well stocked. Customers were coming and going with virtually no let-up, and Alice wondered if the other shops were doing as well as this one. She must find time to do her regular visits and check; the thought flashed through her mind as she carried a tray of flapjacks through to place on the glass shelf beneath the counter.

All day Alice, Sylvia and their team were on their feet and by closing time everyone was exhausted. After the others had gone home, Alice and Sylvia sat in the living room with their feet up on stools and heads resting on the back of their chairs.

'Bloody hell, what a day! My feet are throbbing,' Sylvia moaned.

'Mine too,' Alice said on a breath.

'What did Mom want earlier?' Sylvia asked.

Alice swallowed loudly; she was hoping Sylvia had forgotten about the visit. Lifting her head to look at her friend, she said, 'Your mom is a bit worried. She's afraid Philip might – how did she put it? He might do a moonlight flit.'

Sylvia's head shot up and she howled with pain, bringing a hand to her neck. 'He wouldn't bloody dare!' she growled.

'I said she should stop fretting and that all would be well.'

'But you don't believe that, do you?' Sylvia asked as she rubbed her neck.

'I don't know Philip well enough, socially I mean, to comment one way or the other.'

'Alice, I can see it all over your face,' Sylvia said.

'Doris said it was just a feeling she had and...'

'You have the same feeling?'

Alice nodded. 'I hope I'm wrong, Sylvia, I really do. I could be doing the man an injustice.'

'I'm gonna tell you something now, Alice, I've had the same worry.'

'What? Why didn't you tell me?'

''Cos I'm hoping the same as you, that I'm fretting about nothing. Regardless, there's nothing we can do but wait and see.'

The friends sat for a long time with only the ticking of the clock on the mantelshelf breaking the silence.

* * *

Later that evening, across town, and after dinner, Philip Sanders left his parents' house. They had eaten their meal of roast pheasant, vegetables and potatoes with intermittent strained conversation, Philip wishing he was anywhere else rather than there. William had regaled his wife and son with tales of his dealings with the wealthy merchants of Birmingham. As a financial adviser he suggested ways of cutting costs for these men, as well as better ways to use their substantial fortunes. William Sanders was paid handsomely for the advice he gave and was very well thought of in the town.

Philip and Elise had feigned interest in William's ramblings, but all the time they were waiting for the head of the household to broach the subject of Philip's wedding again. Both were immensely relieved when nothing more was said on the subject.

Walking his horse through the streets, he kept the mare steady when he came to the heath. The last thing he needed was for her to step into a rabbit hole and break a leg.

Finally reaching home, Philip left his trusty steed in the capable hands of the stable boy and strode across the yard into the house. Going to his study, he poured himself a brandy and sat down behind the desk.

A moment later there was a knock on the door and when it opened the maid stood there. 'Can I get you anything, sir?'

'No, thank you. You may retire for the night.'

With a bob of her knee, the maid closed the door with a quiet click.

Philip sipped his drink, enjoying the smooth sensation at the back of his throat. Staring into space, he again considered his father's words. *I will not have you wed to a shop girl... pay her a handsome sum to get rid of it.*

If he did that then he would not have to marry her. He would be free to do as he pleased; maybe he would travel, go to Europe for a few years. A smile lifted his lips at the thought, but then he realised that Joan would never agree to such a thing as removing the child from her life.

Swallowing the last of his drink, Philip stood and brought the bottle to his desk. He had a lot of thinking to do and a brandy or two would help the process along nicely.

8

_____

Joan had requested time off to go in search of a wedding gown which Alice had granted, so Joan and Doris walked down to the railway station early one morning.

The station had been replaced five years previously by a brand-new one, and those who could afford it were quite comfortable travelling on the great steam beast. The station, like those in other towns, had three rails in order to accommodate ordinary gauge which was used for local passenger trains. The long platform was sheltered by a roof and was already filling up with people by the time Doris had purchased their third-class tickets.

Joan nudged her mother then nodded at a couple strolling past. The gentleman wore a dark wool loose jacket which was paired with a waistcoat and contrasting trousers; a shirt and cravat tied at the throat. His beard and moustache were neatly trimmed and on his head sat a silk top hat. Held in one hand was a silver-topped cane and in the other a pair of leather gloves the exact shade of brown as his shoes. The lady at his side was dressed in a scarlet merino wool crinolette skirt, its small steel half-hoops at the back allowing the garment to lie flat at the front. The Zouave jacket, which had gained its name from the Algerian Zouave troops who had fought in the Italian war in 1859, was short and collarless and made of the same material as the skirt. Beneath was a white linen Canazou blouse, previously known as a Garibaldi. The hem of the skirt, the front of the jacket and its rounded borders were trimmed with black soutache braid, giving the whole a startling military look. A matching teardrop hat sat on blonde curls which were gathered up at the back.

Doris and Joan shared a look of '*if only*' before grinning widely when Doris whispered, 'I wouldn't get my fat arse in that anyway.' Their eyes were then drawn to an exasperated woman whose baby was held in a shawl crossed over her chest and tied at the back, her left arm beneath the child for added security. Her other four young children were driving her to distraction as they ran around, doing their best to cause chaos by weaving between passengers.

'I ain't havin' that many,' Joan mumbled as she looked right and left for sight of the train.

'Thank the Lord!' Doris replied with a chuckle.

In the near distance, the steam whistle blew and the train came into view. Slowly it chugged to a halt, puffing out great clouds of smoke. Passengers scrambled aboard as soon as those leaving the train were off, each eager to find a seat.

Joan rolled her eyes as the woman with the children climbed into the third-class carriage at the end of the train. The children threw themselves onto the wooden benches and sat with their legs sticking straight out. As the carriage began to fill, the woman instructed her brood to give up their seats to ladies who were standing. When they complained, she smacked each of them across the back of the head, causing them to wail loudly. 'You'll get another if you don't shut your row!' she growled.

Joan and Doris sighed with relief when the kids snapped their mouths closed and wandered off to find a space where they could look out of the window.

The carriage doors slammed shut and the porter blew his whistle, telling the driver it was safe to go. The loud puff, puff made the children squeal with delight as the engine began to move slowly forward and with each mile they gathered speed.

Doris and Joan watched the landscape seemingly flying past. The scrub of the heath gave way to houses packed tightly together, their chimneys emitting spirals of smoke which drifted away on the wind.

The eight miles to Birmingham passed quickly and the steam whistle sounded as it slowed down, the distance between the clickety-clack of iron wheels on the rails becoming longer. Coming to a halt, people again made a scramble to reach the door, eager to be on their way.

Doris and Joan waited patiently until the rest of the passengers had alighted before doing so themselves. The Birmingham platform was huge and packed with folk jostling to board. Pushing their way through the throng, the women walked out onto the street which, to their dismay, was just as busy.

Arm in arm so as to not get separated, mother and daughter strode quickly towards the shop they had visited when shopping for Sophie's gown. As they entered, they were greeted by the very same saleswoman.

'How nice to see you again,' the woman gushed.

'We've come for a wedding fro... gown for Joan here,' Doris said.

'Congratulations, madam. Do you have anything in mind?' Joan shook her head. 'I see. Well, if Mom would care to take a seat, you and I can browse. Then, if you see something you like, our fitting room is right there.' The saleswoman smiled as she pointed to a door.

'I remember,' Joan said as she followed along to view the dresses on offer.

One after another, Joan tried on gowns, all of which she rejected until she came to one she instantly liked. Silk-lined chiffon, the gown fell to the floor, the hem of which had three horizontal ribbon stripes. The waist was nipped in and the scoop-neck bodice with capped sleeves was decorated with the same ribbon. A veil and coronet were added to the ensemble, as were shoes and long gloves.

Doris nodded as Joan swished around the shop floor, a huge smile on her face. 'You look beautiful,' Doris blubbered, dabbing her eyes with her handkerchief.

'I'll take it!' Joan said, returning to the fitting room to disrobe.

Doris paid for the dress, adding money to the bonus Alice had given her, and Joan bought the veil, coronet, shoes and gloves. With their packages tied with string handles, mother and daughter bid the modiste goodbye and left the shop.

Joan chattered enthusiastically about showing her gown to her sisters and Doris listened with half an ear. Still she could not shake the nagging doubt which loitered in the back of her mind.

Would Joan actually get to wear the dress she was so excited about?

9

The stifling heat in Fremantle was making everyone tetchy and tempers flared at the least little thing. Water canteens were constantly being refilled as the workers couldn't seem to drink enough of the cool refreshing liquid. As soon as their thirst was slaked and they returned to work, the sweat ran down their faces to drip off their chins. Hats and clothes were wringing wet, feeling most uncomfortable on the skin and causing itchy rashes.

Mac was concerned for the men and when one fainted due to heat-stroke, he called a halt to all work. BJ, John and Pete gathered every last man into the yard where Mac addressed them.

'It's too bloody hot to be working so get back to your bunkhouses. We'll pick up again this evening and work through the night when it's cooler.'

Groans of *thank God!* could be heard as the men shuffled away.

Pete joined Mac, BJ and John in the office. 'What should we do about the men out on the prairie?' Pete asked.

'They have the old shack to shelter in so I'm sure they'll be fine.'

'I'll ride out with extra water and just check on them.'

'Thanks, Pete, then get some rest,' Mac acknowledged.

Leaving the office, Pete, BJ and John went to the storeroom and sought out more water skins. BJ and John took them to Cookie to fill while Pete rounded up a couple of not-so-willing helpers. Then the three men, loaded down with cool water, rode out towards where the cattle roamed free.

The static in the air crackled as they trotted along, making the hairs on the backs of their necks stand up.

'Storm brewing,' one said.

'Hopefully with rain,' Pete answered.

Just then, a brilliant streak of lightning shot across the blue sky and shortly afterwards came a loud roll of thunder.

'I hate being out in a storm, especially as we're the tallest things for miles!' the other worker said.

'Let's pick up the pace then. We can rest the horses when we get there and come back when it cools off.' Pete tapped his heels into the mare's flanks, taking her to a gallop.

The sky began to turn grey, enhancing the pink lightning flashes coming one after another. Thunder rumbled in a continuous rolling cacophony and as the men reached the shack, the sky was almost black. Large raindrops pelted down and Pete and his friends lifted their faces to the refreshing splats.

Pete corralled their horses while the others carried the canteens indoors where the drovers were sitting. When Pete joined them, the storm was raging and everyone gave thanks to God for the blessed relief from the heat, even if it was only for a short time.

Back at the ranch, the men poured out of the bunkhouses to

dance around in the rain; the yard soon becoming a quagmire with mud caking their boots. For an hour, the storm moved across the land, spooking cows and horses alike in the corrals before it finally rolled away, leaving in its wake steam rising from the puddles as the heat set in once more.

Indoors again the men changed into dry clothing and lay on their beds, waiting for the sun to go down. As darkness fell, Pete and all of the other drovers rode back to the ranch in time for the evening meal.

Pete reported to Mac, 'The men were all well, but that shack is falling down. It's desperately in need of repair at the least, although a new one would be better.'

'Right, we'll have to build a new one next to it so we can rest up in the old one during the severest heat of the day. I'll get BJ onto it tomorrow.'

Pete left the office and went to eat. Throughout the night, by the light of lanterns, the cattle in the corrals which were due for market, were fed; wood was gathered and loaded onto a cart. This would be transported, come daybreak, to the site where it would be transformed into a new building. The gold, which was also carefully sieved by lamplight, was easier to see as the glow glinted off the shiny particles.

The unusually high temperature so early in the season lasted a week and then, to everyone's relief, fell to within the normal parameters. Life on the ranch reverted back to working in daylight hours and Mac was delighted that everything was back to normal.

After their meal one evening, Mac requested a meeting with BJ, John and Jack Simpkins. 'I've asked to see you because, as you know, Jack, BJ and John will be going back to England soon and I'll be in need of a new overseer.'

'Who, me?' Jack asked incredulously, pre-empting Mac suggesting he take over from BJ.

'Why not? You said yourself you didn't want to go home,' Mac replied.

'I did but...'

'Don't you want the job?' Mac asked. He hadn't even considered the fact that Jack might not want to take on the role offered to him.

'Yes, I'd love it, but how would the men react to me being in charge?'

'I had the same misgivings in the beginning,' BJ put in.

'You'll be fine,' John added.

'Well – all right, if you think I can do it,' Jack said.

'Good because I do. Now, I'd like you to shadow BJ until... the time comes for him to leave. Your wages will rise as of today in accordance with your elevated status, and BJ will inform the workers of what's been agreed. Congratulations, Jack.'

John, BJ and Jack left Mac's office and went from one bunkhouse to another to let the men know Mac's decision. The news was greeted with applause, pats on Jack's back and plenty of handshakes, leaving Jack feeling overwhelmed at the support shown to him by his friends and colleagues.

It was a couple of days later when Mac asked for another meeting in his office, this time with BJ, John, Colin, James and Clem. Sitting behind his desk, he said. 'We're going to town, boys. It's time to book your passages home to England and get you all some new clothes.'

'Really?' James asked tentatively, worried it might be Mac's idea of a joke.

'Truly, James. In a matter of weeks you'll be on your way,' Mac assured him.

To everyone's surprise, Colin burst into tears.

'Colin?' James asked as he put an arm around his friend's shoulder.

'Thank God! I never thought it would ever happen,' Colin said between sobs of sheer relief.

Mac looked at the young man who had gone through so much in his young life, allowing him to bring his emotions under control. Then he said, barely able to hold back his own tears, 'I'll call Rory Cranston in to buy our gold a few days beforehand so you can have your share of the money.'

'Thanks, Mac,' BJ said quietly.

Jumping to his feet, Mac went on, 'We'll have to take the cart because we won't all fit in the buggy.'

'I'll fetch it round to the front of the house,' BJ offered.

After they had all trooped out to wait on the porch, Mac took some cash from the safe and shoved it into his money belt. Then he grabbed the paperwork and strode forth to complete the task he'd been dreading for a long time – to buy BJ his ticket home.

10

The heart of England was being lashed with cold rain, soaking everyone to the skin. Dirty puddles lined the streets, drenching women's skirt hems to the knees, there being too many to step over.

Philip Sanders sat in the office of the estate agents, brooding. He knew Joan would be planning their wedding but he couldn't find it within himself to be excited about it. She had told him the previous evening over dinner at a hotel that she had purchased her gown. He winced as he recalled how he had tried to show enthusiasm as she had chattered on. However, lurking at the back of his mind had been his father's suggestion to pay her off.

Sipping his coffee, he grimaced, it had gone cold while he was considering, yet again, the options open to him. He could do as William had instructed, or he could just up and leave the country; or he could wed the girl and have done with it. The first option would be a nightmare as he was certain Joan would cause a scene, ranting and raving, and her family would be banging on his door, baying for his blood. Going abroad would, of course, be the easiest option. He could simply buy a train ticket to the nearest port, board a ship and sail away to a new life. If he were to marry Joan then she would most certainly disrupt everything. She would move into his house and change the way he had his furniture arranged. He would be unable to go out in the evenings with his friends and come home roaring drunk as was his wont. Joan would have her mother and sisters to visit all the time, and he would come home from work to noise and mess. Then the baby would arrive, screaming at all hours of the day and night, as well as costing him a fortune buying everything a child might need.

The more he thought on it, the further he leaned towards stealing away in the dead of night. He knew he was being a coward but the thought of having a wife and child was abhorrent to him. Philip Sanders liked his life as it was and he didn't want it changed, but in his heart he knew it would be – and soon.

The bell over the door brought him back to the present as his bedraggled colleague rushed in out of the rain. That was another thing to think about. What would happen to his business if he ran away?

Philip didn't hear his colleague blustering about the weather, he just rose from his desk to make fresh coffee for them both. He had more important things on his mind than how heavily the rain was falling. His brain was consumed with what to do about a shop girl he had carelessly seduced and was now about to pay the price for.

Sitting again with his hot drink, Philip knew he should be meeting with the vicar to arrange a time and date for the wedding, but he couldn't face it. Once he did that, he felt his fate would be sealed and it would be impossible to back out.

His friends, once they had stopped laughing at the predicament he'd got himself into, had been no help whatsoever. They had agreed with William, saying Philip should just pay up and be rid of the girl.

Getting to his feet again, Philip donned his hat and coat and grabbed his umbrella, then he walked out of the office, ignoring his colleague's question as to where he was going.

Philip trudged through the rain, cursing his luck. He had brought this upon himself, he knew, but that didn't help. *You're such an idiot, Philip*, he thought as he hurried along, *one day you'll learn your lesson*. But it was too late now, Joan was pregnant because he would not be told no. He had cajoled and pestered, telling her he loved her; he had persevered until, with the promise of marriage, she had given in. Now look where he was, about to become a husband and father.

With a grimace, Philip increased his pace. Coming to his destination, Philip pulled out his wallet, saying, 'One way, first class to Liverpool, please.' A sense of pure relief washed over him as he slid the train ticket into his wallet which he returned to his pocket. Spinning about, he smiled as he hailed a cab. Now it was time to go home and pack his bags.

* * *

Across town, Joan was working in the shop and when she had a tea-break she told Alice about her gown. Alice had popped over to Church Street to see how well the business was doing and to check on Doris.

'It's so exciting!' Alice said. 'Are you having bridesmaids?'

'Yes, my sisters. They said they would be happy to wear the dresses they had for Sophie's wedding, and Sophie and Jake want to sit in the front pew with Mom.'

'You'll need to go and see Ellen and Joyce at Russell Street and order your cake,' Alice said.

'Oh, yes! Can I leave early tonight to go and do it?'

'Of course and tell Ellen I will pay for it, my gift to you and Philip.'

'Thank you, Alice.' Joan gave her friend a hug before returning to her work.

Doris had sat quietly throughout the exchange and only now that she and Alice were alone did she whisper, 'Philip ain't booked in with the vicar yet.'

'What?' Alice was aghast. 'He's cutting it fine, isn't he?'

'Too fine if you ask me and that only adds to my worries,' Doris replied.

'I can understand that. What will you do?' Alice asked with a frown.

'I'm gonna suggest Joan brings Philip to tea on Sunday because he ain't visited us as yet, then I'm gonna put my boot up his arse!' Doris said with a grin.

Alice burst out laughing, despite her concern. 'Doris, you are a tonic. No matter what goes on, you can always see the funny side.'

'Ar, well, let's see if Philip Sanders is laughing when I've finished with him.' Doris became serious again in an instant.

'Doris, did you say Philip has not visited the family yet?'

'Yes, why?'

'So none of you have met him?'

'No, I mean we know *of* him you could say, but we ain't met him officially like.'

'Don't you think that is a little odd, considering he's about to become your son-in-law?'

'Yes, I do, and I think that adds to my worries. Look, Alice, I know our Joan has made a mistake, but I feel for her. She's my daughter after all is said and done, and I love her, same as all the others.'

'I know that, Doris. It's plain to see and those girls adore you, as do I.'

'Alice, I tell you this now and you'd better believe it. If Philip lets my Joan down, there will be nowhere on this earth that he could hide from me! I would hunt him down if it took my last breath!'

Alice felt a shiver run down her spine because she had no doubt Doris would be true to her word.

11

The cart rolled into Fremantle port and on to the stable yard and when it had stopped, Mac and his workers jumped down and strode away towards the shipping office. Inside they were greeted by a tiny man with a bald head who was wearing spectacles.

'Good morning, gentlemen, how can I help you?'

'I need to book five passages on a ship bound for England for some time after 15 October,' Mac said.

'The fifteenth,' Colin muttered. This was the first time any of them had been told the actual date of their release.

'Certainly, sir.' The little man flicked through a large ledger, saying, 'Yes, here we are. Three berths on...'

'No, all five on the same ship, please,' BJ said as he stepped forward.

'Righteo.' Again pages were turned then the clerk smiled. 'Five berths on the *Lady Juliana*.'

'At least it's not the *Neptune*,' James said, reminding them of the ship that had brought them here.

'Three cabins,' Mac said. 'Mr George Newman in one. Mr

Bertram Jordan and Mr John Tobias in another, and Mr Colin Crockutt and Mr James Alexander in the third.' Pushing the paperwork across the desk which contained the men's names, descriptions, reason for deportation and release dates, Mac watched as it was checked, stamped and pushed back. The large ledger was marked as three cabins taken in the aforementioned names and the tickets were issued.

'There you go, sir. Five tickets on the *Lady Juliana* sailing for Liverpool, England on 18 October in the year of our Lord eighteen hundred and sixty-seven.'

'Thank you.' Mac paid the money and placed the tickets with the paperwork and led the others out into the sunshine.

'Bloody hell! We're actually going home!' James gasped. Then he and Colin linked arms and danced a little jig, much to the amusement of the others.

'Come on, to the tailor's first then to have lunch to celebrate,' Mac said with a laugh.

The morning was spent with BJ, John, Colin, James and Clem being measured for new clothes, which were paid for and would be delivered to the ranch when ready. Then Mac took them to a hotel where they enjoyed a lunch of roast pork with plenty of wine. Once the glasses were filled, Clem raised his, saying, 'To Mac, without whom we may never have survived.'

'Mac!' they chorused before sipping their wine.

Excited chatter ensued over their meal and it was then BJ noticed John was very quiet. 'What's wrong, John?' he asked.

'I... I'm not sure where I'll go once we reach England,' John mumbled.

'With us,' Colin put in.

'And where will you go?' John asked with raised eyebrows.

'With him!' James said pointing to BJ, which raised a titter.

'BJ?' John prompted.

'Yes. Well, first I want to find Alice and then my plan is to buy a farm raising cattle and I'll need you to help me.'

Mac grinned then turned to Clem. 'What about you, *George*?'

'I want to find my daughter and once I'm sure she's all right...' He shrugged.

'You can join us too,' BJ finished for him.

'How is Alice going to feel about all of us turning up on her doorstep?' Colin posed the question.

'You won't be. We'll have to book into a guest house while we sort ourselves out.'

Mac nodded. 'That would make sense.' Clearly BJ had thought this through to the last detail, and again Mac felt the sadness settle on him.

'You know, if we all pooled our money we could buy a really big farm!' Colin announced, stretching his arms wide and poking James in the face.

'Watch it! You could have had my eye out, you idiot!' James exclaimed, rubbing the offending area.

'He has a point though,' Clem said.

'That would mean putting all your eggs in one basket,' Mac put in.

'Which means if the farm should fail, we would all lose everything we've worked so hard for,' BJ finished.

'How about you each put in a percentage, that way you would still have plenty to fall back on should the bottom fall out of the market. Although I can't see that happening, not if you're raising beef.' Mac's suggestion was met with approval, everyone agreeing it was the most sensible option. They had all worked with cattle, BJ for seven years, the others not so long, but they were confident they could make the idea work provided they could find and buy either a working farm, or a piece of land large enough to start from scratch.

The conversation continued around the percentage of capital to be put aside, how many head of cattle to purchase in the beginning and men to be hired to work the place. They discussed whether they would be hands-on bosses or gentlemen farmers, letting the hired hands do all the work while they reaped the benefits.

'Well, I'll tell you now, I am *not* working with those beasts!' John said, flapping a hand under his nose, eliciting a ripple of laughter.

'You can keep the books then,' BJ said.

'Oh, goodie.' John's reply was a little sarcastic, again making everyone laugh.

Eventually the time came for them to head back to the ranch and as they walked back to the ostlers they were all were in high spirits.

* * *

The following day, BJ and John eagerly awaited the arrival of the postman. BJ was hoping for a letter from Alice and John the newspapers from England. Both were delighted to receive what they had longed for.

Sitting in the schoolroom, BJ tore open the letter and began to read. Alice's correspondence was full of news about her bakeries and how demand was keeping them busy. She asked after his health, saying she couldn't wait for them to meet in person again after being apart for so long. She told him she was counting down the days until his release, and would begin the count again when he started the long journey home.

Me too, Alice, he thought. As always, she ended with sending her love.

'Well!' John's voice broke BJ's reverie. 'It's about bloody time!'

'It must be important to bring you to cuss over it,' BJ said with a grin.

'It says here that transportation to the colonies could well stop altogether by next year.'

'*Could* stop. It was abolished years ago but they continue to send people over,' BJ remarked. 'Wasn't it the Penal Servitude Act of 1853 that abolished it in 1857?'

'I believe so,' John answered.

'And yet here we are in 1867 and convicts are still coming in.'

'I know. We just have to hope and pray the barbaric practice does end soon,' John said, laying down the newspaper. 'How's Alice?'

'Fine. She's doing really well with the bakeries.'

'Are you going to tell her we have our passages booked?' John asked.

'No, I think I would rather surprise her when I get there.'

'Let's hope she doesn't have a weak heart then because seeing you on her doorstep...'

'Bloody hell, John! You're a little ray of sunshine this morning!' BJ's smile belied his tone which made John laugh loudly. 'You're right though. I'll just write a letter and leave it at that, that way I can still surprise her.'

John nodded and went back to his newspaper as he muttered, 'You'll get there before your letter does, I would imagine.' BJ frowned but found a pen and paper and began to write back to Alice.

Dear Alice,

Thank you for your letter. I'm excited to confirm that my release date is 15 October 1867, so it won't be too much longer before I'm back with you in England.

Filling the rest of the page with news and information about the ranch he also closed with, *All my love, BJ.* Sliding the letter into an envelope which he addressed from memory, he went to place it in the tray on the hall stand. It would be collected by the postman the next time he called.

With a smile, BJ stepped out onto the yard in search of Jack Simpkins to see how he was getting on as trainee overseer. It wouldn't be long now until Jack was starting the job for real.

12

In Church Street, England, an almighty row was going on between Doris and her daughter, Joan.

'I ain't seeing him until Friday night, Mom, I told you!' Joan answered Doris's question about when Philip and Joan were meeting again.

'Don't you yell at me, my girl! Just you tell him to get his arse around 'ere for tea on Sunday!'

'I will. Now for goodness' sake give it a rest!'

Doris harrumphed as she dropped into her armchair and rubbed her belly. She really shouldn't argue on a full stomach, and although she'd enjoyed the evening meal she was now suffering indigestion.

Mary went to the kitchen and returned with a glass of milk. 'Here, Mom, drink this, it will help with the acid.'

'Ta, sweetheart,' Doris said, taking the drink.

'Mom, you should see the doctor 'cos it ain't right you keep havin' the bellyache all the time.'

'I'm fine, lovey, it's just the stress.' Doris didn't see Joan roll her eyes. 'When Sylvia and Joan are wed, this will go away.'

Doris patted her diaphragm. Between sips, she went on, 'We had another order for a wedding cake today. A woman wants a "Peaches and Cream" for May so there's plenty of time to get it made.'

'They're booking in earlier and earlier,' Phoebe said as she walked into the living room with a cup of tea.

'I suppose that way folk can spread the cost,' Doris replied.

'It's certainly keeping us busy and ordering so far in advance of the occasion ensures we stay in work,' Mary put in.

'Are you still enjoying the work?' Doris asked.

'Yes, Mom, we love it, don't we, Phoebe?' Her sister nodded, having just taken a mouthful of tea.

'What's happening about your dresses for our Sylvia's wedding?'

'We all agreed it would make sense to wear the ones we had for Sophie's wedding,' Mary answered.

Doris nodded. 'As long as Sylvia is all right with that.'

'She was the one who suggested it,' Phoebe said.

'And what about for yours, our Joan?'

'I ain't bothered as long as my sisters are there,' Joan replied.

'Well, we might as well get the use out of them,' Mary said, 'they're much too nice to leave in the wardrobe.'

'Good. Then all we need now is Philip to book a date with the vicar,' Doris said pointedly.

Joan closed her eyes then replied, 'I'll tell him to get a shimmy on when I see him on Friday night.'

'All right, cocka, it's just that I don't want you fretting 'cos your frock – sorry, gown – is too tight.'

The conversation continued around the cakes and flowers for both weddings and whether the snow would come early, if at all.

'It's more likely for Sylvia's day,' Mary said.

'Maybe, but we'll need thick coats anyway,' Phoebe added.

'We can't decide anything for you, Joan, until Phi—' Doris began.

'I know! I'm not sure what's got into you, Mom, it's almost like you're in a panic about it all!' Joan snapped.

You have no idea, Doris thought but said instead, 'I'm not, but tell me what you'll do if the babby grows quick and your dress won't fit? We won't have time to get you another.'

'Look, if Philip ain't been to see the vicar then I'll go myself!' Joan jumped to her feet. 'I'm going to bed.' With that, she flounced from the living room, leaving Doris feeling wretched for mithering the girl.

'Take no notice of our Joan, it's 'cos she's pregnant,' Phoebe told her mother, 'and God knows you know what that's like.'

Doris grinned. 'I do. Your poor father couldn't put a foot right while I was carrying.'

'Tell us about it, Mom,' Mary encouraged. The rest of the evening was spent reminiscing about their dear departed dad and was filled with laughter and tears.

* * *

Whilst Joan had been arguing with her mother, Philip was sitting in his study, staring at the train ticket lying on his desk. On his return from the railway station, he had gone straight to his room and packed his clothes into a trunk which sat in the corner.

Philip's mind was in a whirl as he considered; he should see his mother before he left. Elise, he knew, would try to talk him out of going away and leaving her to cope with the aftermath alone. Should he speak with Joan? No, not a good idea. She would probably crown him with the heaviest object close to hand.

Grimacing, Philip picked up his glass and swallowed the last of his brandy. He was very much aware that he was about to take the coward's way out, but the thought of being saddled with a wife and child made his blood run cold. He simply could not envisage himself as a husband and father, so it made sense not to put himself in that position. Especially when the solution was a little piece of paper sitting on his desk. Picking up the ticket, he looked at the thick black writing. *Liverpool – one way.* Tucking it back into his wallet, Philip's mouth twitched at the corners. It was not quite a smile; that would come later when he had boarded the train. Once he was on his way then he would permit himself the pleasure, in fact he could well find he might laugh all the way to the port.

Firstly, however, he must visit his mother to explain his intentions, and pray she would understand why he had to do this.

* * *

The following morning, Philip rode over to see Elise. He had determined that no matter what she said, he was going to Liverpool where he would book a passage to some far-off country. The tall ships sailed all over the world in this modern age so he could take his pick as to a destination. He could even to go to Australia where, he'd heard, the weather was very clement and a man might make a fortune.

Walking his horse through the streets, he felt the cold bite his nose and he shivered. Inwardly he nodded, he would be glad to be in more favourable temperatures where the ladies weren't covered up to their chins.

Steering his mount into the driveway, he led her around to the stables at the back of the house. Leaving the mare with the groom, he wandered across the yard, looking up at the big house in front of him. He wondered if he would still inherit it if he chose to run away from his responsibilities. Truth be told, he didn't much care because he had seen his mother's will, and she had decreed all of her substantial fortune would go to her only son – Philip Sanders.

All right, Mama, let's see what you think of my plans, he thought as he entered his parents' house – maybe for the last time.

13

___

'Philip, have you gone quite mad?' Elise snapped after she'd heard what her son had to say.

'Mother, I can't go through with it!' Philip replied and even to his own ears he sounded like a petulant child.

'Darling, you cannot leave Joan to deal with this all on her own.'

'She's not alone, she has her family around her.'

'I'm sorry but that's not nearly good enough! You are the father of the child and you should own your mistake and take responsibility for its upbringing.' Elise was furious that her boy could even consider running away. 'God only knows what your father will say.'

'He won't care, Mother, he said he will not discuss the matter further.'

'Oh, he will when he hears what you have planned.' Elise sighed loudly. 'Philip, I love you with all my heart, but you can be such a fool at times.'

Philip, suitably chastised, looked down at his riding boots, noting they needed a good polishing. 'Whatever you and Father say, I've made up my mind. I *will not* marry Joan Wilkins and that's an end to it!'

'It most certainly is not! If you choose this path then you must explain to the girl yourself.'

'I can't do that! Her family will lynch me!'

'It's no more than you deserve.' Elise stared at her son with fire in her eyes.

'Mama, please, you have to help me!'

'I don't, not if you desert the girl you made pregnant! You should be more like your father.' Elise snapped her mouth shut, realising she may have said too much.

'What do you mean?' Philip asked, suddenly interested in the conversation again.

'Nothing, just that you are so pig-headed. Stubborn to the bone.'

'Oh,' Philip replied, his interest waning once more.

Elise let out a relieved breath as she saw Philip accept her explanation. 'We have to discuss this with William when he gets home.'

'You can if you wish but I won't be here. I'm not waiting around for him to berate me yet again.'

'Philip!'

'No, Mother. Look, yes, I made a mistake but instead of trying to help, Father just yells and lays down the law. I'm tired of it and I do not intend to listen to any more of it.' Philip got to his feet and turned to leave just as William walked through the door.

'Philip.' William's greeting was sharp.

'Father. I was just going.'

'Sit. I need a word.' William instructed and only when Philip dropped back onto his seat did he acknowledge his wife.

'M'dear,' he said as he kissed her cheek. His attention returned to Philip as he asked, 'Well?'

Philip frowned. 'Well what?'

'Is it done?'

Philip knew what his father was speaking of but decided to play the innocent, giving him time to build his confidence to deal with the storm about to erupt. 'I'm not sure what you are referring to.'

Drawing a huge breath, William's anger began to build. 'The girl! Have you seen to it?'

'Oh, you mean Joan. No, Father, I haven't.'

Elise closed her eyes for a moment, waiting for her husband's wrath to burst forth. 'Why in heaven's name not?'

Philip shook his head. 'I've been – busy.'

'*Busy*! Philip, this is not something that can wait. It has to be done sooner rather than later!' William exploded.

'That's up to Joan. You see, Father, I'm not going to be here for some considerable time. I'm going abroad.'

William looked from son to mother and back again, his mouth open in complete shock.

'William, we have to discuss this calmly,' Elise said quietly.

'Clearly there's nothing to be said because it seems he's made up his mind to run off and leave us to clean up his mess,' William replied.

'I've told him he has to face up to it and—' Elise began.

Sarcasm dripped from his words as William went on, 'No, Elise, Philip wants to go abroad and get some other young woman in the family way. Then he'll write, asking us to bail him out of that too.'

'I want nothing from you, Father!' Philip yelled.

'Good because that's just what you are getting – nothing!' William shouted back.

Elise brought her hand to her mouth as the argument raged on.

'You've never given me anything!' Philip said with a little laugh.

'You don't deserve it, you ungrateful cur!' William lambasted.

'You still don't see it, do you? All I ever wanted from you was your love!' Philip's voice cracked as he spoke.

Elise screwed up her eyes, praying for this to end before words were spoken which could never be taken back. She was to be sorely disappointed as William boomed out, 'How can I love another man's child?'

A sob escaped Elise's lips, breaking the silence which had dropped like a ton weight.

William threw back his head, dragging in a ragged breath. From the day of Philip's birth, William had held his tongue and now because of his temper the truth had spilled out. Turning to his wife, he muttered, 'Elise, I'm sorry.'

Tears ran down Elise's face as she growled, 'It's too late for that now.'

Philip watched in a state of shock as William knelt before his wife, mumbling an apology over and over again.

Elise pushed him away. 'I knew this would happen one day. I've waited for it for years and now it has simply because you couldn't hold your temper.'

'Elise, I didn't mean to tell the boy,' William wailed.

'Well, now you've started, you should tell *my* son all of it,' Elise said through clenched teeth.

'No. It's not my place—'

'Ha! You should have considered that before you hung out my dirty washing for my boy to see!'

'Darling...'

'Don't you call me that; I'm not, nor was I ever, your darling!'

'Mother, what the hell is going on?' Philip found his tongue at last.

'William Sanders is not your father,' Elise said. 'He married me out of pity for being pregnant before being wed!'

'Bloody hell!' Philip gasped.

'That's not fair, Elise. I've loved you since long before you found yourself—'

'Pregnant!' Elise yelled in his face. 'Why are you so afraid to say it?'

'Elise, please,' William begged.

Shaking her head, Elise turned her eyes to her son.

Philip recalled the last time they discussed his predicament and William saying, *this time, Elise, your son has gone too far!* Suddenly the words slipped into place. It was then he asked, 'So who is my father?'

14

BJ was frantically scribbling on a piece of paper when John asked, 'What are you doing?'

'I've just worked it out. We won't be home for Christmas, it will be sometime in February.'

'Oh, marvellous, one of the coldest months of the year.'

'Bloody hell!' Colin said as he strolled over to BJ's bed in the bunkhouse. 'That's forever away.'

'Colin, we've been here almost seven years,' James put in, 'another few months won't make much difference, especially as we'll be sailing towards England rather than away from it.'

'I s'pose,' Colin mumbled.

'I wonder what the crossing will be like,' John mused.

'Choppy, seasickness, bellyache, rotten food...' BJ said, watching John almost turn green at the thought. 'But at least we'll have a cabin this time.'

'Such sweet mercies,' John returned.

'God, do you remember that storm? I thought we were all gonna die,' James said, recalling their journey on the open sea.

'All right, I think I might just stay here after all,' John said with an exaggerated shiver which caused the others to laugh.

'It will be fine,' BJ tried to assure them. 'I believe the ships have doctors on board now.'

'They have shanty singers an' all but they won't be any good if you're drowning,' Colin retorted.

'Oh, I don't know, they could sing us into our watery graves,' John said.

'Bugger off, John, say summat nice or shut your cake-hole,' Colin said playfully.

'Maybe I might meet a nice young sailor,' John said dreamily.

'And maybe the captain will chuck you overboard for distracting the sailors from their work,' James laughed.

'Ooh, I can just imagine it – "Bonjour, Matelot."' John wiggled his fingers in a little wave.

'What?' asked Colin.

'Hello sailor in French,' John supplied the answer.

'Dear God, what next?' Colin grinned widely.

'Possibly I should aim higher – to the captain, perhaps.'

'Colin, you just had to ask, didn't you?' BJ said before they all roared with laughter.

Work on the ranch continued as usual with cattle being bought and sold. The new patch of land that Mac had acquired some years previously was still producing gold, much to everyone's delight. The underground water source filling the castellum put in place by the workers under the supervision of Alex Gough, the engineer, worked beautifully.

Often, as he sat in the big house alone at night, Mac would wonder if he and BJ would ever see each other again.

He thought it would be most unlikely. BJ would soon be halfway across the world, the perilous voyage taking months.

Ships were lost all the time in the raging storms, and Mac prayed BJ's crossing would go well and he would reach his homeland safely.

They would, of course, write to each other but even with so many ships undertaking the dangerous journey, it would be at least half, or if he was very lucky, a quarter of a year before Mac received word from his friend.

Mac had stopped taking on new convicts some time ago but it would be a few years yet before all of his would be repatriated. Only then would he be able to supplement his workforce with local men looking for work. So for the moment he was content that his ranch was running smoothly and he was making a reasonably good profit, and a lot of that good fortune was down to the management of his favourite convict – BJ.

BJ's mind was also full of mixed emotions. He was excited to be going home at last, but sad at leaving the ranch. He was happy he would see Alice quite soon but knew he would feel bereft at never being in Mac's company again.

For now, both men squashed these thoughts as each day that passed brought them closer to the moment they had to say goodbye.

* * *

Early one morning Pete, the chief drover, came galloping up to the big house. The horse skidded to a halt and Pete leapt down, running indoors and yelling for Mac.

'What's going on?' BJ asked John as they finished their breakfast.

'We should probably go and find out,' came the reply.

Leaving the canteen, they shot across the yard just as Mac and Pete emerged.

'Saddle up, we have a problem,' Mac instructed.

Racing around to the stables, three horses were made ready and along with Pete they rode to the perimeter of Mac's land. John, who was not much of a rider, somehow managed to stay in his saddle, bringing up the rear.

Coming to the newly built corral, the four men dismounted, tying the reins to the hitching post.

'Show me,' Mac said.

'There, the darkest of them,' Pete answered, pointing out the steer in question.

They walked around the log fence to get a better look and then Mac sighed. 'Yes, it looks like it to me.'

'What?' BJ asked.

'These are the cattle I bought two weeks ago. Look at the mouth, see the blisters?'

BJ nodded and John muttered, 'Oh, no.'

'What?' BJ asked again, feeling thoroughly frustrated at not knowing what was being spoken about.

'They're infected with foot and mouth disease,' Mac said as he hung his head. 'They will all have to be destroyed.'

15

William Sanders sat quietly, his chin on his chest as his wife spoke.

'Philip, what you have to understand is—'

'Mother, just tell me who my real father is!'

Taking a deep breath, Elise nodded. 'When I was a girl, I was courting a young man from a high society family. His name was Carter Wainright-Jones.'

'Carter Wain...' Philip muttered.

'He and I were pledged to marry but were not yet engaged. I made a mistake, Philip, and gave in to the pressures he put upon me.' Philip grimaced, beginning to wish he'd never asked. 'Don't look like that, especially as you now find yourself in the same position!' Elise snapped. 'Well, you know the outcome. When I told him he was going to be a father, his family called off the pledge. Carter was immediately shipped off to the Americas where I guess he remains to this day.'

'Why didn't he marry you straight away?' Philip asked.

'Because he didn't love me,' Elise said, her voice cracking. 'I was just a dalliance for him and my family were not really good enough. The engagement had been agreed to because Carter wanted it at first, his parents giving in to him. He was very spoiled, you understand.'

'What about your parents, what did they say?' Philip asked.

'My father railed against the injustice of it all but it was done. Carter disappeared overnight and I never saw him again.'

'How did Father – William – come into it?'

'William and I had been friends since we were children, and when I told him of my predicament he went to my father to ask for my hand.'

'So you knew before you married Mother?' Philip directed his question to the man he'd thought was his father all of his life.

William nodded. 'I've loved your mother since I was a boy, and I still do. The problem was – she didn't love me the same way.'

'So you have a marriage of convenience,' Philip said.

'You could put it that way,' Elise took up. 'I will always be grateful to William for sparing my family from the shame of having a pregnant unwed daughter.'

'Now you want me to do the same thing, except the child is actually mine.' Philip shook his head. 'Everything is clearer now; why you, William, never treated me as you would had I been your son.'

'I'm sorry, lad, truly I am,' William said sadly. 'It has been unbelievably difficult for me over the years, watching you grow into the image of your birth father.'

'I can imagine,' Philip said, now beginning to feel sorry for the man who had given him his name and raised him as well as he could under the circumstances. 'Why did you not tell me all this before?' Philip asked his mother.

'For this precise reason,' Elise said, spreading her arm out.

'Look at us, we're fragmented now. That's the last thing I ever wanted and I beg of you not to make the same mistake as your father.'

'So what do you think I should do about Joan Wilkins?'

'Let's all sleep on it then tomorrow we can discuss it more calmly,' Elise suggested. 'I'll have your room made up.'

Philip nodded, still trying to come to terms with all he'd heard. 'I'm seeing Joan later, maybe I should tell her I don't want to marry her.'

'It will break her heart, Philip, believe me, I know,' Elise said, her voice full of sorrow.

'Mama, I have to! I can't go through with it and be chained to her for the rest of my life!'

'The choice is yours, son,' William put in.

'Please don't call me that, I am not your son,' Philip said.

'As you wish.' William stood and walked from the room, closing the door behind him with a quiet click.

'Philip, William took me on when I had nowhere else to go. He's treated me with the utmost respect all these years and he tried his best to accept you as his own.'

'I know and I'm sorry but it doesn't change the fact that I'm not his.'

The clock on the mantelshelf chimed the hour and Philip got to his feet. 'I'll see you later.'

Elise watched her boy go and only then did she allow her tears to fall.

* * *

Over in Church Street, Joan was getting ready for her evening out with Philip.

'Don't forget about Sunday tea,' Doris reminded her.

'I won't,' Joan replied as she donned her coat.

'Where are you off to?'

'The Theatre Royal, so I won't be late.' Joan kissed Doris's cheek, grabbed her bag, checked her hat was on straight and rushed out to meet her betrothed.

The streets were dark save for the pools of yellow light shed by the gas lamps. The temperature had dipped and Joan shivered as she walked, rubbing her gloved hands together. Her breath plumed as she breathed and her nose tingled. There were not many people abroad on this cold night, most electing to stay indoors by their firesides.

Reaching the Five Ways, Joan turned into High Street, passing a public house which was lit up brightly. Eventually she came to the theatre where she waited for Philip to arrive. Feeling the cold wind bite, Joan mounted the few steps to stand in the doorway.

'Come on, Philip, I'm freezing my arse off here!' she muttered under her breath. She nodded to people entering the building and slowly a feeling of despair began to creep over her. Philip was late and she started to worry he might have been in an accident.

The theatre's outer doors were closed by the porter, denoting the performance was about to start, and Joan's feeling of foreboding heightened as she stamped her feet to beat off the cold. As the church clock struck, Joan realised she had been waiting an hour. Descending the steps, she walked home, wondering what on earth had happened to Philip.

Joan had no way of knowing that Philip was at that very moment sitting on a train heading for Liverpool.

16

_____

'You're back early. What's happened?' Doris asked, seeing Joan's face as she walked into the living room.

'Philip didn't come. Mom, I'm worried something might have...'

'Now then, sit by the fire and calm down,' Doris instructed.

'He could be lying hurt somewhere!' Joan railed.

'He ain't, he's probably fallen asleep in front of his own fire,' Doris said, trying to placate her daughter, but inside she was also in turmoil. Had Philip finally done what she suspected he might all along and ran away?

'Why don't you pop round to his house and see if he's there?'

'I... erm... I don't know where he lives,' Joan confessed.

'What? You've been courting all this time and you ain't never been to his house?' Doris was aghast.

'No. We always met outside like the theatre or the... park. That was where...'

'I don't wish to know where you got pregnant, Joan. D'aint it ever occur to you to ask to see where you'd be livin' once you were wed?'

Joan shook her head. 'Oh, Mom, I'm scared!'

'It's all right, lovey. We'll go round to the estate agents tomorrow and you'll see he'll have a perfectly good reason for keeping you standing in the cold. Then you can give him a piece of your mind.'

Joan gave a tight-lipped smile. 'I will, don't you worry about that.'

Later that night, when everyone else was in bed, Doris sat alone watching the flames dancing in the hearth. She was convinced Philip had done a runner, although she couldn't say why. It was just a feeling she'd had from the very beginning when she discovered Joan was pregnant. Maybe she was wrong and the fellow did have a good excuse but somehow she doubted it. Looking back, she recalled her conversation with Alice about Philip not visiting her house once and now Joan was telling her she didn't know where his residence was. The whole thing had a bad smell about it, and Doris's anger began to build the more she thought on it.

'You've buggered off, ain't yer, you swine?' Doris muttered quietly. 'If so, you'd best pray I don't find you 'cos if I do, I'll rip that todger clean off! You won't be fathering any more kids, believe me!'

After a restless night, Doris and Joan wrapped up warmly and set out for the estate agents' office. Walking in, they were greeted by a young man. 'Good morning, ladies, how can I help you?'

'Where's Philip?' Doris asked without preamble.

'He's not in this morning as yet.'

'Where does he live?' Doris asked.

'I'm afraid I can't divulge—'

'Look here, sonny, this here is his fiancée. They were supposed to meet last night and he d'aint turn up, so she just wants to mek sure he's all right.'

'Oh, I see. Well, it's all very irregular but under the circumstances I suppose it would be all right.' The man wrote down the address on a scrap of paper, thinking it strange that Philip's fiancée would not know where he lived. With a shrug, he held the paper out.

Doris snatched it and she and Joan walked out, leaving the man wondering if he had done the right thing.

Hailing a cab, Doris called out the address. The driver nodded and the women climbed aboard. A short journey later, the cab stopped. Doris and Joan alighted and checked the number on the door was correct before Doris hammered loudly on the knocker. A moment passed before the door was opened by the maid.

'We're here to see Philip Sanders,' Doris said curtly.

'I'm sorry, Master Philip isn't here. He left last night on the train to Liverpool.'

Joan let out a howl which made the maid jump before she closed the door quickly in the women's faces.

'Mom!' Joan cried.

'Come on, let's go home.' Doris pushed her weeping daughter into the cab they had only just left, calling out her destination before climbing in herself.

Joan sobbed all the way back to Church Street. Doris told her to go indoors while she paid the cabbie. 'Do us a favour and whistle for a runner,' Doris said.

The cabbie nodded and did as she asked, then he moved off. In an instant, a child in a ragged coat appeared. 'You need a runner, missus?' the boy asked.

'Ar. You know Alice's Bakery in Union Street?' When the

boy nodded, she went on, 'Here's a tanner. Ask Alice Green to come here as soon as she can.'

'Will do. Ta, missus.' The boy sped away, the sixpence clutched tightly in his dirty hand.

Doris went into the house where she found Joan still crying. Taking off her coat, she then went to wrap her arms around her daughter.

'Oh, Mom, what am I gonna do?' Joan managed between sobs.

'First of all, do you want to have this babby?' Doris asked. The two locked eyes and Joan's shocked expression was evident. 'Look, if you don't want to have it – there are ways... Or you can put it up for adoption after you give birth.' Doris was trying to be practical and said so. 'You have to decide, my wench, and soon.'

'What if I don't have it and Philip comes back?' Joan muttered.

'Sweetheart, we both know that ain't gonna happen. That bugger has done a runner 'cos he can't face up to his responsibilities.'

Joan nodded. 'You know, Mom, I was frightened this might happen because he wasn't excited about the pregnancy.'

'He didn't see the vicar either about arranging a date for your wedding,' Doris said. 'I have to admit I had the same misgivings.'

'You never said...'

'I wasn't sure, darlin', it was just a feeling. I thought it strange as well that he never came to meet the family. In fact, I talked about it with Alice.'

'What did she say?' Joan asked.

'Much the same as me, lovey. Now you sit quietly while I

make us a cup of tea then we can talk some more.' Doris went to the kitchen and, picking up a cup and saucer, she noticed her hands were shaking. Placing the crockery on the table, she clenched her hands tightly, a look of absolute fury on her face. Shaking the anger from her body through her arms, she then set about making the drink.

Doris and Joan were sipping hot tea when they heard the frantic call.

'Doris? Doris, are you all right?' Alice's voice preceded her into the room.

'Yes, lovey. Come in, we have something to tell you.' Doris related what she and Joan had discovered about Philip, and Joan was sad to notice that Alice wasn't taken aback.

'I'm sorry, Joan, but I can't say I'm surprised,' Alice said as gently as she could. 'So, what are you going to do now?'

'I'm going to be a mother and I'm looking forward to it.'

Joan's statement came as a shock because Doris and Alice had expected her to want to be rid of the child now she had been abandoned by its father.

'You know what you're letting yourself in for as regards the gossip?' Doris asked.

'Folk can talk all they like, I don't care; I'm the victim here. Philip Sanders left me pregnant when he ran off, and anyone who calls shame on me will know because I'll tell them what he did!' Joan's sorrow was turning to anger and both Doris and Alice knew then that Joan was strong enough to deal with anything that came her way.

'Right, young lady, you get back to work while I make Alice a drink, then I'll nip to the market for some wool. I've got some knitting to do,' Doris said.

Joan smiled and went through to the shop. Doris and Alice

shared a look of *we saw this coming* as Doris again went to the kitchen. The two chatted quietly over their drink.

'Joan is determined to see this through, Doris,' Alice said.

'Yeah, in a way I wished she'd chosen the other route.'

'Why?' Alice asked.

'Every time she looks at that child she'll be reminded of its swine of a father. She'll relive this for the rest of her days.'

'Oh, Doris! I never thought about it that way, but Joan's made up her mind so we will have to support her as much as we can.'

With a nod, Doris pulled on her coat, then they left the house together.

As they walked, Doris spoke quietly. 'I'll kill that man if I ever set eyes on him again.'

'Somehow I don't think Philip will be coming back, Doris,' Alice replied.

'Strange, ain't it? That we both had the same feeling about him.'

'Not just us, Doris, Sylvia did too.'

Doris's head swivelled towards Alice. 'Really?'

Alice nodded. 'We kept quiet because we were hoping we were wrong.'

'I'd bloody love to know where he's going. It's my guess he's after a ship to take him abroad,' Doris mused.

'It seems likely if he took the train to Liverpool as the maid told you,' Alice responded.

'Well, I don't wish him any harm, but I hope that ship sinks and the bugger drowns!' Alice couldn't help but snigger at Doris's words. 'I'll come with you and tell our Sylvia what's happened, then I'll get down the market.'

'I think Joan has a hard road ahead of her,' Alice said.

'True, but she's got all of us around her so she'll be fine. With family and friends like you, how can she go wrong?'

Alice looped her arm through Doris's as they walked on towards the bakery. *I hope you're right, Doris*, she thought.

17

The heat in the bunkhouse over in Fremantle was making everyone sweat.

BJ marked off another day on the makeshift calendar he had drawn up, and placed it back into the cupboard next to his bed which held his spare clothes. Lying on his bed, he thought of Alice and what it would be like seeing her again. Closing his eyes, his mind drifted back over the years to when they first met.

Alice had run away from a father who hated her after her mother died and she was just a kid trying to survive on the streets for the first time in her life. They had immediately become friends and had set up home on the heath like brother and sister.

BJ had taught her how to pick pockets, and at first Alice had been adamant she wouldn't do it. However, BJ had stressed how important it was because it could mean the difference between life and death. Alice had relented and in the end had become quite proficient at stealing the odd thing here and there.

He smiled as he remembered the shelter they had built

together and he wondered if it might still be standing after all these years. The children had made a life for themselves and the local market had been a useful source of food and money. As well as pilfering, BJ had shown Alice how to exchange information between the traders for food and other goodies. It was a hard existence but they were happy enough until BJ's mistake had resulted in his transportation. But Alice and BJ had never given up on each other.

As soon as they were able, they began to correspond and had written letters regularly. Now the time was fast approaching when he would be leaving Australia bound for England.

Many times he had imagined the scenario of them coming face to face once more, and each time it was different. Perhaps they would just stand and stare at each other; maybe Alice would run to him and throw her arms around him. How ever it came about, BJ couldn't wait to find out.

A few more weeks on the ranch, then around one hundred and twenty days on the ship, which would seem like forever. Docking at Liverpool, it would then be a train journey to Wednesbury, and finally a cab to a fine guest house or hotel. Once booked in and after he had stowed his things in his bedroom, he would take another cab to Alice's Bakery.

The snores from his friends in the bunkhouse broke his reverie and he realised the huge grin was still plastered on his face.

Feeling the need to relieve himself, BJ stole quietly from the room and walked towards the latrine block. Then he stopped as something caught his eye. Squinting into the darkness, he watched as a pinpoint of light seemed to hop about.

Turning on his heel, he ran back towards the bunkhouse, yelling for everyone to get up. Curses came his way and grumbling filled the air until BJ called out, 'Someone is stealing our gold!'

The men jumped to their feet and began to clamour towards the door.

'Stop!' BJ said sternly. 'We need to do this carefully if we are to catch whoever is on the patch, otherwise they will run and we will lose them!'

'What do you suggest?' John asked.

'Rouse the others but quietly. We need to surround the fencing so the thief or thieves can't get out. Then we'll take them to Mac in the big house. Take some lamps but keep them shuttered until I give the signal.'

One by one, the other bunkhouses were alerted, and silently men poured out, making their way to the gold-laden area with its chain-link fence. Slowly, covered by darkness, they crept forward until everyone was in place.

BJ listened to the scraping of a shovel on the earth and then the light was lifted to reveal two men laughing.

'Hey there!' BJ yelled and one by one the lamps' shutters were opened, bathing the ground in light.

The two men dropped the shovels and turned around in a circle, only then realising there was nowhere to run. The chain-link fence enclosed them on all four sides.

'Come out – *now!*' BJ's booming voice carried on the silence as he stood by the gate.

The men returned to the spot where they had cut the fence and scrambled through. There they were grabbed and held until BJ walked over to them. He held out his hand and the men reluctantly gave him what they had dug up. BJ looked at the three tiny gold nuggets then said, 'And the rest.' One man pulled a small glass bottle with a cork in the neck from his pocket and handed it to BJ. 'Bring them,' he instructed as he led them all back to the big house. Over his shoulder he yelled, 'Somebody get that fence fixed, please.'

Banging on the door, BJ waited and watched as lamps were lit before Mac appeared in just his trousers.

'BJ, what's going on?' Mac asked sleepily.

'Sorry to disturb you, Mac, but we found these two pinching our gold.'

The offenders were dragged forward to face the ranch owner.

'BJ, John, Pete, Clem, Colin and James, bring them into the living room. The rest of you stand guard in case they attempt to flee.' Mac then followed them into the large living room where he lit the lamps.

'This is what they got,' BJ said, handing over the nuggets and bottle full of gold dust.

Holding the bottle up to the light, Mac said, 'It looks like this isn't the first time you've been on my land and stolen from me.' Mac then glared at the men facing him. Simultaneously the men dropped their heads, suddenly finding something interesting to look at on the floor. 'Well? What have you to say for yourselves?' Mac asked.

Shaking their heads, the men said nothing.

'How did you know about this?' Mac held up the bottle.

'We watched you,' one said.

'Who else knows?' Mac probed.

'Nobody,' the other man said quickly.

Mac looked at BJ. 'What should we do with them?'

'Word will get out about our gold if we call in the police,' BJ replied.

'That's a very good point,' Mac concurred. 'We could string them up.'

The thieves' heads shot up in alarm as the buzz of agreement sounded. 'We're sorry, we won't do it again,' the first said, his friend nodding wildly.

'How do we know that is the truth?' Mac asked. 'You've been caught stealing, which is bad enough, but... you've stolen from convicts.' Mac paused as his words sank in then he went on, 'There are burglars here and murderers too. How do you think they will feel about you pinching their hard-earned gold?'

'Look, mister...'

'Please, mate!' The men began to gabble and Mac shook his head.

'Who are you and where are you from?'

'Joseph Archer.'

'Eric Ryder. We live over west in the shanty town.'

Mac shot a quick glance at John, who grimaced. 'Do you have family?' Mac's attention was once more on the men, who nodded vigorously.

'I have four kids,' Joseph answered.

'And I have two, another on the way,' said Eric.

'I take it you can't find work?' Mac asked.

'No, sir.' Their answers came in unison.

'Well, boys, there will be no more pilfering from my land so what will you do if I let you go?' Looking down at their tattered boots, neither spoke. 'I see, steal from someone else, eh?'

'Look, mister, we've tried everywhere to get work and can't so we're reduced to pinching so we can feed our families!' Joseph said indignantly.

Mac saw the fierce pride in the man's eyes and knew what he'd been considering would be the right thing to do. 'If I offered you a job, could I trust you?'

'Yes, sir!' Eric replied quickly.

'Can you work with cattle?' Pete asked at a nod from Mac.

'We'll soon bloody learn!' Eric's statement made everyone smile.

'Fair enough. Be here at seven on the dot each morning and report to Pete. BJ here,' Mac pointed to his friend, 'will pay your wages every Friday evening. I warn you, any thieving and I'll let the men deal with you, is that understood?'

'It is, sir!'

'Mac's the name. Joseph, Eric, welcome to the ranch. *Do not* make me regret this decision.'

'We won't, sir – Mac – honest to God!' Eric blabbered, feeling overcome with emotion.

'BJ, fetch me the tin from the office, please.' BJ knew Mac meant the tin box in the desk drawer where the petty cash was kept. Taking a lamp with him, BJ walked off and a few minutes later was back, passing the box to Mac. 'I'll give you a couple of pounds each to see you through until pay day. Take it home to your wives to feed your children.'

'Thanks, Mac,' Eric said, taking the money. 'We don't deserve your kindness.'

'Oh, you'll be making up for it, don't you worry. Pete will work you hard and the other blokes will be watching you both like hawks.'

'Right enough,' Joseph agreed.

'All right, go home and don't forget – seven sharp tomorrow.'

'Thank you, Mac,' Joseph said and both tipped their hats as they walked out followed by Mac, BJ and the others.

The workers were still waiting in the yard as the men came out onto the porch and Mac took a breath and yelled, 'Joseph and Eric are joining our team as of tomorrow.'

Grumbles of disbelief echoed on the night air and Mac held up his hands for quiet. 'I'm giving them a second chance, fellas, just like I gave some of you. And if they let me down, they know we'll comb the shanty town looking for them.'

Again the buzz of conversation rippled through the gathered crowd and Mac knew this time it was different. The men were thinking... *There but for the grace of God!*

The crowd parted, allowing the two new recruits to walk between them before disappearing into the darkness. Then they all drifted back to their beds.

18

In the bakery living room, Sylvia was livid after hearing about Philip running out on her sister. 'I bloody knew this would happen!' she growled. 'How's our Joan?'

'She ain't good, but she's made up her mind to have the babby,' Doris replied.

'Christ, what a mess! I could kill that man!' Sylvia clenched her fists as she spoke.

'We should forget him now and all rally around Joan,' Alice said, hoping to calm Sylvia's anger.

'Yes, poor kid. The gossip will be rife.'

'Not when folk know he's absconded, leaving Joan to deal with the aftermath all on her own,' Alice reminded her.

'Well, people will know, believe me!' Sylvia's anger bubbled up again. Then on a thought she said, 'Alice, you'll need to fill her place at the bakery when she's due.'

'We'll worry about that when the time comes. For now, Joan needs all the support we can give her.'

'Maybe we could ask everyone to knit summat for the little 'un,' Doris suggested.

'Good idea,' Alice concurred. 'I'm sure she'd appreciate that.'

'I'd better get off then. I'll see you later,' Doris said with a sigh before leaving Alice and Sylvia to their work.

* * *

Philip had boarded the train and heaved a sigh of relief as it trundled out of the station. Throughout the journey, he stared out of the window but saw nothing of the passing landscape and dirty houses shoved close together. He had some misgivings about what he was doing but not enough to return and face the music. He did feel bad about leaving Joan but he put his own happiness first. He thought long and hard about what his mother had finally divulged about his parentage and wondered what Carter Wainright-Jones was like. Clearly he was a cad, and they were made of the same stuff if the man had disappeared, leaving Elise in the same condition as Joan was now. Yes, it was his family who had made the decision, but had Carter cared enough he would have fought to marry Elise. Although Philip didn't know his birth father, he knew they dealt with sticky situations in the same way.

Philip heard the steam whistle blow and felt the train begin to slow down. Liverpool station was just ahead; one leg of his journey was complete.

Donning his hat and coat, Philip moved towards the carriage door as soon as the train came to a halt. Alighting, he directed a porter to lift down his luggage. Paying the man a coin to mind his trunk, Philip looked around for the shipping office.

'That way, sir, if you need to book a passage,' the porter said, pointing to the end of the platform.

'Thank you. Bring that if you would be so kind.' Philip nodded to his trunk. Pushing his way through the gangs of rowdy sailors, Philip cursed under his breath.

The porter led the way off the platform and out of the station. 'Just along the road and it's on your left.'

Thanking the porter, Philip dragged his trunk, wishing he'd only brought a valise instead. Finally locating the right office, he walked in and on towards the ticket window. 'I'd like a passage to America on the next available ship, please.'

The ticket officer checked his ledger. 'There's one leaving on the morning tide but you'll have to be quick, sir.'

Philip paid his money, grabbed his ticket and hurried in the direction pointed out to him. Coming to the jetty, he showed his ticket and was led to a rowing boat. 'That will take you to your ship, sir,' the inspector said.

The men who rowed lugged his trunk aboard, swearing loudly as the boat sank lower into the water. 'Come on then, get in!' one said.

Carefully Philip stepped into the vessel and immediately sat down on the small wooden seat at the far end.

The men began to row and the boat sped across the water where it reached a huge tall ship gliding gracefully alongside.

'Up you go,' one of the rowers said, pointing to the rope ladder hanging over the side.

'Where's the gangplank?' Philip asked.

'What would it rest on – water?' the other rower laughed. 'Go on, we ain't got all bleedin' night!'

Philip scrambled onto the ladder and climbed up; he was helped aboard by a sailor. 'Good evening, sir, sorry about that but we moved from our berth an hour ago because we are getting ready to leave in the morning.'

'Oh, I see. Thank you.' Philip watched his trunk being roped and hauled aboard.

'If you'll follow me, sir, I'll show you to your cabin,' the sailor said jovially. Philip did as he was bid and frowned when he stepped into the tiniest room he'd ever seen. 'There you go, your luggage will be along shortly.' The sailor knuckled his forehead and walked away, leaving Philip to glance around him. There was a small bed which fitted neatly into an alcove, a tiny table and a chair. An oil lamp, which was already lit, sat on the table with a box of Swan Vestas matches.

Philip groaned as he sat on the hard bed. This was to be his home for God only knew how long.

There was a knock on the open door and a young boy dragged Philip's trunk inside. With a grin, the boy left, pulling the door closed behind him.

'Whatever am I doing?' Philip whispered into the silence of the cabin. Then he jumped as he heard footsteps on the deck above him. Putting his head in his hands, he wanted to weep. He just knew this was going to be a nightmare voyage and he was feeling extremely sorry for himself.

After a short while, Philip pulled himself together and stripped off his over clothes. Finding no wardrobe, he draped his garments over his trunk. He did, however, see another door, which he opened tentatively, where he discovered a sink and a toilet which proved to be no more than a seat over a bucket.

Closing the bathroom door with another sigh, he climbed into his bed and, seeing his feet cramped against the wall, he swore profusely before pulling up his knees and turning over.

Not realising he'd been asleep until he woke with a jolt, Philip felt the ship moving and, getting out of bed, he glanced through the little round porthole window. One minute he saw a grey sky and the next the dark blue water. Philip went back to his bed as his stomach lurched in time with the roiling of the ship.

'Dear God, save me from this voyage and – from women!' he muttered, pulling the blanket over his head.

19

'Shanty towns have sprung up all over the country around the major towns and cities where men come looking for work dragging their families along with them. When they arrive, they have nothing, so can't afford housing of any sort. That's when they throw something together out of anything they can beg, borrow or steal,' Mac was explaining.

'Bloody hell, it's just like home, the no work problem, I mean,' Colin said.

'I expect it's the same everywhere if you did but look,' Clem agreed with a nod.

'The shelters are made from wood, tin or in the direst cases, cardboard. The people live cheek by jowl and, as you can imagine, sickness is prevalent in the shanty towns,' Mac continued.

'Can't the government help?' BJ asked.

Mac shrugged. 'I've no idea, I don't know anything about politics. Suffice to say nothing is being done to help those poor buggers.'

'That's why you gave Joseph and Eric a job,' James put in.

'Yes,' Mac answered.

'Won't they tell the others who live there? You could have folk crawling all over the place if they do,' Colin said, looking rather worried.

'I doubt it. What little I know of that community is that they keep themselves to themselves where money and work is concerned. When they do get a job, they don't want anyone else moving in and taking it from them so they keep tight-lipped about their good fortune.'

'That's understandable,' BJ muttered. 'I wonder if we will see them in the morning.'

'I think we will. In fact, it would be my guess they'll be here before Cookie gets breakfast started,' Mac said with a laugh. Then, glancing at the clock, he added, 'Which isn't that far off so I suggest we get some sleep.'

'I'm going for a pee first because that's how come I was up in the first place when I spotted our would-be thieves.' BJ stood and raced off to the latrine, the others ambling back to the bunkhouse.

As they left, Mac thought, *I hope I haven't made a mistake here tonight, because I don't fancy trying to hunt those fellas down. It probably wouldn't be worth the effort anyway.*

However, Mac's hunch proved right when, only a handful of hours later, Joseph and Eric were waiting in the yard ready to start work.

BJ took them to the canteen to eat while John sorted out some better clothes than those they stood up in. After breakfast, the two new additions to the workforce were added to a group who were mending fencing. Realising how lucky they were, Joseph and Eric worked hard all day, knowing there were many eyes on them the whole time.

Come finishing time, Mac instructed Cookie to box up some food for the two men to take home for their families.

That, along with the advance on their wages, would help tide them over until pay day and ensure their children didn't go to bed hungry.

As the week went on, Joseph and Eric proved their worth working in the hot sun, even emptying the latrines, without complaint. Needless to say, Mac was relieved that trusting his instinct had not let him down.

One afternoon a few days later, Pete and the drovers returned to the ranch earlier than usual. Sliding from his horse, Pete tied his reins to the hitching post and ascended the steps to the big house. Knocking on the office door, which was ajar, he stuck his head around it. 'Big storm coming in, Mac.'

'Thanks, Pete, best let everyone know.'

'Will do.' Pete strode away to find BJ, John and Jack Simpkins who would send messages to those working further afield to get back to the ranch and help batten down the hatches.

When Pete found BJ and warned him about the coming storm, BJ asked, 'How are those cattle that had foot and mouth?'

'It's not looking good. I'm thinking Mac may have to put them down.'

'That's a shame.'

Pete nodded. 'It's a lot of money to lose as well.'

Going their separate ways, they saw men rushing about, moving or tethering down anything that could fly away in a high wind. The shutters on all of the buildings were secured and the corral gates were checked to ensure they were fastened tightly. The horses were in their stalls and the cattle out on the plain would find their own safe haven. All that could be was done; now everyone settled down to wait out the bad weather.

Overhead, the sky turned grey as the wind began to gather speed. Slowly the clouds changed to a charcoal colour before they became almost black, bathing the ranch in an eerie darkness. Large raindrops splatted onto the dry earth, kicking up dust as they landed. Suddenly silver-white forked lightning split the sky and almost immediately a loud clap of thunder boomed. The rain fell in earnest, quickly turning the yard into a quagmire, the wind blowing it nearly horizontally.

The men sat indoors watching as the lightning, streaking in different places, shot between the spaces in the shutters. The thunder rolled while the rain hammered the roofs. Occasionally peeping out of the door, they saw the yard fill with water as the rain fell too fast to drain away. The buzz of conversation mainly centred on how they would be up to their knees in mud when work resumed after the storm abated.

All night the wind howled as it slammed against the buildings but by morning all was calm once more. The sun was strong and bright when the men rose for breakfast, although the grumbling was loud as they trawled through the mud on their way to the canteen. It would only take a couple of days for the earth to be baked hard again, but in the meantime a lot of boot polishing would take place.

Mac asked Pete to ride into town and request the veterinarian to make a visit with a view to culling the diseased cattle. Mac would have the paperwork ready for the man when he arrived, detailing when and where the cattle were purchased, and most importantly, who they were bought from. This was necessary for the veterinarian to follow up in case the vendor had more sick animals which would need to be put down.

Glad now that he always kept his new stock corralled away from the main herd, Mac hoped this was a solitary case and had not spread to other ranchers. He also prayed the person who had sold them in the first place was unaware of the sickness. There would be hell to pay if they knew and were getting rid of the diseased animals in the market regardless.

By that evening, Mac's sick beasts had been killed by order of the vet. They were burned and the ashes and bones were buried in a trench at the edge of Mac's land. The rest of the herd had been inspected and pronounced fit and well by the vet before he left to chase up the seller from the information Mac had provided.

BJ tapped the open door of the office and walked in. 'Sorry about the cattle, Mac.' Mac nodded then indicated BJ take a seat. 'On a brighter note, the rain washed away a lot of loose dirt on the field and revealed a lot more gold. The men are out there even now with lamps ready for when they're needed.'

Mac grinned. 'I guess they won't be seeing their beds tonight then, eh?'

'It's looking that way. In fact, I think I may go and give them a hand,' BJ said.

Mac jumped to his feet, saying, 'And I think I may join you!'

20

Doris checked the table in the large bakery kitchen one last time. Dishes of food were set out and covered with clean cloths. Cutlery and condiments sat at one end next to the pile of plates. With a nod of satisfaction that she'd done all she could for Sylvia's wedding reception, Doris went to the living room to have a moment's rest. Absent-mindedly she rubbed her abdomen as she listened to the excited giggles coming from the bedrooms.

'It's mad up there!' Jake said as he entered the room, fiddling with his cravat.

'Come here, son, let me do that for you,' Doris said. Tying her son-in-law's neckwear, she patted his chest. 'There you go.'

'Thanks. Oh, look at the time! The cab will be here in a minute.'

'I wish our Sylvia was going to the church from here,' Doris said.

'This isn't her home, though, Doris. Union Street has been for years now,' Jake said gently, not wishing to upset the woman he thought the world of.

A knock to the door heralded the arrival of the cab which would take Jake to the Union Street bakery, from where he would escort Sylvia to St Bart's church.

Donning his overcoat, top hat and gloves, Jake kissed Doris's cheek. 'See you at the church.'

Sophie, Joan, Phoebe and Mary rattled down the stairs one after the other, all with radiant smiles.

'You all right, our Joan?' Doris asked quietly as she fussed with her daughter's hair.

'I am, Mom, I'm so happy for Sylvia.'

With a nod, it was all Doris could do to hold back her tears as she watched her daughters put on their outdoor clothes.

'Mom, cabs are here!' Phoebe yelled as she glanced out of the window.

Some brides preferred to walk to their weddings, but Doris had booked cabs; she wanted her family to arrive in style.

'Right, you lot, let's get gone.' Doris ushered the girls out of the room towards the front door.

'Oh, look, it's raining,' Mary said, holding out her hand to catch the huge drops.

'Ar, bloody typical! Get aboard, Mary!' Doris said as she locked the door behind her.

The journey to St Bart's was short as the church was at the top of the street known as Church Hill, and on arrival the women alighted and stepped smartly into the building.

The medieval church dates back to the sixteenth century as the date on the pulpit testifies – 1611. In 1855, the upper part of the spire was completely rebuilt and its eight bells were recast. A further two new bells were added as well as a new clock and weathercock.

Inside, the light shone through the stained-glass windows, shooting fingers of coloured rays like a rainbow. The pews were filling with family and friends, all eager to see the bride on her special day.

Alice was already there so once Doris had quietened the bridesmaids, she went to join her friend. 'Bloody hell, it's cold in here!' she said, making Alice smile. 'Is our Sylvia all right?'

'Yes, she looks beautiful, Doris. She and Jake should be along any minute.'

Doris crossed the aisle to where Grayson was nervously waiting.

'Doris, this is Samson Fowler, my best man.'

Doris's eyes widened as she shook hands with the handsome young man with a face as black as coal.

'I'm very pleased to meet you, Mrs Wilkins,' the man said, his smile showing even white teeth.

'Same here,' Doris replied.

'Samson kindly offered to step in after Philip...' Grayson began.

'That's very good of you,' Doris cut in with a smile.

Guests chatted quietly as they claimed a seat or changed with someone else so they could sit with friends or colleagues, then the organ struck up a jolly tune.

'Right, won't be long now. Good luck, son.' Doris returned to sit next to Alice, whispering, 'Have you seen him? Grayson's best man.'

'I have, isn't he good looking?' Alice replied with a chuckle.

Doris nodded. 'Bit of a shock though.'

The woman playing the organ suddenly slammed her hands on the keys and everyone stood and turned to watch the bride begin her walk down the aisle. Sylvia's arm was threaded through Jake's as they slowly moved forward, followed by the bridesmaids. Everyone had broad smiles, including Grayson, who turned to watch his bride-to-be coming towards him. It was all he could do not to cry with happiness and he was comforted by a reassuring hand on his shoulder from his best man.

Sylvia was excited and couldn't wait to reach her intended but she maintained her composure as she glided along.

'Oh, look at her!' Doris sniffed, accepting the handkerchief Alice held out to her.

Coming to a halt in front of the vicar and next to Grayson, Jake stepped back and the service began.

Paul, you would have been so proud – of all of your girls, Doris thought as she dabbed away her tears of joy.

Everything went smoothly as Sylvia and Grayson said their vows loud and clear for everyone to hear. Sylvia beamed as the ring was placed on her finger and then came the time for the wedded couple to share a kiss. Grayson placed his lips on hers and Sylvia closed her eyes, savouring her first embrace as a married lady. Thanking the vicar, Grayson turned his new wife to face the congregation where spontaneous applause rang out. Then Mr and Mrs Atherton walked happily, arm in arm, towards the vestry to sign the register before going to the cloak-room to collect their coats. Rushing to the waiting cab to get out of the rain, they then set off for their reception. As one cab moved off, another took its place until everyone was being ferried to enjoy what promised to be a fine feast.

Back at the bakery the beer, gin and wine was flowing freely and the kettle was kept on a low heat for those wanting tea. Doris and Alice removed the cloths from the table, revealing sandwiches of ham or cheese next to plates of pork pies and sausages. Out of the oven, pots of faggots in gravy and stew with dumplings were brought steaming to the table. Fresh bread was sliced and buttered and everyone tucked in hungrily.

The wedding cake made by Alice's Bakery sat in pride of

place on a side table where it was safe from people moving around the kitchen.

All the staff from the bakeries were there as well as neighbours and old friends of the family. Doris noticed, as did others, how Samson Fowler and Phoebe spent a long time chatting. Feeling a shiver run down her spine, Doris shook it off; she knew she was meeting trouble around the corner, fretting about the future for them both. Clearly the two were taken with each other and Doris began to worry. If they were destined to be together then she would not stand in their way but she knew they would face hardship along the way. A black man and a white woman were bound to be talked about, even possibly ostracised. Doris also took note of the glares Mary was sending her sister. *There could be trouble there*, Doris thought as she watched her daughters.

'Come on, Doris, sing us a song,' someone called out, breaking her train of thought. After a little cajoling, Doris agreed but only if the rest of the guests promised to join in with the chorus.

The more alcohol was imbibed, the noisier the guests became, until raucous singing and dancing broke out. Doris took centre stage, lifting the hem of her skirt and kicking out her feet as she sang at the top of her voice – badly.

The day turned into night and finally people began staggering away with thanks and a piece of wedding cake after seeing Grayson and Sylvia off on the first step of their married life. They had decided to live in Grayson's house, which was a three-bedroomed place across town, but for now they were journeying to their honeymoon. In time-honoured tradition, no one asked where they were going, and only the best man knew that the newlyweds were having a week at the seaside.

Joan, Sophie and her husband Jake, along with Alice, Mary

and Phoebe set to clearing away and washing dishes and Doris collapsed into her armchair and was snoring gently almost immediately.

Finally ready to return to the living room, Alice felt someone catch her arm.

'Alice, I'm worried about Mom,' Phoebe said.

'Why?' Alice asked, noting everyone who had stayed to help stopped to listen too.

'She keeps getting bellyache and I don't think drinking milk is helping any more.'

'Has she seen a doctor?' Alice asked.

'No, she won't go.' It was Sophie who answered.

'Then call in the doctor to see her,' Alice said.

'She'll go bloody mad!' Mary put in.

'Maybe but it will be too late then, and at least we'll know what the problem is,' Alice said simply.

'I'll go first thing in the morning,' Jake said. 'She won't suspect because she'll think I'm off to work.'

'Let me know the outcome, please,' Alice said as she reached for her hat and coat.

'I'll walk you home,' Jake offered.

'No need, I'll get a cab, but thank you.' Alice gave everyone a hug and, seeing Doris was asleep, she left quietly.

Stepping out into the cold dark night, Alice shivered as a cab rolled slowly towards her. Was her friend very ill; moreover, was she going to die? Stemming the threatened tears, she climbed aboard, calling out her destination in a croaky voice.

21

_____

'What are you doing here?' Doris asked the man standing in front of her the following morning.

'Jake fetched me,' Dr Robinson answered.

'What for? Who's poorly?'

'You are, by all accounts,' the doctor said kindly, laying down his little bag. 'Now let's take a look at you.'

Jake ushered everyone out of the living room, giving Doris some privacy.

'Jake tells me you have bellyache all the time,' the doctor began.

'It's only indigestion,' Doris cut across him.

'Oh, so you're a doctor now, are you?'

Doris blew out her cheeks before submitting to a thorough examination and answering a lot of questions.

'So what's up with me?' she asked eventually.

'In my opinion, you have what we commonly refer to as a bad gut,' Dr Robinson answered as he called in the rest of the family.

'Charming!' Doris spat.

'What that means is – look, all you have to do is to change your diet and you should be fine.'

'Diet? I don't have a lot to eat as it is!'

'Change *what* you eat, Doris!' The doctor shook his head and turned to Jake and Sophie. 'Your mother must cut out tea and coffee. She's allowed boiled water flavoured with ginger or honey or chamomile. Avoid milk, sugar and fatty foods. Bananas, white rice, toast, crackers and broth are to be encouraged as well as oatmeal and plenty of fresh vegetables.'

'What?' Doris was aghast. 'Cake?' she asked hopefully.

'Certainly not,' Dr Robinson said. 'Follow these rules and you'll start to feel better very soon and it will help you gain the weight you've lost.'

Jake paid the doctor's fee and saw him out with his thanks. He returned to hear Doris arguing with her daughters. 'All right, that's enough!' Jake's voice boomed, bringing everyone to silence in an instant. 'We'll have no more of this. Mom, you'll do as you're told because we're all very worried about you; none of us can stand to see you poorly.'

Heads nodded in agreement and Doris looked around at her family. Finally she acquiesced with a nod and they all breathed a sigh of relief. 'Bloody hell, I could kill for a cup of tea,' she muttered, prompting a ripple of nervous laughter.

'One honey tea coming right up,' Mary said.

Doris grimaced at the thought but as the pain ripped through her stomach she knew it was all for the best. A little while later, she sat down to a bowl of oatmeal sweetened with honey and a cup of ginger tea. 'You know what, I could get used to this,' she said, pushing her empty bowl away.

'Bloody good job because you're going to have to!' Phoebe said, grabbing her apron ready to start work.

Moving to the bakery kitchen, Mary said, 'I'll nip up to

Alice's and let her know what the doctor advised. We'll have to keep an eye on Mom to start with because you know what she's like for her cake.'

'As if we don't have enough to do,' Sophie muttered.

'Oi, you! Whatever's got into you?' Phoebe asked sharply.

'Nothing, sorry.' Sophie's words were not strictly true; she couldn't say anything to anyone as yet but in a couple of weeks' time she would be able to share her news. Sophie was sure she was pregnant but until it was confirmed by the doctor, she would keep it to herself. She was worried how Joan would feel once she found out; however, Sophie had faith that her sister would be happy for her and Jake.

Throughout the day, one or another of the staff took it in turns to go through to check on Doris, and only once did Mary find her trying to sneak a slice of cake. Doris was told in no uncertain terms to munch on a piece of toast.

It was Jake who went to inform Alice of the doctor's diagnosis; she was pleased that Doris's ailment could be kept at bay by a good balanced diet, so she decided whenever she called round she would take a couple of bananas, if she could get them, instead of a pastry.

Life went on as usual in Wednesbury for some weeks, then one morning the postman arrived with a letter for Alice and she was excited to see it was from BJ. Unable to contain herself, she went to the living room to read it. She learned of someone trying to steal something from the ranch, but BJ didn't articulate what it was. She was disappointed that he had not mentioned anything about when he would be leaving Australia or landing in England. Surely it couldn't be too much longer now. These last weeks of waiting for word of his return had dragged by interminably slowly, and with each correspondence her frustration grew.

Tucking the letter into her apron pocket, Alice went back to the kitchen. She determined when she wrote back she would ask BJ outright when he would be home; she just hoped he would receive it before he left the ranch.

* * *

Over at Church Street, Phoebe was in a world of her own. She had spent a little time at Sylvia's wedding chatting to Samson Fowler and was really quite taken with him. He had also shown an interest in her and now she was daydreaming about how it would be to walk out with him. She had learned he wasn't married, which had pleased her immensely, but when she might come into contact with him again was anyone's guess. What she was sure of was, should they ever be in the position where he would ask to see her, she would jump at the chance. For now, however, she had to content herself with hoping they would meet again soon. What she didn't know was Mary was harbouring the same feelings for the handsome young man.

22

The end of another week in Fremantle saw an unusual sight – a wagon arrived at the ranch stacked with barrels of beer. As they were unloaded and stored in the barn, BJ went to search out Mac. Finding him in his office where he spent most of his time, BJ asked, 'What's going on?'

'We're having a party,' Mac responded without taking his eyes from the paper held in his hand.

'What for?' BJ pursued.

'For you and your pals. You'll be on your way in a week and the blokes wanted to give you a good send-off – as it were.'

'Oh, what a lovely thought. That's great. Mac, are you all right?'

Mac held out the piece of paper for BJ to read. 'Bloody hell!' he exclaimed before returning the letter to his employer and friend.

'Indeed.'

'What happened?' BJ asked.

'I haven't a clue. All I know is what's in here.' Mac flapped the page in the air. 'Joe Burton has died and the funeral is tomorrow, after which I have to meet with his solicitor.'

'Probably for the reading of his will,' BJ remarked.

Mac nodded. 'Why have I been notified though? We've been sworn enemies for years.'

'Maybe he's left you something – you know, like a sheep,' BJ teased but when Mac didn't laugh, he went on, 'but you'll find out tomorrow.'

'Fetch John and tell him you're both coming with me,' Mac said, laying the letter on his desk and stabbing a finger on it.

After a moment's thought, BJ asked, 'Tomorrow – isn't that a bit quick?'

'The letter is a week old, judging by the date.'

'So, who has been running the sheep station in the interim?'

'My guess would be that swine of an overseer, Eli Kane,' Mac answered with a snarl of utter distaste.

BJ left the office calling out for John, knowing he would be, as usual, in the schoolroom reading. He explained the situation and John frowned.

'What's wrong?' BJ asked.

Taking a breath, John began. 'Many years ago, Mac met a lovely lady by the name of Amelia Winters. He instantly fell in love with her and they became betrothed.'

BJ listened intently as John continued. 'However, Joe Burton knew of this relationship and decided he too wanted the hand of the beautiful Amelia, because with her came a lot of money from her father – a dowry of sorts, you could say.'

'Why do I think this isn't going to end well?' BJ muttered.

'Probably because it didn't. Joe and Amelia were married very quickly and when Mac found out he was, as you can imagine, furious.'

'What did he do?'

'There wasn't much he could do, BJ. It was done; his heart was broken.'

'What happened to Amelia?'

'Apparently she was so desperately unhappy, she hanged herself in the middle of the night on Joe's porch six months later.'

'Good grief!' BJ exclaimed.

John nodded. 'He's never really gotten over losing the love of his life. Needless to say, Mac has hated Burton from that day on.'

'So that's why he said he and Burton were enemies. Poor Mac,' BJ whispered, unable to comprehend the years of sadness his friend had endured.

BJ and John quietly speculated on the reason Mac had been invited to the funeral, and more so to the meeting afterwards with the solicitor. Unbeknown to them, Mac was doing the same thing, sitting in his office staring at the letter.

The following day, Mac, John and BJ travelled in the buggy to Burton's sheep station. On the way, Mac said, 'We are not attending the funeral this morning.' John and BJ exchanged a quick glance. 'John, you know about Amelia and I'm supposing you told BJ.' Mac was aware the man driving the buggy was all ears. 'And it's for that reason I will not see that man laid to rest because I hope he never finds it. In fact, I hope he spends eternity in the lowest fiery pit of hell!'

Neither BJ nor John spoke as they watched Mac wrestle with his anger.

Drawing a breath, Mac continued. 'So, we are only

attending the meeting with the solicitor to see what he wants and then we go home.'

Nothing more was said as the buggy rattled over the dusty dirt track leading to the sheep station.

On arrival at the front of the house, they alighted from the buggy and Mac knocked loudly. After a moment, it was Eli Kane who opened the door. The two men glared at each other before Kane stood aside to allow Mac to enter, but he put out his arm to stop BJ and John. Mac turned and, seeing what was happening, he swiped the edge of his hand down across Kane's arm, causing the man to yelp. BJ and John smiled as they strode past the man clutching his sore arm.

Entering the living room, they saw a man sitting in an armchair, a small briefcase on his lap. 'Thank you for coming,' the man said, 'my name is Terence Barclay of Barclay, Barclay & Barclay, solicitors of law.' Kane sniggered but the fellow chose to ignore him. 'I'm sorry you weren't greeted by the maid, but she quit her employ on Mr Burton's demise. Very wise in my opinion, with so many men on the station.'

Mac introduced himself and his companions as they took a seat.

Opening his case, Barclay pulled out a sheaf of papers and an envelope which he passed to Mac. 'This was addressed to you. Now let's get down to business, shall we? I am about to read the last will and testament of Joseph Burton and I would appreciate you keeping any questions until I have finished.' Looking over the top of his glasses and seeing them all nod, he continued, 'To my overseer, Eli Kane, I leave one hundred pounds...'

Kane gasped then a broad grin spread across his face as he sneered at Mac and his friends.

'The sheep station and all that goes with it I leave to Gerald McNally to do with as he sees fit.'

BJ and John shot a shocked look at Mac, who closed his eyes for a moment then let out an audible sigh.

'Please sign these documents, which are a transfer of deeds into your name,' Barclay instructed.

Mac duly signed the two papers, one of which he kept, the other he returned to Barclay.

Pushing the papers back into his case, he snapped it shut and got to his feet. 'Thank you, gentlemen. That concludes my business.' With that, Barclay walked from the room, closing the door behind him.

Mac got to his feet slapping a bag of coins on the table and, turning to Kane, said, 'Get your stuff and get off my station.'

'But...'

'*Now!*' Mac yelled. Watching Kane virtually run from the room, Mac then retook his seat. He sat staring into space then muttered, 'Why have you left all this to me, Joe Burton? Moreover, what the hell am I going to do with a bloody sheep station?'

The three men exited the house just in time to see Eli Kane, knapsack over his shoulder, being jeered off the property by workers who had clearly heard Mac's shouts from outside.

Mac walked over to where the emaciated convicts were shouting and whistling, which stopped the moment he raised a hand. 'As of this moment, I am the boss, so go and round up anyone who is not here. I want to speak to you all.' The men scrambled away, kicking up dust as they went. Turning to BJ and John, Mac said, 'The first thing is to get these fellas fed properly. Once that's done, we need to sort out showers and clean clothes for them.'

'It's my guess there won't be any showers judging by the

state of that lot,' John said, tipping his head towards the men beginning to gather again.

Eventually, when a large crowd of men was standing quietly in front of the big house, Mac spoke. 'My name is Gerald McNally but you can call me Mac, and I am now the owner of this place.' He paused as the muttering began. 'First of all – where is the canteen?'

'That building there, sir – Mac,' a forward young man spoke up.

'What's your name?' Mac asked, beckoning the young man to him. The fellow was dirty, in bare feet and stick thin. Mac inwardly shuddered at the thought of this workforce being underfed.

'Jim Cartwright, Mac.'

Mac nodded then turned to the crowd. 'First of all, I'm going to organise a decent meal for you all, then we'll decide what's to be done with this place.' He swung his arm out to encompass the station. 'I will take care of you if you are good and loyal workers. Any of my men will tell you that I'm good to my word.'

To the young man, he said, 'Right, Jim, come with me. You others go and find some shade and rest.' Turning to BJ, he said, 'See if you can find somewhere for them to wash. John, have a look for a storeroom, and hopefully a change of clothes for them all, please.'

With a nod, BJ and John went about their allotted tasks while Mac and Jim strode over and into the canteen.

'Here, what's going on?' the cook exclaimed as Mac marched into the kitchen to check the larder. Seeing it was full, he said, 'I'm Mac, the new owner. I want all the men fed – properly – as soon as possible.'

The cook threw down the cloth he had been holding. 'I can't feed all of them...'

'You can and you will or I will find someone to replace you and you can see to the sheep. Is that clear?'

The cook shivered then nodded before yelling for his assistants.

Mac and Jim returned to the yard where BJ and John were waiting. 'Any luck?' he asked.

Shaking their heads, they chorused, 'No.'

'Christ!' Mac hissed, dragging a hand through his hair. 'This would happen just as you're about to go home!'

23

'BJ, could you please ask our driver to go to the ranch and bring Alex Gough here? This place is sorely in need of an engineer to rig up some washing facilities.' Nodding, BJ did as he was bid. When he came back, he said, 'I asked him to load a cart with clothes and bring them as well.'

'I forgot about that, well done, lad.' Turning to Jim, he asked, 'How's the water level, any idea?'

'No, but I can check.' The young man walked away and before long he returned saying, 'The tank is full, Boss – erm, Mac.'

'Good, that's one thing we don't have to worry about.' Just then, Mac heard a shrill whistle and, turning, he saw the cook on the doorstep of the canteen. Stamping across, he eyed the man. 'When you wish to speak with me, you come and find me. You do *not* whistle me like your pet dog!'

'Sorry.' The man looked suitably chastised. 'The food is ready.'

Mac nodded then went to the men sitting in the shade. 'Please form an orderly queue and get your lunch.' He smiled as they jumped to their feet and stood one behind the other, eager to be fed. Mac preceded them into the canteen to see what was on offer. Lifting the lid of a huge cooking pot, he ladled the contents onto a dish. Looking at the cook, he threw down the ladle in disgust. Turning to the assistants, he said, 'Take this and pour it into the latrine pit!' Seeing them look to the cook, he snapped, 'You obey me now, not him!'

BJ and John chanced a glance at each other then watched as Mac rolled up his shirt sleeves. 'BJ, make some coffee for everyone if you would. John, give me a hand. Jim, get that lot sat down, and you...' he pointed to the cook, 'will help prepare a decent meal. There will be no more slop served to these workers!'

Applause rang out as the workers heard Mac's words, and the message was passed back down the line to those who were wondering what was going on.

It took some time to cook enough lamb, potatoes and vegetables with gravy to feed every man, but they enjoyed their drink while they waited. As the time passed, watching Mac directing the kitchen staff, the rumblings of conversation turned to joking and laughter.

Finally, Mac, BJ and John sat with more coffee as the men tucked into the first hearty meal they'd had in a good while. Then, when they had finished, Mac stood to address them again.

'Gentlemen, I'm going to be relying upon you to run this station until I can get a manager in place because I know bugger all about sheep.'

Titters broke out before someone yelled, 'That may be so, but you can sure cook a great meal!' to which they all applauded once more.

'I'm in cattle, so beef will be on the menu too from now on,'

Mac yelled over the noise which had escalated to deafening proportions. Holding up his hands, he went on, 'An engineer called Alex Gough is on his way and he will need some help setting up some showers for you.' He smiled at the cheers and whistling. 'I take it you all know Jim Cartwright?'

'Ar, gaffer, he's a good bloke,' a voice shouted.

'Good because he is the new overseer and the first job in his new role is to pull up and burn the whipping post!' Mac grinned as the men got to their feet and began to dance around.

'Gentlemen!' Mac bawled out. One by one the men sat down again. 'I need to know how this station works so we can run it properly.'

'I'll take you round and show you, Mac,' Jim said, 'just as soon as these lazy blighters get back to their jobs.' He ushered the men out, a big grin on his face at their good-natured grumbling.

Mac, BJ and John were in one of the shearing sheds when Alex, sitting next to the driver, arrived on a laden cart.

Mac quickly filled the engineer in on his inheritance and what was needed. Introduced to Jim, Alex was shown around the buildings including the castellum.

'Right,' Alex instructed, 'anyone not shearing will be working on the showers, so...' Jim saluted and ran off before the engineer could finish his sentence.

It seemed to Mac that all of a sudden there was activity where before there had been only lethargy. Sawing and hammering, whistling, singing and laughing resounded across the land and in the meantime BJ and John inspected the bunkhouses. Mac was asked to take a look at what they found. Wooden beds with thin straw mattresses alive with lice; no lockers, curtains or lamps.

'Bloody hellfire!' Mac yelled. Outside again, he called to a couple of men who were carrying the fleeces to the store shed. 'When you've done that, please take all the mattresses out and burn them – over there.' He pointed to a patch of scrubland.

'Sir – Mac – that's the graveyard,' one of them said quietly.

'Oh, there are no markers... All right, find somewhere away from the buildings.' Watching the men go off to complete their task, Mac took a deep breath.

'You all right, Mac?' BJ asked.

'I can't believe all this! What the hell was Burton doing with his money?'

'Let's have a look at his books and we might find out,' BJ said, raising his eyebrows.

Striding into the house and on into the office, BJ immediately began searching until he finally found the ledgers in the desk drawer which he passed to Mac.

Sitting, Mac placed the books on the desk and opening the first he found the last entry. With a gasp, he looked up at John and BJ, then he turned it for them to see.

'Good God above!' John whispered, bringing a hand to his chest.

BJ looked at Mac, saying, 'He had half a million pounds!'

'It looks that way, and these poor men being fed just enough to keep them alive.' Mac slammed the ledger shut, making BJ and John jump. 'John, I want the bunkhouses thoroughly cleaned out; burn the men's clothing, they can run around naked if they have to until they get scrubbed clean, otherwise the lice will transfer to their new clothes. BJ, get somebody to break into that safe, we'll need some money for new bedding.'

BJ had been glancing through the other ledger and said, 'No need, the combination is here.' In a trice, he had the safe open and was pulling out its contents to place on the desk.

Piles of money lay in front of him but Mac's eyes only saw one thing – a photograph. Amelia Winters smiled back at him from her cardboard tomb and suddenly Mac was undone.

Covering his face with his hands, he cried out his heartache for all the world to hear.

24

Doris Wilkins stepped out of her front door to see what all the shouting was about, and when she saw the line of men stretched across the road, she knew. There was a street race about to begin. The contestants in their shirt sleeves, despite the biting cold, stood bent at the waist with their weight on the back foot, ready to push off. The invigilator in his smart suit, whistle clenched between his teeth, held up his hand.

'Come on out of it, Fred Wattle, you'm too old for all this now!' a woman yelled.

'You bugger off, I ain't done yet!' came the reply from the white-whiskered man.

'Ready! Steady! Go!' The whistle blew and they were off. Hobnailed boots slammed onto the cobbles as the men raced to the end of the street, swung round the lamp post and ran back to where they had started.

The women in the bakery queue clapped and called out encouragement and before long the winner sped across the finishing line. The invigilator noted the times of each participant, including Fred Wattle, who staggered in last.

Street racing was a time-honoured tradition in the Black Country, and for those quick enough could lead to better things like a hefty winner's purse at the properly organised races.

For now, however, the men donned their jackets and retired to the nearest public house to enjoy a pint of porter.

Doris returned to her living room and her warm fireside, her memories of when Paul, her late husband, used to take part still fresh. Thin as a whippet, he could run down a rabbit in a field, forcing it to give up and just sit, completely exhausted. The thoughts brought a smile to her lips as she recalled how the older girls would shout for their daddy to win the race. Closing her eyes, Doris lost herself to remembering years gone by.

* * *

Alice, meanwhile, was visiting Ellen and Joyce at Russell Street. The order book for wedding cakes was filling up nicely, and Alice was delighted to be told the shop was being widely recommended. Church Street and Union Street bakeries were selling out quickly and the staff could only just about keep up with demand.

Mary and Phoebe were loving working with Ellen and Joyce and their cake-decorating skills were improving by the day.

It was happenstance that Samson Fowler called at the shop whilst Alice was there. She watched quietly as Samson and Ellen conducted the business of his choosing a cake for his sister's wedding. Once he had paid, Samson greeted Alice with a smile and a handshake.

'It's very nice to see you again, Mr Fowler,' Alice said.

'You too, Miss Green.'

'Well, I must be off. Please excuse me, Mr Fowler.'

'Miss Green, may I escort you to your destination?'

'Thank you but I'm only going back to Union Street.'

'Please share my cab,' Samson said, 'there is something I would like to speak with you about.'

'I'll just get my coat then.' Alice wished everyone goodbye and left the shop, being helped into the waiting cab by Samson.

Once settled and they were on the move, Samson said, 'Forgive me but I saw at the wedding that you are a great friend to the Wilkins family.'

'Yes, they are like family to me.'

'I wonder if I may ask your advice on a rather delicate matter.'

'Of course, if I can help in any way you only have to ask,' Alice said.

'Miss Phoebe and I...'

'Ah, do I detect a romance in the offing, Mr Fowler?' Alice's smile lit up her face.

'I do hope so. However... I'm just not sure how Mrs Wilkins will feel about it.'

Alice frowned. 'I'm not sure I understand.'

'Miss Green...'

'Alice.'

Samson inclined his head. 'Please call me Samson. Alice, it cannot have escaped your notice that my skin is black.'

'Samson, Doris won't mind a bit about that, I can assure you.' Alice drew in a breath and went on. 'I take it Grayson told you about Philip Sanders leaving Joan in the family way before absconding as you so kindly stepped in as best man.'

'He did and I have to say it was a dastardly thing to do. The man should be horse-whipped.'

'Then you will understand that Doris will be worried for both Phoebe and Mary.'

'Of course and rightly so,' Samson concurred.

'If I were you, I would go and visit Doris. Speak to her and let her know your intentions. I will warn you, though, Doris is a straight talker.' Alice grinned and was heartened to hear him laugh loudly.

The cab halted and Samson helped Alice to the pavement.

'Thank you, Samson.'

'No, thank *you*, Alice. I'm going to see Mrs Wilkins right now before I lose my nerve.'

'Good luck,' Alice said. She waved him off and went into the bakery, hoping her advice was sound and the outcome would be a happy one for all concerned.

Throughout his journey, Samson's nerves jangled. Then, as the cab drew to a halt, he straightened his shoulders before stepping down onto the pavement. He entered the bakery and as the crowd of waiting customers stared, he said confidently, 'I'd like to see Mrs Wilkins, please.'

Doris was very surprised when Joan led Samson into the front room.

'Mrs Wilkins, thank you for seeing me. My name is...'

'Samson Fowler. Yes, I remember. Take a seat, lad, and tell me what I can do for you.'

With a smile and a nod of his head, Samson said, 'Thank you. Alice said you were a straight talker.'

'She's right. Tea, Mr Fowler?'

'Samson, and yes, please, Mrs...'

'Doris.'

Doris made tea for Samson but stuck with her new regime of honey tea for herself. 'Bloody doctor said I have to drink this muck!' she said as she retook her seat. 'I appear to have a *bad gut*, so he tells me.'

Samson's laughter boomed out. 'I know a drink I think you

would like much better. It's made from sorrel flower, orange peel, ginger, cinnamon, cloves, brown sugar and lime.'

'Now that sounds lovely.'

'I will bring you some next time we see each other.'

'Ta very much. Now then, to business, lad.'

'I wish to know how you would feel about your beautiful daughter, Phoebe, walking out with me.'

'I see, and what does our Phoebe say about it?' Doris asked.

'Alas, I have not, as yet, asked her as I thought it important to speak with you in the first instance.'

'Look here, Samson, I have one daughter in trouble by a man...'

'Doris, let me state here and now that my intentions are entirely honourable. I know of Joan's... predicament, and how she was left by that cad. I swear to you that Phoebe will come to no harm from me or any other as long as I have anything to do with it.'

Doris looked him directly in the eye for a long moment then said, 'Fair enough. If our Phoebe agrees, then you have my blessing.'

'Dear lady, I cannot thank you enough.'

'You can. Just send me some of that drink you mentioned 'cos this is shit!'

They burst out laughing and Samson and Doris knew they were going to get along very nicely indeed.

25

Doris and Samson talked for a long time about how Doris had lost her husband and how her daughters had rallied around her. Samson explained he had come over from Africa and how it had taken him an age to get used to the cold weather. He said his parents were both deceased and his siblings still remained in the country of his birth. He told her of how he had studied hard to learn the language and to become successful in his work.

Doris suddenly said, 'You do know you'll both have to put up with dirty looks and snide comments, what with you being black and our Phoebe being white.'

'I realise that and I can weather it. I just hope Phoebe can.'

'The remarks won't be said to your face, Samson, but they will be within your hearing. Not everyone is as forthright as me.'

'Would that they were. The last thing I want is for Phoebe to be upset.'

'So, you said you studied hard, what do you do for a living, Samson?'

'I'm an accountant.'

'Like Grayson.'

'Yes, we are in partnership, Atherton & Fowler. We joined forces only last year and fortunately we are doing very well. In fact, I really should be on my way to doing some work.'

'Thanks for calling round and being so upfront and honest,' Doris said. 'Come to tea this evening and you can speak to our Phoebe then.'

'I look forward to it. Until later,' Samson said, picking up his hat and coat.

Doris saw him out, thinking what a nice young man he was. It was then she recalled the black looks Mary sent her sister at the wedding. *Black looks*, Doris tittered at her own wit, then instantly realised how it could be interpreted by other people. *I'll have to be very careful about that.*

She went to the family kitchen to prepare a roast dinner: a joint of pork with all the trimmings. Once the meat was in the oven, she nipped to the bakery for a Victoria sponge and a chocolate cake.

'Is this for tea?' Sophie asked.

'Yes. We're having a visitor,' Doris answered.

'Oh, who?'

'Samson Fowler. He's coming to ask our Phoebe if she'll court him.'

'What?' Sophie's eyes widened in surprise.

'Is that going to be a problem?' Doris asked sharply.

'No, I just wasn't expecting it.'

'Speaking of expecting,' Doris whispered as she pulled Sophie to one side, 'I'm thrilled for you, sweetheart.'

'Mom! How did you know?'

'Lovey, I've had five of my own. I won't say a word; you tell everybody when you'm ready.' Doris smiled warmly and, taking the cakes, she retreated back to her own kitchen.

Two grandchildren on the way, Doris thought proudly as she set the table. *Sylvia could be next.* A warm glow spread through her as she pottered about.

Phoebe and Mary were the last in from work and Doris called them both into the living room. She told Sophie and Jake, Phoebe and Mary about their visitor who would be arriving shortly, and, seeing the look on Mary's face, said, 'There's someone out there for you, darlin', you just ain't met him yet. So be happy for your sister and don't break your heart over summat you can't have.' Doris hugged her daughter tightly.

'I know, Mom, I was just hoping...' Mary left the sentence hanging. Then, turning to Phoebe, she said, 'I am happy for you. I hope it all works out well and we can have another wedding!'

Phoebe's face was a picture of surprise as Mary hugged her, which then turned to a big grin.

'Right, come on and get washed and changed. Samson will be here in a minute.' Doris smiled as Jake stood back while the girls made a dash for the stairs in order to change out of their work clothes. 'I'll have a wash in the kitchen, Doris.'

Exactly on time, Samson arrived with flowers for Doris and was made welcome. Doris ushered Jake, Sophie and Mary into the kitchen to help dish up the food, leaving Samson some privacy to ask Phoebe to be his sweetheart.

A short while later, Doris called for everyone to come to the table and, judging by the smiles, she knew Phoebe had said yes. Plates of steaming hot food were placed in front of those sitting and once the food was consumed, the conversation began. Mary was a little quiet at first, her disappointment evident, but after a while she began to tease Phoebe about choosing a wedding date. She couldn't help but laugh at the shock written on Samson's face.

'You'll get used to this lot before too long,' Doris said, tilting her head towards her daughters, 'just give as good as you get.'

'I'll do my best,' he replied.

'Thank God there's another bloke here now, I was being suffocated by all these women,' Jake joked.

As the evening wore on, the banter became louder and the house was filled with happy noise, much to Doris's delight.

By contrast, over in Union Street, Alice was eating alone. She had forgotten how it was to live on her own, and now that Sylvia had wed and moved out Alice felt the emptiness keenly. She found she was talking to herself and realised it was almost like she was suffering a bereavement. After washing the dishes, Alice sat down to write to BJ. The pen hovered over the paper as she wondered again if he would receive it, or whether he would have left the ranch before it arrived. Putting the pen down, she sat back in her chair. Staring into the fire, she knew all she could do now was wait to hear from him. It was already October so surely he would write her one last letter if only to let her know when to expect him home. A shiver of excitement made the hair on the back of her neck stand on end. BJ would be coming back soon, maybe he would arrive in the next few weeks. He could already be on his way!

The same questions came to mind as they had so many times before such as where would BJ live? He couldn't reside under her roof; they weren't children any more, innocently cohabiting under a shelter out on the heath. They were adults now and the gossip could ruin her reputation and bring shame on them both. No, he would have to find a boarding house until other arrangements could be made. He would also have to look for a job, though the poverty was so high in the town that it told its own tale; there was no work to be had.

Slowly the fire in the grate died down and Alice did her rounds, checking all doors and windows were secured, the ovens were safe and the guard was placed in front of the fire. This nightly ritual had stemmed from when a fire destroyed the bakery in which she was staying. Jethro and Josie Green had taken her in when BJ was deported and Jethro had taught her all he knew about baking. One night, she woke smelling smoke and she tried desperately to rouse the Greens but unfortunately they had already perished and Alice only just got out in time herself. She had lost two very dear friends whom she loved and she thought of them every night as she went through this routine. Then she turned off the gas lamps and went wearily to bed.

Tomorrow was another day closer to seeing her beloved BJ once more.

26

While Alice had been wishing her life away in her eagerness to see her childhood friend again, BJ was being kept busy helping Mac sort out the sheep farm.

Alex, the engineer, had men working on building showers at the back of the bunkhouses; Mac had asked his driver to take John to town with the cart to fetch what new mattresses they could get and order more. Whilst there, John was to place a regular order with the grocer for fresh food to be delivered every few days, with the invoices to be paid monthly.

Mac sat in his new office, now staring at the photograph of Amelia, the woman he had loved and lost. Then he opened the envelope given to him by the solicitor. Pulling out the letter, he read on.

Dear Mac,

I want you to know how sorry I am for buying Amelia from her father. I knew you loved her, which I can now admit I never did.

Mac clenched his teeth hard enough to break them before reading further.

> *I had no idea Amelia was so unhappy, Mac, I swear it, not until I found her lifeless on the porch. Passing my sheep station on to you is my way of trying to make up for what I did. I know I don't deserve it but I hope one day you can find it in your heart to forgive me.*
>
> *Your one-time friend, Joe*

Mac screwed up the letter into a tight ball as he thought, *there is no way I could ever forgive you, Joe Burton, for what you've done, and I hope you burn in hell for all eternity!*

Mid-afternoon, John arrived back, saying there were some mattresses on order and the ones the merchant had in stock were now piled on the cart. Also on there were lamps and oil but before they were put in place John wanted to check the sleeping quarters had been scrubbed and disinfected against lice.

BJ had commandeered a couple of carpenters to knock together lockers for each convict, and a couple of hours later a cheer went up as the first shower was finished.

Mac went outside and was met by Alex. 'The showers are only rough and ready but they'll work so at least the men can get clean.'

'Thanks, Alex.' Mac's eyes swept over the land. 'I've just realised what's been troubling me. Where are all the sheep? The ones not being shorn, I mean.'

'Good question. I hadn't thought about that,' Alex answered before following Mac who had stepped off the porch to find his new overseer. 'Jim, where are all the other sheep?'

'Out in the pasture. Do you want to go and see?'

Mac nodded. 'Where are the horses?'

'There's only the one that pulled the boss's buggy.'

'Christ! This gets worse at every turn. Come on, you and me in Joe's buggy it is then.'

Mac drove and when they reached the pasture he was dumbfounded. 'When were these poor beasts last shorn?' Jim shrugged, saying he didn't know.

Sheep barely able to walk because of their heavy fleeces were ambling about or lying down bleating loudly. Mac swung the buggy around and headed back to the farm. Jumping down, he said to Jim, 'Round up some men and fetch those sheep to the shearing stations. I want them relieved of their fleeces by morning.'

Jim sped off and Mac watched as a handful of men walked off the yard with their overseer. 'Why the hell were those sheep not shorn?'

'Maybe Burton forgot they were there, or perhaps he just lost interest in the place,' BJ remarked. 'It's ramshackle, every-thing is falling down.'

'It's possible, I suppose,' Mac muttered.

'This is madness, Mac, all these men underfed and with nothing to do when the shearing was finished so they tell me,' BJ said.

'There will be plenty of work for them now because I'm selling the sheep off.'

'Oh, when did you decide this?'

'Just now. I know nothing about sheep and I'm too old now to learn, BJ, I'm a rancher, always have been and always will be. I'm turning this into a cattle ranch so get somebody to take down that sign.' Mac pointed to the name board over the gates, *Burton's Sheep Station*, 'and get a new one up. In the next few days, I'd like the sheep and fleeces gone to market. The shearing sheds can be pulled down and the wood used for corrals.'

'These men know nothing about cattle, Mac,' BJ proffered.

'They soon will. I'll ask some of my ranch hands to come over and teach them.'

'Mac, there you are,' Alex said as he wandered over. 'I can pipe water here if you wish; same as on your ranch.'

'Where from?' Mac asked as he glanced around.

'There.' Alex pointed to the trees in the near distance. 'I've checked it out and it won't be as much work as it was before as it's nearer. We can use the same system laying pipes to a castellum to be filled, then more pipework to the station. Exactly the same because I'm fairly sure the pressure will be sufficient to fill the tanks.'

'Good on yer, mate,' Mac said with a grin. 'I've just told BJ the sheep are going, to make way for shorthorns.'

Alex nodded and walked away.

As the sun set around 6.30 p.m., BJ and John ensured each bunk had a mattress which had been delivered an hour earlier, having been brought directly from the manufacturer. The rest of the bunks were coming the following day which the men were looking forward to. All work halted for the men to eat a good healthy meal for which the cook was praised by Mac. Then the shearing resumed, by the light of oil lamps placed strategically and safely around the sheds, each man taking a turn before the animals were released to spend the night crowded into pens.

Hours later, with only the moon and stars lighting the way, Mac, BJ, John and Alex sat on the cart as the driver took them home, tired and still somewhat shocked from the whole day's proceedings.

'Tomorrow night we're having a party,' Mac said, 'to say

goodbye to you and your friends, and I think it might be nice if those fellas could come and join in.' Mac threw a thumb over his shoulder, indicating the men on the sheep station.

'We have enough carts to transport them,' BJ said, suddenly feeling sadness bite as the day of his leaving drew nearer.

'So be it.' Mac lay down on the cart and watched stars blinking alight. *I hope you are up there, Amelia. Wait for me, sweetheart, I'll try not to be too long.*

* * *

The following day, Pete chose a few of his drovers to join him in herding some of the sheep to town for sale. The fleeces were ready to go as well, stacked in bundles on a cart. Pete was also tasked with buying some horses; the men on the new ranch would need to learn how to ride. It was going to take many days to shear the hundreds of sheep still left on the station so as soon as a decent number were relieved of their heavy coats, they would be taken to market.

Jim organised a team who would pull down the shearing sheds once the sheep were finally gone, and Alex was busy with calculations and diagrams. BJ ensured those working on the showers knew what they were doing, while John checked the cook and his assistants were happy in their jobs.

BJ was walking back to the big house when a man called out to him, 'Sir, I wonder if I might have a word.'

'I'm BJ, not sir.'

'I am Dr Wynne Jones and I'm from Wales.'

'Doctor? What happened to bring you out here?'

'Theft, I'm afraid. You see, the hospital I worked in at home was hoarding money rather than spending it on the patients. So

I stole it and bought medicines to give to those poor devils who needed them.'

'You were reported, I take it?' BJ asked.

'Indeed I was and now I'm here. So, I was wondering...'

'If you could set up a hospital?'

'Yes, but there are no medical supplies or equipment. There are bound to be accidents at some point as well as diseases, coughs and colds, etc. I would imagine it would take a long time for a doctor to get here in an emergency.'

'I agree. Get the last bunkhouse on the row turned into a hospital and you're in charge. You might want to sound out anyone who might be interested in learning the basics of medicine who could help out if needed.'

'Thank you, BJ.' Dr Jones dashed off, grinning for all he was worth.

Pete and the drovers returned just in time for lunch, with each man leading two horses which were put in one of the empty sheep pens.

After their food, dozens of tired men climbed to sit on the empty carts now arriving from the ranch. Happy that the shearing had finished for another day, they watched as the carts rattled away. One by one, the convoy wound its way over uneven ground towards Mac's home.

The tantalising aroma of roasting beef drifted on the gentle breeze as the spit was turned by one of Cookie's assistants. From the canteen, the smell of freshly baked bread wafted across the yard and in the barn a table loaded with glasses was set up in front of the beer barrels.

Cookie made sauces, gravy and salad, and one of his helpers was frying a massive pan of chopped onions. The ranch hands had organised games with lariats which could be looped and tossed over short poles hammered into the ground, each one representing a steed, and those musicians who had instruments arranged themselves on the hay bales.

As they arrived, the men from the sheep farm stared at all the activity, but as they climbed off the carts they were greeted with respect. Slowly they were drawn into the crowds where they integrated with smiles and handshakes.

Once everyone had gathered, Mac stood on a box and whistled loudly. 'Tonight's celebration is in honour of BJ, Colin, James, Clem and, last but not least, John, who will all be leaving us next week. Colin, James and Clem I've only known for a relatively short time, but they have proved their worth on my ranch, and they're nice blokes to boot. John has been here since what seems like time began.' Pausing at the laughter coming from the men, Mac then went on. 'He has been my right-hand man since he arrived and has been like a brother to me. I will miss him greatly but he knows, as do the others, that there will always be a place for him here should he wish to return.' Mac saw John's handkerchief swipe the tears from his cheeks and hurried on.

'Then we come to BJ. This young man has been invaluable to me; he found fresh water on the ranch and was instrumental in getting it piped in. Not only that but he found gold here too, which has made all of you very wealthy men.' A rousing cheer went up and BJ smiled timidly. As the noise died down, Mac resumed his speech. 'This young man has become like my son, and...' Mac cleared his throat. 'I don't know what I'll do without him. So please raise your glasses and toast with me. My friends, may your journey be short and your lives happy and long.' The toast was made before applause broke out, which was deafening as men cheered and clapped, then the music started – the farewell party had begun.

27

Sophie Harris walked away from seeing the doctor happier than she had ever been; her pregnancy had been confirmed. She and Jake had discussed the possibility in great detail and had even chosen names in readiness. Not wishing to say a word to anyone until she had told her husband, Sophie worked through the day with difficulty. She was desperate to share her news and couldn't wait for Jake to come home from work.

With the bakery closed for the evening, Sophie was helping Doris with the evening meal when Jake walked in. Immediately his eyes went to hers and she nodded. Rushing across the kitchen, he picked up his wife and swung her round before giving her a kiss.

'Hey up!' Doris said with a smile.

'Mom, we're going to have a baby!' Sophie's excitement spread through the whole family and Doris, Phoebe, Mary and Joan hugged her then Jake.

'A springtime babby!' Doris gushed. Of course, Doris had already guessed as she had told Sophie, but she had kept her tongue behind her teeth. She didn't want to spoil Sophie's surprise.

'Yes, around the same time as you, our Joan,' Sophie said.

'Bloody hell, I think I'll ask Alice if I can move in with her if we're having two screaming kids!' Phoebe joked.

'I could be joining you,' Mary added.

'You'll have to decide on names,' Doris said.

'We have already. If it's a boy we're going to call him Paul after Dad.'

'Oh, sweetheart.' Doris dabbed her eyes with the hem of her apron.

'If it's a girl, we thought Esther.'

'Two Biblical names, lovely,' Doris blubbered.

'I had thought Paul if I had a lad, but I'll have to rethink now,' Joan said, not unkindly.

'Oh, Joanie, I'm sorry,' Sophie whispered.

'Don't be. Dad will be honoured by one of us and that's all that matters. As for a girl, I wondered about Elizabeth.'

'Oh, yes!' Doris said. 'I like that as well. What about William?'

'Billy Wilkins...' Joan tried out the name. 'Yes, that sounds right to me.'

'We'll go and tell my parents after tea,' Jake said.

'Right, get sat down and I'll dish up.' Doris hummed a little tune as she piled the plates with potatoes, vegetables, lamb chops and gravy.

When Sophie and Jake had left to see his parents, and the dishes were all washed, Doris, Joan, Phoebe and Mary sat by the fire. Doris picked up her knitting and asked when Phoebe was seeing Samson again.

'Tomorrow night. He's taking me out to dinner.'

'Lovely,' Doris muttered as she glanced at her pattern

balanced on her knee. 'You've been out quite a lot lately, how's it going, sweetheart?'

'Mom...' Phoebe drew out the word in a way which made Doris lift her eyes from her needles. 'We get a lot of strange looks from people.'

Putting her knitting down, Doris gave her daughter her full attention. 'I guessed you would. In fact, it was something I talked with Samson about that first time he came to see me.'

'What did he say?'

'He said he could weather it and hoped you could an' all,' Doris replied. She smiled when she saw her girl nod.

'I wouldn't give a tinker's cuss!' Mary put in.

'Nor me,' Joan added.

'Look, lovey, if it came to pass that you and Samson make a go of it and should wed, you'll have folk talk; probably behind your back. There will come a day when you overhear it and it will hurt like the devil, especially if you have kids. Now I would suggest you think about it long and hard and if you ain't sure you can face it, then tell Samson now before it's too late.'

'I don't care about myself. It was you – my family – I was concerned about.'

'Don't you go worrying about us, darlin', you concentrate on yourself and that nice young man of yours.' Doris smiled again as she went back to her knitting, which would be keeping her very busy over the next few months.

They all settled down in front of the fire and chatted happily about the forthcoming additions to their family.

* * *

The following day, Sophie went to tell Alice and Sylvia her news and was hugged until she ached. After she left, Sylvia said, 'Alice, why don't we make Joan and Sophie a christening cake?'

Alice's mouth dropped open. 'What a marvellous idea! We could ask Ellen and Joyce to organise it, once we know whether they have boys or girls. I'll pop round this evening and discuss it with them.'

'You never know, other customers might be inspired to order christening cakes too.'

'Sounds like we could be extending our fancy cakes with a baby range then,' Alice said with a grin.

'That would be so nice,' Sylvia said wistfully.

I think Sylvia is getting broody, Alice thought with an inward smile.

That evening, while Alice, Ellen and Joyce discussed Sylvia's idea, Samson arrived at Church Street to collect Phoebe. Having been invited in, he presented Doris with a box, inside which were tiny linen parcels. 'Sorrel tea in those,' Samson pointed out, 'tamarind in those, and these are mango. Steeped in hot water or cold, they are all delicious.'

'Ooh, thank you!' Doris said, grinning all over her face.

'Should you decide you like them I can put in an order from my supplier on your behalf.'

'Very cloak and dagger,' Doris said with a laugh.

'Not at all, it will save you the walk across town is all,' Samson replied. Turning to Phoebe, who had just walked into the room, he gasped. 'Oh, my! You look beautiful!'

With a fierce blush, Phoebe thanked him. 'I won't be late,' she said to her mother as the happy couple said their goodnights.

When they had left, Doris hurried into the kitchen to make tea for Joan and Mary and a 'special' for herself. Sitting before the fire, Doris sipped her drink. 'Oh, this is bloody lovely!' she said. 'Here, have a try.' She passed her cup to Joan who took a sip and nodded and then Mary did the same.

'It is. Maybe Samson could get us all some,' Mary said.

'I'll ask him when he brings our Phoebe home.' Without her realising, Doris's taste buds had gone on a Caribbean journey, leaving her feeling warm and content – with no bellyache.

28

On the morning of 15 October 1868, Mac sent for BJ, Colin, James and Clem to present them with their Certificates of Freedom. John, although he'd received his years ago, joined the little coterie.

'There you are, you're all free to go now.' Mac felt the tug at his heart, knowing that in three days' time he would be waving them off from Fremantle port. Big grins adorned the faces of the men Mac now thought of as his friends while he shook their hands one by one. 'Another few days and you'll be sailing for home.'

'I can't believe we've survived it!' Colin said. 'Seven years!'

'We just have to manage the voyage now,' BJ said, teasing his pal.

'Oh, God! The seasickness,' James wailed.

'With luck it will be all smooth sailing,' Clem added. 'Mac, you made this possible for me and I'll be forever grateful.'

'All I ask is that you each drop me a line to let me know you've arrived safely, and a note every now and then telling me about your lives in England.'

'Provided you do the same,' BJ said.

As they trooped out of his office, Mac said, 'We'll finish off the beer tonight.'

Keen to keep themselves busy and repay Mac for his kindness, BJ and John took the buggy over to the new ranch to see how things were progressing while Mac had a horse saddled and rode into town. He had to see Rory Cranston about selling their latest haul of gold so he could pay out to those who were leaving. BJ and his friends were set to receive a very large amount of money for all their hard work, and Mac decided money belts would be a wise idea, so he decided to purchase some after seeing the gold buyer.

BJ had placed his Certificate alongside Alice's letters in his locker beside his bed before he'd set off to the sheep farm.

His mind was on Alice as he watched the workers building corrals and clearing land of debris.

'BJ, have you come to lend a hand?' Alex's voice snapped him back to the present.

'You want me to work on my release day?' BJ replied, grinning.

'Oh, my boy, congratulations!' Alex shook BJ's hand, a beaming smile on his face. 'You'll be going home then?'

'Yes. Three more days and then back to cooler climes.'

'That will take some getting used to again, I'm sure,' Alex said.

'Yes, I'll bloody freeze in the winter months!' He laughed along with the engineer as they watched the work being done.

'Are you digging out a castellum?' BJ asked.

'Indeed. As before, digging and pipe laying – all jolly good fun.'

'For you maybe, but I remember how hard it was on the muscles,' BJ said.

'Ah, but look at them now.' Alex laughed as he play-punched BJ's arm. 'Best get back to it or that lot will have reached England before you do.'

BJ watched the engineer walk away, recalling the days and weeks they had worked together. Again a sadness touched his heart at leaving all this behind. This time next week he would be on the ocean, probably comforting Colin or James as they hung over the side of the ship, a green tinge to their faces. At least on this voyage they would be a little more comfortable, having a cabin rather than a hammock in the hold. They would be months at sea and he wished he could just click his fingers and be home. Maybe one day someone would find a quicker way to travel such great distances, but for now the only way was by tall ship gracefully negotiating the vast expanses of water.

As the sun began to set, BJ and John set off back to the cattle ranch, both ready for a cool drink and a hearty meal. Then, after dinner, Mac presented the five free men with their money belts. 'I've been to see Rory and he's coming the day before you leave so you'll each have your share to take with you. What I will say is that you are all very, very wealthy men.'

The next couple of days passed in a blur for BJ until finally he and his friends were called to the office with their money belts to join Mac and Rory. He watched Rory weigh the gold on his small set of scales before making his calculations. His eyes widened as the money was counted out onto Mac's desk.

'As you know, I would normally pay by bank draft, but Mac told me you fellas are leaving tomorrow and would need cash,' Rory said.

'Thanks, Rory, it's much appreciated,' Mac said.

'Best of luck to you blokes,' the gold buyer said as he left Mac's office to return to town.

Mac checked each man's chit and divided their share, which

was placed in their money belts and put into the safe until the following morning. 'You can collect these after breakfast, then it will be off to your ship,' Mac informed them. 'It would probably make sense to say your goodbyes this evening.'

'It's finally happening,' Colin whispered.

'I don't think I'll really believe it until we set sail,' James added.

'Tomorrow – breakfast then shower, shit and shave, then away we go!' Clem's comment made them all roar with laughter and the tension was broken.

None of the five men due to leave the ranch slept that night. Instead they crowded around BJ's bed and spoke in whispers. They discussed, yet again, what it would be like back in their hometowns; what the weather would be like and how they would cope with it after the searing heat of Australia.

James spoke of finding himself a wife, which Colin agreed would be sensible for him too. Clem, who would miraculously become George Newman the moment they arrived to board the ship, could talk about nothing other than finding his daughter. BJ was excited about seeing Alice again but John didn't seem to be caught up in the joy the others were feeling. When his friends asked him why, his reply was simple. 'I'm scared.'

BJ frowned in the darkness of the bunkhouse. 'Why? What of?' he asked.

'Because England will be alien to me. I've been here for so long I feel part of the land.'

'John, you don't have to go if you'd rather stay here.' It was Colin who spoke.

'I know, but I'd like to see England again before I die.'

'Bloody hell, John!' James said.

'What I mean is, if I hate it back at home, I can always come back here.'

'Well, there is that,' BJ concurred. 'The way I see it is this – tomorrow is the start of yet another great adventure, and we should make the most of it.'

'I recall you saying much the same thing about our coming over,' James said. 'Blue skies, watching the birds and fish, strolling on the deck in the sunshine. What did we get? A hammock alongside fifty other men down in the belly of the ship!'

Their quiet titters were muffled to avoid them waking the others who were sleeping peacefully but the gentle buzz of their conversation continued until the sun's first rays lit up their excited faces.

29

Alice tore open the letter postmarked Australia and quickly scanned the contents. BJ was free at last, but how long would it take for him to come home? It would be months surely, she thought. She tried to work it out but she really had no idea. She paced the living room in frustration. He would most likely land at Liverpool then travel to Wednesbury by train.

Sitting once more, Alice burst into a paroxysm of tears; pent-up anger at the Justice of the Peace who had sent BJ away, sadness at being unable to see him and missing him for all these years, and relief at him finally having completed his sentence pouring forth like a dam bursting.

Sylvia's voice cut through her emotions. 'Morning, Alice.' Coming to where Alice sat, she saw her friend sobbing. 'Whatever is the matter?' she asked, rushing to wrap Alice in her arms.

Alice passed the letter over for Sylvia to read. 'BJ's coming home! That's fantastic!'

Alice nodded as she dried her eyes. 'I'm not sure when though.'

'He's been away seven years and you've coped. Look around you and see what you've achieved in that time. Three bakeries working flat out; a business which is going from strength to strength. You have a new family in the Wilkinses, and you are respected in the world of business.'

With a sad smile, Alice nodded. 'I just want BJ back safe and sound.'

'I know and he will be. Just a little while longer and he'll be knocking on your door, a big grin on his face.'

Alice's smile lost its sadness and a new joy radiated out as she thought about Sylvia's words.

'That's better. I'll make you a cuppa before the others come in, we have another busy day ahead of us.'

Sylvia was proved right as customers came and went in a never-ending stream. Trays of rock cakes, lemon curd tarts, shortbread, gingerbread, seed cakes and a host of other delicacies were selling out faster than ever. Small threepenny loaves had all gone by lunchtime, as had the coffee cake and chocolate cake.

During the early-afternoon lull in trade, Sylvia said, 'Alice, this is ridiculous! We really can't go on at this pace.'

'I know but what can I do?' Alice was up to her elbows in flour as they talked.

'It's a shame that place next door ain't up for sale because you could extend into there.'

As they continued to work, Alice mulled over the idea Sylvia had put into her head. The building she had referred to housed a business selling everything from buckets to tea cloths, tap washers to oil lamps. Alice wondered how well the shop was faring with these things available to buy cheaper on the market.

Over the following days, the seed Sylvia had planted in

Alice's mind grew until she finally decided to have a word with
Grayson. He would, as her accountant, be able to tell her how
much she could afford to pay if she could persuade her neigh-
bour to sell.

Discussing this with Sylvia quietly a week later, when the
work day was at an end, Alice was pleased when Sylvia said,
'Come to dinner tonight and chat with Grayson then.'

'Thank you, I'll look forward to it.'

Later that evening, dressed smartly, Alice hailed a cab and
rode to the Athertons'. Greeted warmly, Alice explained Sylvia's
idea over their meal.

'You have more than enough money in the bank to
purchase the premises, Alice, but getting the fellow to sell to
you could be the stumbling block,' Grayson advised.

'That's my concern too. For all I know he could have a
thriving business and not want to part with it.'

'I suppose the only way to find out is to ask. Of course, you
would have to decide how much you would be willing to pay
should he agree.'

'There again, without seeing it, I wouldn't have a clue,' Alice
admitted.

'If it would help, I'd be happy to accompany you.'

'That would be a great help and I'd be ever so grateful.'

'I can manage tomorrow at two o'clock as I've had a cancel-
lation in my diary.'

'Great, I can too, the shop is a little quieter early afternoon,'
Alice said.

'Oh, you two just swan off and leave all the work to me,'
Sylvia teased.

By the time Alice left that evening, the arrangement was
made that Grayson would come to the bakery at two on the dot
and they would approach the owner of the shop next door

together. In the cab on the way home, Alice was feeling excited at the prospect of extending into the building next to her bakery. She just hoped the man was amenable to her proposal, and if so he wouldn't ask an exorbitant amount.

Home safely, Alice went straight to bed and in the darkness of her room she thought, *If I can buy that property then setting it up and staffing it will keep my mind off worrying about BJ*. With a smile, Alice closed her eyes and fell instantly into a deep sleep.

* * *

The following day, Grayson arrived exactly on time; Alice had washed and changed and was waiting, a box of cakes in hand. Together they left the bakery and entered the shop next door. The little bell announced their arrival and a voice yelled, 'I'll be right there.'

Alice took a moment to look around her. The shop was dark despite the light trying to come in through the window. There was a counter along one wall behind which there were rows of shelves reaching to the ceiling stacked to capacity with all sorts of things: tins of furniture polish, boxes with labels dirty with overuse. The other walls were the same, and there were stacks of buckets, brushes and mops cluttering the floor space.

A short man Alice guessed was in his fifties hobbled through from a back room and promptly sat on a stool behind the counter. 'Arthritis, you know,' he said. 'Now, what can I do for you?'

Sell me this place, Alice thought, but said instead, 'I'm Alice Green from the bakery—'

'I know who you are, my dear. I'll bet there ain't a person round here who doesn't.'

Feeling a little disarmed, Alice blushed. 'I was wondering... that is... I'm sorry, this is Grayson Atherton, my accountant.'

'Aha!' the man said. 'Pleased to meet you, sir, my name is Ezra Connors. I have a feeling you're not interested in buying *from* my shop, but maybe the shop itself.'

Alice glanced at Grayson, not knowing what to say.

'Miss Green would be very pleased to discuss the possibility if you decided it would be worth your while to sell up.'

'I see. Well, may I call you Alice?'

'Please do.'

'Be a dear, Alice, and lock the door, then follow me. I think tea is called for. You can't negotiate with a dry throat.'

Alice passed over the box she had brought with her. 'Maybe a little cake with our tea?' she said with a cheeky grin. Then she went to the door and shot the bolt before following Ezra into the back room.

'Tea first, then we can talk,' Ezra said, limping away to the kitchen.

Alice gave Grayson an excited look and with his hands out he raised and lowered them, gesturing for her to calm down. With a nod, Alice took a deep breath. The next hour or so would decide whether she'd be the owner of another bakery – or not.

30

'I'm surprised you agreed to speak with us so readily, Mr...'

'Ezra.'

Alice inclined her head.

'It's like this. As I said, the old arthritis is playing me up something chronic now so I've been thinking maybe it's time. I've been here for – God knows how long and there's nothing I'd like more than to move to Brighton where my sister lives. She's getting on a bit now, as am I, so for us to be together at the end would be nice. We're the only two left of eight siblings, therefore I'd be glad to spend some time with her before we pop our clogs.'

'I understand but I'm sure you would be at the seaside for many years to come.'

'That remains to be seen. If I were to agree to sell to you, what would happen to my stock?'

'Naturally I would compensate you for any you don't sell,' Alice said.

'I suppose I could have a half-price sale while it all went

through,' Ezra said thoughtfully. 'I tell you what, while I enjoy some of this cake, why don't you two go and have a look around. That way you'll know if the place will be any good to you.'

'Thank you, Ezra,' Alice said as she and Grayson moved to the kitchen which she was surprised to find was far bigger than she'd expected. A small scullery led to the yard with its own standpipe. Off the living room the staircase took them to two bedrooms which Alice considered would make excellent storage space.

Downstairs once more, Alice smiled as Ezra smacked his lips. 'I might just stay here and live on your cakes.'

Alice laughed. She liked this man with his twinkling blue eyes and easy manner.

'Now let's get down to brass tacks,' Ezra said. 'Is it what you're looking for?'

'Yes, it would be ideal,' Alice replied. 'I'm working flat out next door and we still can't keep up with demand so I need somewhere that can be used as a bakery only rather than a shop.'

Ezra said, 'So if I have this right, cooking here and selling from...' He nodded in the direction of her building.

'Yes, although we will still bake there as well.'

'Hmm.' Ezra picked up another cake from the box on the table and took a bite. His mind whirled as he chewed and considered; it wouldn't take long to get the paperwork drawn up and signed. The money would be transferred by the bank and he could then just get on the train to Brighton. He could leave all his cares behind and enjoy life by the sea with his sister, who he hadn't seen in an age. He eyed the young woman sitting opposite him as he munched. She must be a shrewd businessperson as he had seen the queues of women waiting to be served at her premises. Swallowing the last bite, he took Alice by surprise when he asked, 'How much?'

The discussion continued for quite a while until at last they reached an accord. Alice and Ezra shook hands on the deal and Alice said, 'I'll get a solicitor to draw up the agreement.'

'There ain't no need for that, Alice. You give me the money and I give you the deeds.'

'We should have proof of sale nevertheless,' Alice said.

'I can do that and you can both sign; I will witness the documents, then you can have a copy each,' Grayson said.

'Excellent. When do you want me out?' Ezra asked, but seeing Alice's face fall, he added, 'Sorry, what I meant was when can I go and see my sister. I'm rather keen to be off now it's all agreed.'

'I'll bring the documents around tomorrow for you to sign,' Grayson said.

'And I'll see the bank manager for a banker's draft in the morning,' Alice added.

'As for me, I'll buy a train ticket to Brighton!' Ezra said as he got to his feet and danced a little jig before dropping into his armchair with a loud groan. 'These bloody old bones!'

'The sea air will do you a power of good. Ezra, thank you.' Alice, without thinking, gave the older man a hug.

'Ooh, if I were thirty years younger,' Ezra said, giving Grayson a wink.

Leaving Ezra to his planning, Alice thanked Grayson, who raced off to draw up the sales documents, then she rushed into the bakery to tell Sylvia the good news.

'That's wonderful, Alice! I did wonder how it was going because you've been there a long time.'

'I know, I'm sorry...' Alice began.

'No, don't be, because evidently it was worth it. I expect that place will take some clearing out though, goodness knows what's in there.'

'It's so cluttered, Sylvia, I think it will need to be gutted, cleaned and re-equipped.'

'I'll bet Mom would help with that,' Sylvia suggested.

'She has enough to do,' Alice said.

'Alice, she's bored out of her mind. She takes orders for wedding cakes then has nothing to do for the rest of the day. Our Joan says she's popping into the bakery kitchen every five minutes, driving everyone mad!'

'I didn't realise. I'll have a word with her and see if she would be interested in helping out then.' Alice determined she would visit Doris that evening as she set to with her baking once more.

After closing up for the night, Alice wandered through the market on her way to Church Street.

'All right, Alice?' a man called from his stall selling tools.

'Hello, Jack.' Alice took a few steps then stopped. Going to the stall, she briefly explained about the stock in the shop next to the bakery and how it was to become hers.

'Ar, I know the place. All sorts of stuff.' Alice nodded. 'You want me to come and have a look? I could maybe sell some of it on your behalf or I could buy it from you.'

'Thanks, Jack. I'll let you know the best time to call.' Alice resumed her journey to seek Doris's help next.

Reaching her destination, Alice was made welcome as always. Once the tea was made, Alice told Doris all about her plans. 'Bloody hell, wench, ain't there any stopping you?' Seeing Alice smile, she went on, 'I'd love to give you a hand, it will get me out of these four walls.'

'You'll be taking on more staff then when the place is ready,' Joan said.

'Yes, hopefully it will alleviate the stress in our kitchen. How are you coping here?'

'We're managing but it would help enormously if all the wedding stuff could be moved over to Ellen and Joyce in Russell Street.'

'That's a very good idea, in fact, I'll see to that while I'm out tomorrow.'

'Will that mean Phoebe and I will work at Russell Street then?' Mary asked.

'Yes, how would you feel about that?'

'I'm not bothered,' Mary answered.

'Nor me,' Phoebe added.

'Good. I'll let Ellen know so she can sort out an area for you both to work in.'

Eventually Alice said goodnight and walked home. It was still cold and dark and she wished she'd left a light on at home. Going indoors, she wandered through to the kitchen and shed her coat and hat. She lit the gas lamp then opened the range door which filled the room with comforting heat. Too tired to cook, she toasted some bread on the flames and made a cup of tea. As she ate, she thought how she liked living there but sometimes the loneliness threatened to suffocate her. Then she thought of Ezra who also lived alone. If only she'd known before, maybe they could have been company for each other every now and then.

Feeling her eyelids begin to droop, Alice made sure everything was locked up and safe, then she dragged herself to bed, feeling weary to the bone. All this dashing about and stress was taking its toll on her; she needed to slow down and recoup her strength and wellbeing. She didn't want to look like a worn-out dish cloth when BJ got home.

An image of her friend in her mind brought a smile to her face in the darkness of her room. It wouldn't be too much longer now before she would see him in person.

31

Breakfast in the canteen was a sombre affair and hardly anyone spoke as BJ, John, Colin, James and Clem sipped their tea. Everybody knew these men were leaving the ranch today; some men were envious, others sad to see BJ going. He had been a hard-working, fair-minded overseer who had implemented a change in working conditions for every one of them. And no one could forget that he was the one who had found the gold which had made them all rich beyond their wildest imaginings. Not to mention, it had been his idea to pipe fresh water to the ranch, saving Mac a lot of money in the long run.

Dressed in their finest clothes, their full money belts hidden beneath, BJ and the others stood to leave. Suddenly spontaneous applause broke out with loud shouts of 'Good luck.'

BJ, feeling choked, waved and left the room, afraid his emotions would betray him and he would cry.

Mac was waiting on the driving seat of the buggy and BJ climbed up next to him. The others sat in the back with their bags which contained a winter coat and hat, toiletries and a couple of changes of clothes and underwear, as well as anything else they wished to take as a memento. BJ's bag contained Alice's letters, which were very dear to him. Their Certificates of Freedom were in their jacket pockets for easy access if needed.

The yard quickly filled with men keen to wave off their friends, and BJ noted handkerchiefs were being used to mop up tears or blow noses. Swallowing hard, he waved once more as Mac shook the reins and the horse walked on. The journey to the port was quiet as each man felt mixed emotions tugging at their hearts.

Mac drove the buggy almost to where the gangplank rested but as they alighted there was a shout. 'Oi! You can't leave that there!' An officious little man came bustling up to them, waving his arms around. 'Did you hear me? You can't...'

Mac stepped forward, towering over the man, and growled, 'Do not start with me today, not if you value your life!'

BJ and John exchanged a glance, wondering how the scenario would play out.

'But it's my job...' the man whined, instantly intimidated by Mac's size as well as his mood.

'It won't be if you're dead, will it?' Mac took another step forward.

Stumbling back, the man said, 'Well if you're not going to be long then...' He spun on his heel and rushed away.

Mac turned to see BJ grinning despite the sadness in his heart. Colin, James and Clem, who they all had to remember was now George, shook hands with Mac, giving their thanks and best wishes before walking up the gangplank, bags in hand.

John threw his arms around Mac and openly wept.

'John, if you want to, please come back anytime. I'm gonna miss you, pal.'

'Oh my God! Get me on that ship before I drown in my own tears!' John wailed, letting go of the man he'd known and loved, as a boss, for a great many years.

Mac shook BJ's hand with his tears rolling down his face unashamedly. 'I've loved you like a son and now my heart is breaking.'

BJ was undone at the words and between sobs he managed, 'I love you like a father too, Mac. I will miss you so much.' The two hugged tightly before finally BJ let go to join the others. Going immediately on deck, they stood in a line at the rail as the plank was drawn in.

Mac went to sit on the buggy, thinking he could be here a while yet. His eyes never left the men standing on the ship looking down on him as his tears rolled down his face. Around him the port was as busy as ever with cargo being loaded or unloaded; sailors were cleaning ships before they would be allowed shore leave. Vendors shouted out their prices for food sold from handcarts, the aroma drifting on the wind, and doxies roamed the street in search of anyone willing to spend their wages for an hour in a seedy room somewhere. There was the creak of a gangplank being lowered before hitting the land with a loud bang and the sound of horses and carriages rattled along after collecting passengers to be taken home. Aboard one of the vessels, someone sang a sea shanty as the work around him went on. Mac didn't see or hear any of this as he stared up at his friends, his neck beginning to ache.

Above him the men felt movement as the ship slipped her mooring, but they kept their eyes on Mac sitting alone in the buggy they had ridden in so often.

BJ and Mac stared after each other long after they were out

of sight until finally Mac turned the horses, feeling lost already without BJ and John. He cried all the way back to the ranch.

On the ship, George was shown to his tiny cabin, his bag there waiting for him, and he sat on his bunk. He took a moment to pray that his daughter was still alive, that she would be happy to see him, and that when he landed he could find her.

Colin and James shared a cabin with two small bunks, there being no more room for anything else. They chatted excitedly about how long they would be on board the *Lady Juliana*, and when they might sight England again.

BJ and John sat on their bunks, staring at each other. 'Well, we've done it; there's no turning back now,' John whispered.

BJ nodded. 'I suppose we ought to look on this as an adventure, maybe that way we won't feel quite so bad.'

'You think?'

'We should try if only for the sake of the others,' BJ replied but with no enthusiasm.

'You're right, of course,' John sighed loudly.

'Come on, let's go up top, it's too stuffy in here.'

Stepping through the door, they came face to face with Colin and James, and a moment later George joined them.

'Stroll on deck, gentlemen?' BJ asked.

'Why the hell not?' George responded, slapping BJ on the shoulder hard enough to send him staggering.

Despite themselves, all five friends burst out laughing. As they made their way up to the deck, each had the same thought – their voyage home had begun.

32

True to his word, Grayson arrived at the bakery the next day with documents in hand. Alice had been to the bank first thing in the morning and had the banker's draft in readiness. Alice and Grayson went next door and Ezra put the kettle to boil before he and Alice signed the papers, while Grayson witnessed the transaction with his own signature. Once they had exchanged the money and the deeds, Ezra went to make the tea, an excited lilt to his hobbling walk.

On his return, he said, 'I have my train ticket and I'll be off as soon as I pack a bag. I've arranged storage for everything else which I can send for when I'm settled.'

'Will you be sorry to leave the place?' Alice asked.

'In a way; I've been here for what seems like forever. It's been good to me over the years,' he said wistfully, 'but on the other hand, I'm more than ready to retire, and now I have some money I won't have to worry about living hand to mouth.'

Ezra went to the sideboard and from a drawer he pulled out a set of keys. Handing them to Alice, he went on, 'These are the spares, I'll leave mine here on the table when I go.'

Alice took the keys. 'You'd go without saying goodbye?'

Ezra smiled. 'All right, I'll pop them into you in exchange for a cake for my journey. How does that sound?'

'Fair exchange is no robbery.' Alice smiled at Ezra's cheeky grin.

Leaving the older man to his packing, Alice returned to the bakery and Grayson to his office with Alice's thanks.

'Sylvia, I have to see Ellen and Joyce about moving the wedding business to them from Church Street. I'll try not to be too long,' Alice called out.

'All right, we can manage for a while.'

Alice hailed a cab and set off for Russell Street. It was cold in the carriage and Alice rubbed her gloved hands together, wishing the better weather would hurry up. Asking the cabbie to wait, she hurried inside the shop, pleased to see it was as clean as a new pin. A queue of women wrapped in shawls against the chill waited patiently and Alice exchanged a word with a few.

'I hope as you've got some of them there sweet buns left by the time I get served,' an older woman said.

'I'm sure there will be,' Alice responded with a glance at Ellen for confirmation and smiled at her nod before she went through to the back room.

Explaining why she was there, she asked, 'Would you be able to cope with the extra work?'

'Yes, because Phoebe and Mary will be here to help,' Joyce answered.

'Don't forget the christening side of the business too though,' Alice reminded them.

'If it gets too much, we'll let you know,' Ellen said. 'Oh, while you're here...' Ellen picked up some sketches and passed them to Alice.

'Ellen, these are amazing!' Alice gushed as she leafed through them. Cake designs, in full colour, of baby carriages with pink or blue blankets were laid out before her. There were babies in white swaddling clothes, their tiny eyes closed, all made from modelling paste. 'My goodness, you are incredibly talented.'

'We thought we could use the same ingredients as we do for wedding cakes,' Joyce added.

'Joyce, you are a treasure,' Alice praised her friend. 'Well done, both of you.'

After a well-deserved cup of tea, Alice left her delighted staff and returned to Union Street where she immediately got to work. There were lots of customers who were waiting in line, but happy to use this time to gossip.

* * *

A couple of days later, Ezra brought round his keys to Alice. 'I wish you every success,' he said as he accepted a box of cakes and pastries.

'And I wish you a long and happy life with your sister.'

After shaking hands, Alice watched Ezra climb gladly into a cab, and as it moved off, a hand holding a Queen cake waved through the open window.

Alice laughed and went back indoors. Now the hard work next door could start. Ezra's shop needed to be emptied, cleaned, painted, refitted and re-stocked. Alice gave herself a mental reminder to ask Janet Howard, the cleaner, if she would be willing to help out for a bonus in her wages, of course.

On Sunday morning, Jack from the market knocked on Alice's door. She was surprised to see him standing there because she had quite forgotten to give him a time to call.

'Sorry it took so long, but the market has kept me busy,' he said.

'I'm grateful, Jack. I'll just get the keys.'

They went to Ezra's shop and Jack gasped. 'Bloody hell! Oh, begging your pardon, Alice, but...' He gazed around at the shelves, full to overflowing. Stepping around a pyramid of buckets, he wandered in and out of the clutter before he blew out his cheeks. 'I can take some of it which I can sell, but the rest I have no use for.'

'I understand,' Alice said.

'I tell you what, I'll come back this afternoon with my lad and shift what I can. As soon as I sell it, I'll bring you the money.'

Alice nodded gratefully. 'That would be a great help.'

'Might I suggest you have a sale with whatever is left? Folk love a bargain and every item that sells is a penny in your pocket.'

'That's a good idea, thank you, Jack.'

Once he had gone, Alice set off for Church Street. She knew this was something Doris could advise her about and with luck her friend might even be able to run the sale for her.

Doris, just as Alice had hoped, jumped at the chance to be a shopkeeper once Alice explained about Jack and his idea.

'I'll come first thing in the morning and see what's what,' Doris said enthusiastically.

'Thank you, Doris, you're a life saver.' Alice and Doris hugged and took the time for a good natter and a catch-up before Alice left to go home.

Later that day, a horse and cart drew up outside Alice's new premises and Alice opened up for Jack and his son.

'Right, let's get cracking,' Jack said.

'I'll make some tea and fetch some cake, then I'll give you a hand,' Alice said.

All afternoon they toiled, sorting, carrying and loading the cart until Jack said, 'That's about the lot, Alice.'

'I really appreciate everything you're doing.' A huge box of cakes and a bag of bread was passed over by way of thanks. 'They'll need eating right away,' she said with a smile.

'Oh, they won't last long in our house,' Jack's son said, earning him a clip across the head from his father.

Once Jack and his son had gone, Alice looked around her. There was certainly more space now but there were still a lot of things to be rid of. Brushes and brooms, tins of polish, knick-knacks, baskets, doormats, the list seemed endless. Alice locked up feeling tired to the bone, her feet and arms aching.

Sitting in her kitchen in front of the range, Alice thought about her achievement. *I can tell BJ in my next letter.* Then she remembered she wouldn't be able to; if everything had gone to plan, he could be on the high seas even now.

33

BJ and his friends were indeed on the ocean, their tall ship pitching and yawing as she sped across the waves. The crack of the sails luffing was loud and on deck sailors were busy going about their tasks.

The young boy who had brought their luggage aboard now showed the men the privy. 'It's in the bow, or to you, the front.' A tiny cabin with slots cut near the floor allowed the normal wave action to clean it out. 'That there is the tow-rag.' The boy held up a long piece of rope which was tied securely next to a slot, the end of which was frayed. 'After you've wiped your arse, drop it back into the water. The sea will clean it.'

'Oh, dear God! I should have stayed on the ranch!' John wailed at the thought of the whole process.

'You'll be fine – just don't fall over.' The boy laughed before returning them to the deck. 'Now if you want to be sick, go to the rail at the stern.' Seeing John frown, he clarified with, 'The end.' He pointed to ensure they all understood. 'If you do get sick, drink water, otherwise you'll dehydrate and then you really will be in trouble.'

'Argh...' Colin groaned, already looking a bit green.

'Stay up top for the fresh air,' the boy said, then left them to their own devices.

'I'll never make it,' Colin said.

'Colin, we've only just set off,' BJ said with a grin, 'we have a few more months of this yet.'

This was too much for his friend. Colin rushed to the place pointed out to him and hung over the rail, much to the amusement of the crew.

'Get back to work, you lazy lubbers!' the Bosun yelled. Waiting for Colin to stand erect again, he walked over to him. 'May I suggest you stand feet well apart, sir, it helps with balance.'

'Thanks,' Colin said as he parted his feet. 'It does!'

With a nod, the Bosun wandered away to supervise the crew.

That evening, the first of their long voyage, everyone was given a drink of lime juice with a little sugar topped up with fresh water. 'It helps with the sickness and bellyache,' the on-board doctor told them.

'It's refreshing too,' John said, quite surprised that he liked it.

After dinner, the friends again went on deck. 'Look at all those stars,' James whispered.

Oil lanterns fore and aft were lit and swung gently as the ship moved.

'That's how they navigate at night,' BJ said, recalling his lessons with John. 'It's beautiful.'

'We didn't think so coming over,' Colin put in.

'That's because we couldn't see them. We were stuck down below, remember?' James asked.

'Oh, yeah.' The others laughed before Colin went on, 'I do

recall freezing my arse off at some point.'

'That would have been as you travelled through the Southern Sea rounding Cape Horn,' John suggested.

'Will we go that way back?' George asked.

'Most likely. My guess would be the Southern Sea, Cape Leeuwin, Cape Horn, Cape of Good Hope.'

'How do you know that?' BJ asked.

'I asked the captain.' John laughed loudly as his friends jostled him.

After a while of enjoying the sea air, they retired to their cabins, all hoping they would manage to sleep despite not being used to the roll of the ship as yet.

Over the next days, they all became accustomed to the ship's rocking motion, at least as far as being able to stay on their feet was concerned. Colin was still suffering with seasickness and stayed on deck as much as possible. He ate little but sipped water constantly.

Eventually John suggested Colin keep a diary of his journey; more to give him something to do to keep his mind off being ill. Amazingly it worked and Colin could be found on deck every day sketching seabirds and dolphins.

BJ noticed the further they went the more the temperature began to drop, and he realised before too long they would be crossing the Southern Sea with the strong westerly winds of the Roaring Forties. This would then bring them into the ice zone, which he vividly recalled from their outward voyage.

In the evenings, he and his friends often chatted with off-duty sailors, and on occasion they listened spellbound to someone singing a sea shanty.

John's time was taken up with reading the books he had brought with him stuffed into his trunk. James became a competent card player, joining the games of the crew, and

George spent many hours looking for sight of England, despite knowing it would be many months yet. BJ read and re-read Alice's letters until he knew them word for word, and at other times the five of them would sit quietly talking about their time on the ranch.

They all wondered how Mac was getting on with refitting the old sheep farm, and whether it was up and running yet. Each in their own way missed being a part of it, but the call of home was strong. They also knew that if their own country was no longer to their liking, they could always brave the voyage back to Fremantle.

Being gentlemen now, they were not expected to help on board, but now and then BJ would practise his knot-tying, much to the surprise of the tars. How he'd learned he kept to himself, saying only he'd worked on a cattle ranch. He had no intention of telling them he had been taught on the voyage over when he was a convict being transported.

Day by day, the *Lady Juliana* glided across the sea, bringing the men ever closer to home, and with each new morning BJ's excitement grew a little more.

34

Whilst BJ was aboard ship, Doris had opened Ezra's shop on Alice's behalf and held a half-price sale. Word soon travelled that a bargain could be had and Doris was kept busy shifting what was left of the stock.

After a couple of days, the place was virtually empty and Doris began, with Janet the cleaner, to give the whole building a thorough bottoming. The floors were swept and walls were washed down. Alice had decided to leave the shelves behind the counter in place so she could display some coloured glass bottles and pretty crockery.

Jake and his friend had given the shop a coat of whitewash and the big window was cleaned inside and out with vinegar-soaked newspaper. Doris then hung some curtains which were tied back to give the shop a homely look.

The unwanted furniture from the bedrooms was carried down and placed in the street with a notice saying, *FREE, Please help yourself*. Doris watched as each piece was held onto by a woman as her husband borrowed a cart to transport it. Wardrobes, chests of drawers and washstands disappeared as the grateful poor shouted their thanks. Now the bedrooms were empty, they would be used for storing sacks of flour, urns of milk and baskets of eggs, as well as extra baking tins and utensils.

Doris was thrown back into her life at Church Street, knitting baby clothes for Sophie and Joan once the shop was complete, and she was feeling redundant. Fed up to the back teeth, one day she decided to call on Alice, who always had an ear to lend to her friend.

'I need summat more than knitting, Alice,' she said over tea, having brought a pouch of sorrel with her which helped enormously with her stomach problems.

'I don't know what to suggest, Doris.'

'I'm climbing the walls! I have to find something to occupy my time.'

Suddenly Alice had a thought. 'Doris, do you think we could turn Ezra's into a shop again, this time selling cakes?'

'I don't see why not. The kitchen is big enough for a couple of bakers, which is what you'd planned anyway, and the front is lovely now it's all cleared out.'

'How would you fancy being shop manager there if I get a girl to help?'

'I'd bloody love it!' Doris enthused. 'So how do we go about this?'

Doris and Alice thrashed out some ideas about hiring new staff and equipping the kitchen, and by the time Doris went home, both women were excited about the new development.

Sylvia was delighted when Alice told her what she and Doris had decided. 'It was your idea in the first place,' Alice said, 'and a very good one at that.'

'You'd best get off to the Servants' Registry then and get

some new staff organised, because if I know Mom she'll be chomping at the bit to get started!'

'I'll call into the mill and grocer to increase our orders too,' Alice said as she grabbed her hat and coat.

When Alice arrived back at the new shop after completing her errands, Doris appeared. 'I'll need the keys if I'm to open up early every day.'

'Of course.' Alice went to the kitchen drawer and pulled out the keys which she handed to Doris. 'You should interview the ladies coming for the jobs as well. The only thing I ask is that they stick rigidly to my recipes.'

'Naturally because they'm winners. Look at how far you've come in the last how many years?'

'Seven. I started not long after BJ was deported.' The reminder of her years away from BJ stung yet again.

'Ar, well, he'll be back soon. Have you thought about what will happen then?'

'Often, Doris. Each time the scenario is different, but I'll be so glad to see him safe and well.'

'Has he mentioned in his letters what he'll do for work?'

Alice shook her head. 'No, but it might be he'll look for a job on a farm. He was on a cattle ranch out there so working with cows would seem the obvious choice.'

'That makes sense. Now, I'm going next door to make a list of what's needed for the kitchen. Then, if you like, I can go to the market and get it bought.'

'Excellent, thank you, Doris.'

And so it was Doris Wilkins became the manager of the new shop, adding to the string known by all around as Alice's Bakeries.

* * *

As time passed and Joan's pregnancy began to show, the snide comments started. Nothing was said to her face, as Doris had forewarned, but people's attitude towards her changed. Eyes that usually found hers moved to her belly before frowns formed. Heads shook in disgust as women left the shop, gossiping about Joan's plight.

At first Joan ignored it, determined to be strong and not let it get to her. But slowly it wore her down, leaving the poor girl in tears every evening. Doris held her daughter as she cried, trying to soothe the hurt Joan was feeling, but she knew it would never go away completely. Even when the child was born, folk would talk, trying to work out who the father was and why he hadn't done the decent thing and married Joan. At school the other kids would ask where the baby's daddy was. They would taunt the child when they found out, which would cause ructions in the school yard as well as between Joan and other parents.

One morning, Joan, looking paler than usual, said, 'Mom, I'm bleeding!'

'Oh, Christ! Right, back to bed while I fetch the doctor.'

Joan obeyed, feeling relieved she would not have to face the malevolent stares from customers.

The doctor accompanied Doris back to Church Street and went straight upstairs to Joan's room. Doris refused to leave as he examined her daughter. 'Complete bed rest if we are to save this child,' he ordered.

'I'm not sure I want to,' Joan mumbled.

'What a wicked thing to say!' the doctor boomed.

'Oi!' Doris intervened. 'Don't you speak to her like that! She's got enough to deal with.'

'I am sworn to save life...' the doctor began.

'Now you look here! Do you know what it's like having a

babby? No, of course not. My wench was abandoned after the father found out she was pregnant.'

'The man should have been made to—' Again the doctor tried to speak.

'He did a moonlight flit!' Doris raged.

'I see.'

'I don't think you do! Our Joan was impregnated by Philip bloody Sanders who turned tail and ran!' Doris was fuming and the words were out before she knew it. Turning to Joan, she said, 'I'm sorry, love, I didn't mean to tell, but I'm so bloody angry!'

The doctor quickly headed for the door, repeating, 'Bed rest.' Then he was gone, foregoing payment in his haste to be out of the place.

Doris sat on the bed, looking at her daughter.

'Well, that told him. I'm glad you're my mom and not my enemy. Did you see his face? You scared the hell out of him!' Joan said, whereupon both women burst out laughing.

35

The doctor returned to his surgery, still fuming from being spoken to as he was by Doris Wilkins. Of course the nurse was very interested in what was going on and eventually the doctor answered the nurse's questions about his visit to Church Street bakery. Naturally, with such gossip virtually burning the end of her tongue, the nurse couldn't wait to blab to everyone she met, telling them who the father of Joan Wilkins's baby was, and how he'd deserted her.

Over the next week, while Joan lay abed, the news travelled fast and eventually reached the ears of Elise and William Sanders. They found themselves being shunned at the high-class restaurants and functions. Of course they had no idea where their son was, only that he had disappeared in the middle of the night. No matter how much they protested their ignorance of his whereabouts, the upper echelon of society refused to accept it.

Over the following months, William's business suffered and Elise stopped going out of the house, unable to face the back-lash of her son's actions. Eventually, when Elise suffered a complete mental breakdown, they put the house up for sale and moved away down south to Cornwall, where they would live out their days in peace – or so they thought. It would be a little while in the future that their relationship would break down beyond repair and they would part company.

After her bed rest, and with the blessing of the doctor, Joan returned to work and was gratified to see that attitudes towards her had turned again. However, the pity on people's faces was almost as bad as their disgust, so she was still very unhappy.

One evening, as she sat by the fire with Doris and Mary, Phoebe having gone out with Samson, Joan said, 'Mom, something doesn't feel right.'

Doris looked up from her knitting to see Joan lay her hand on her stomach. 'What do you mean, love?'

'Well, I don't know. Shouldn't the baby be moving by now?' Doris nodded after a quick mental calculation. 'Well, it's not.'

'Get your coat on, we'm going up the hospital. Let them check you out.'

'What about the doctor?'

'That quack? Don't get me started – just do as I say. Mary, hail a cab.'

Both women were worried but on the short journey, Doris did her best to quell Joan's fears. On arrival, Joan was shown into a room where she could be examined. A little while later, Doris was called in to see Joan sobbing.

'Mrs Wilkins, I'm afraid I cannot find a heartbeat; I'm very sorry but it seems the baby has died in the womb.'

Doris dropped into a chair next to the bed Joan was lying on. 'Oh, my wench, I ain't half sorry.'

'We will have to take Joan in and deliver the child,' the doctor went on. Doris nodded. 'We don't have a bed for her right away so she must come back in the morning...'

'Thanks, doctor, I'll bring her myself.' Doris cut across his words. 'Come on, love, let's get you home.'

Doris and Joan left the hospital, Joan in tears and Doris in a daze. When they got home, Mary made tea before being told the outcome of the hospital visit. Mary cried as she hugged her sister.

'Mom, why is this happening?' Joan asked through her tears.

'I don't know, love. Maybe God has taken it unto Himself because something wasn't right.'

'I'm scared to go back to the hospital tomorrow,' Joan admitted.

'I know, but I'll be there with you. It has to be done, sweetheart, otherwise you could be very ill. Now go and pack an overnight bag.'

Joan and Mary disappeared upstairs, leaving Doris gazing into the fire, mentally cursing Philip Sanders. *I hope you rot in hell for all eternity for what you've put my girl through!*

After an evening at the music hall, Sophie and Jake arrived home just as Phoebe and Samson were saying goodnight. Exchanging pleasantries, Samson left and Jake led his wife and sister-in-law indoors. They knew something was amiss as soon as they entered the living room. Doris's scowl said it all.

'What's happened?' Sophie asked as she took off her coat.

Doris related all that had happened and Phoebe and Sophie rushed upstairs to be with their sister. Jake dropped into a chair. 'I'm sorry, Doris. I don't know what to say.'

'Ain't nothing to be said, son,' Doris replied. Sitting in silence, they both watched the dancing flames in the hearth, unknowingly thinking the same thing – if Philip Sanders ever showed his face again, he would not survive very long.

The following morning, after Joan and Doris had departed

for the hospital, Mary went to tell Sylvia and Alice what was happening.

'Oh, no! Poor Joan,' Alice said, her heart breaking for her friend.

'I know it sounds callous, but I'm thinking it might be for the best in the long run,' Sylvia said quietly.

'I suspect Mom thinks the same,' Mary said.

'If there's anything I can do...' Alice began.

'Thanks, Alice, I'll tell Mom.' Keen to keep herself busy, Mary left them to go on to Russell Street to start work.

'Sylvia, I'm going to the hospital to be with Doris, she shouldn't be alone at a time like this,' Alice said.

'I thought about going too but I'm not sure I could face it, and I think the others are the same else they'd be there now. I fear our sadness would make things even harder. I know Mom would appreciate your company.'

Alice donned her hat and coat, grabbed her bag and rushed outside to hail a cab. At the hospital, Alice found Doris sitting in the waiting room, twisting a handkerchief between her fingers.

'Doris, Mary told us... how are you?'

'I'm all right, it's our Joan I'm worried about.'

'Do you need anything?' Alice asked.

'A cup of proper tea.'

'I'll see to it.' Alice walked away in search of someone who could provide them with tea. Then she returned to sit next to Doris. 'Tea is coming.'

'I wish Philip would come back,' Doris whispered.

'Why?'

Alice was shocked when Doris said, 'So I can bury him!'

36

Aboard the *Lady Juliana*, Colin's seasickness abated just in time for them to experience again the ferocious winds of the Roaring Forties. Sailors fought with sails and rigging as the captain bellowed orders at the top of his voice. Dressed in capes and sou'westers, which had been coated with linseed oil and lampblack to make them waterproof, the crew worked hard in the icy rain which lashed down.

BJ and his friends stayed below deck, all cramped together in one cabin as they silently prayed that the Lord would bring them safely through the tempest.

'I wish more than ever now that I'd stayed on the ranch!' John wailed.

'We'll be all right, the captain knows what he's doing,' BJ said, hoping to goodness he was right. 'He does this journey twice a year.'

The ship rocked from side to side alarmingly and BJ glanced through the small round window, one minute seeing the sea and the next the dark roiling clouds. They looked up at the ceiling as footsteps hammered on deck.

'Cold food tonight,' James said.

'Yes, the captain won't allow a fire on board in this,' BJ agreed. 'I'm sure whatever we get will be delicious though.'

'Can we not discuss food, please?' Colin begged, feeling his queasiness returning.

'Why is it always so rough here?' George asked.

'Because we are approaching Cape Horn. The winds are the turbulent cyclones coming off the Andes mountains, and with the relatively shallow water it makes this part of the journey violently hazardous. Then we'll be in the ice zone,' John reminded them, which made everyone shiver. They had been in temperatures so hot it could kill, and now they would be passing into weather that was so cold it could freeze the sea. Their bodies could go into such shock they could drop down dead, but no one chose to think about that. All they were concerned with was getting through this latest leg of their very long voyage.

Slowly, over the next few days, the ship began to settle and everyone, including the captain, breathed a sigh of relief. Now the sails were trimmed so that the *Lady Juliana* could coast gently, the crew avidly watching out for icebergs.

The captain issued big fur coats and hats to his passengers, who were allowed on deck at last. A weak sun sat in a blue sky, casting its light on the water, glinting like diamonds.

'Iceberg ahead!' The shout came from the sailor in the crow's nest high above the deck. Everyone looked in the direction he was pointing and they felt the ship begin to manoeuvre away from the silvery-blue ice which could sink her.

BJ gasped as they passed by at a safe distance. 'Look at that!'

'Yes, but it's only 10 per cent of it that we can see, the rest is below the water, that's what makes them so dangerous,' John instructed.

The massive pale blue block seemed to float away as the ship reverted to her original course. Birds dipped and dived overhead, screeching loudly as they performed their aerial acrobatics.

'Cape Horn, gentlemen,' the captain called out, 'it should take us about fourteen days to go round her then it will be plain sailing to the Cape of Good Hope.'

'Fourteen days! I'll freeze my arse off!' Colin said.

The captain's laugh boomed out, echoing across the water. 'There's plenty to see like the Rockhopper penguins and fur seals. You might even catch sight of humpback whales.'

'Bloody hell!' James said. 'John, what's a humpback whale?'

BJ couldn't help but laugh but listened well as John explained, then told them of the storm petrels flying overhead.

Each day they went on deck to spot for whales, the smell of the sea strong in their nostrils. Plenty of hot stew filled their bellies in the evenings before they snuggled up in their bunks, the fur coats over the top of their blankets.

The captain or crew members were happy to answer any questions their passengers might have, and the wondrous journey became an education in itself.

Early one morning, James spotted his first whale. 'Look, look!' he yelled excitedly as spray leapt into the air from its blowhole. Then it breached, showing its tail before diving again. John explained how these huge creatures could sleep while swimming and how in force they would bubble feed. 'Working as a co-operative, they swim in circles blowing bubbles, which drives the fish to the surface – then they dine.'

All five of them watched in awe as the massive whale breached and dived over and over again, enjoying its freedom in the vast expanse of ocean, until it finally swam away.

'This is something we'll remember for the rest of our lives,' George said reverently.

'Indeed. Imagine if we hadn't been transported; we would never have seen all of this,' BJ added.

'I'm sure there will be more to see as we sail on,' John informed them.

Eventually, as days passed, BJ noticed the weather was getting warmer, and at a yell from the Boatswain the sailors hoisted the mainsail which luffed before it filled with wind. The ship seemed to lurch forward and before long she was speeding her way to the next cape – Good Hope.

John brought an atlas on deck one day to show the others. 'There's Australia,' he said, 'and we came here round Cape Horn. This is the Cape of Good Hope on the tip of Africa.'

'Then where?' Colin asked.

'Head for home, I should imagine,' John answered as he tapped a finger on Great Britain.

No one asked how long it would take; they felt better about not knowing in case inclement weather intervened.

BJ looked from the map to the horizon. *I'm coming, Alice, it won't be much longer now.*

37

Alice and Doris sat by Joan's bedside. She was still a little sleepy from the anaesthetic but shook her head when Doris asked if she was in any pain.

'It's gone, Mom, the baby, I mean,' Joan said tearfully.

'I know, love, and maybe it's for the best because now you can get on with your life.'

Joan nodded before drifting off to sleep.

Doris and Alice crept out of the room quietly. Outside the hospital, Alice hailed a cab, and they rode to Church Street, talking about how Joan would be feeling when she came home.

'I think she'll be sad but relieved,' Doris said, to which Alice agreed. 'She'll probably be off men for a long time an' all.'

'The only thing we can do for her now is show support,' Alice said.

'It'll be hard for her when Sophie gives birth though.'

'I expect so.'

'Then if our Sylvia has kids, then Phoebe and Mary, it will just keep getting more difficult to cope with.'

'Joan could meet and marry a nice young man in the mean-time though,' Alice said reassuringly.

'True but somehow I don't think she will. I have a feeling our Joan will be single for the rest of her life.'

'Oh, Doris, I hope not!' Alice exclaimed.

'We'll see. First we have to get her home and well.'

* * *

Joan lay in her bed, finally awake and thinking about what she'd been through. Of course it wasn't all Philip's fault, after all, it took two to conceive a child. She did blame him, however, for running out on her after promising they would be wed. Would he do this again to some other poor unsuspecting girl? She certainly hoped not. Maybe he had learned his lesson, she thought, but she didn't really believe that. Philip Sanders could just run away time after time, leaving a trail of miserable women behind him. His upbringing was such that he thought he could do whatever he liked and not have to face the conse-quences, of which Joan was one.

Well, Philip was gone and so was his child, so it would be up to Joan to rebuild her life. She would weather whatever came at her in the future, but for now she needed rest and recu-peration.

All of the family visited Joan in hospital, each having five minutes alone with her on the ward sister's orders. She was pleased to see them, assuring everyone she was fine, saying she was eager to get back to work. The walls of the long corridors leading to the wards were painted green and cream and the floor covered in linoleum. The ward itself was a huge room with high windows which let in plenty of light. There were ten beds on each side, most containing ladies of various ages. At one end sat a nurse at a desk working quietly on her paper-work. Just outside the door was the sister's office, a small room for any private consultations with visitors or her staff. Other nurses in their pristine white uniforms were bustling about, making up the empty beds in readiness for patients coming in. The whole place was sparkling clean and smelled of disin-fectant.

On the day of Joan's release, Doris collected her in a cab and once home fussed over her with tea and cake. Sophie came through from the bakery kitchen to give her a hug. Joan laid a hand on her sister's extended belly and smiled, which was all it took for Sophie to burst into tears. Joan had shown Sophie she was happy about the baby and could cope with losing her own.

Sophie didn't see the look of sadness flash across Joan's face as she returned to the kitchen – but Doris did. Her girl was putting on a brave face for the sake of the family but how long that would last was anyone's guess.

Again gossip flared as people learned that Joan had lost her baby, and once more looks of pity came her way when she finally went back to work. Joan did her best to ignore this but beneath her bravado her heart ached for what she felt she would never now have.

One evening, as the family sat around the fire chatting, Sophie said, 'I have something to tell you.'

All eyes turned to her and, patting her stomach, she said, 'The doctor says I'm having twins!'

Jake choked on his tea and Mary thumped his back as he coughed and spluttered. It was Joan who was the first to congratulate the parents-to-be, despite Jake still being in shock. This had not escaped Doris's notice and she worried about how it would affect Joan.

'The doctor heard two heartbeats through his little trumpet thingy,' Sophie went on.

'Of course he did, one was yours,' Mary said.

'Besides mine, you ninny.'

'Oh, Lord! That means you'll need two of everything,' Doris said, holding up her knitting.

Joan and Doris were the last to go to bed that night and Doris asked, 'You all right, lovey?'

'Hmm.'

'What's up?'

'It doesn't seem fair, does it?' *Here it comes*, Doris thought. 'You know, our Sophie having twins and I couldn't even manage one.'

'Joan, life ain't fair, bab, I don't need to tell you that. You having Philip's babby wasn't meant to be.'

'It was my baby as well,' Joan whispered.

'Maybe God has another plan for you, and being a mother at this time wasn't in it.' Doris was trying her best to console her daughter, but she knew Joan was grieving her loss.

'I wonder if I was having a boy or a girl.'

'Look, Joan, you have to stop fretting about what's past!' Doris said rather sharply. 'It ain't healthy. Now is the time to look forward; decide what you want to do with your life.'

'I work in a shop, Mom!'

'And what, may I ask, is wrong with that? Besides, you'm the manager.' Joan laughed but it lacked mirth. 'I can't imagine what it's been like for you, sweetheart, but what I can say is we all love you very much.'

With those few words from her mother, Joan was undone and she leant forward in a paroxysm of tears. Doris was by her side in an instant, wrapping her sobbing daughter in her arms. 'Cry it out, my little wench. Get rid of all the hurt and anger 'cos it's weighing you down.' Her own tears sliding down her cheeks, Doris kissed her child's head and rocked her back and forth, murmuring words of love softly.

Joan slowly brought her emotions under control but she stayed in Doris's arms. She felt like a kid again as she breathed in her mother's unique fragrance. She felt warm and safe and wanted to stay there forever.

With gentle care, Doris let go and pushed Joan's hair away from her face. 'You'm so beautiful, Joan, inside and out, and I'm proud to be your mom.'

'I couldn't wish for anyone better,' Joan replied with a genuine smile, 'and I love you.'

The two sat for a while longer in silence, just happy to be enjoying each other's company.

38

Doris interviewed and hired two bakers and a serving girl for what everyone continued to call Ezra's shop. Ingredients were delivered and new equipment was bought from the market and the money from Jack selling Ezra's stock, less his percentage, was paid to Alice, who was delighted.

At the bakery in Russell Street, Phoebe and Mary had become experts in the field of piping icing and making paste flowers under Ellen's tutelage.

Still living with Doris at Church Street, Sophie and Jake were happily planning for the arrival of the twins, and had asked Joan to help, which had been an enormous relief to Doris.

Sylvia and Grayson were enjoying married life, and Doris was looking forward to the grand opening of the new shop with her as the manager.

Although Alice was kept on her toes with her business, the nights for her were long. She missed having a lodger and she felt the loneliness keenly. She couldn't even write to BJ any more as she felt certain he would be on his way home by now.

There were times she wished she had someone to talk to as the evenings dragged slowly by. This living on her own was not all it was cracked up to be.

Alice began to realise that even when BJ was back things wouldn't really change for her. She would work and sleep, much as she had always done. She had no social life or a friend to go out with. A trip to the music hall would be wonderful, but women didn't enjoy these things on their own.

Glancing at the clock on the mantelshelf for the hundredth time, Alice sighed loudly into the quiet of her living room, thinking time was standing still.

Where are you at this minute, BJ? she thought. She wondered what he was doing and if he was thinking of her. She tried to imagine him on the deck of a tall ship gazing across the sea as if looking for her.

Stop it, Alice! she admonished herself as she stood to make a hot drink. *Fantasising is doing you no good!*

However, once the tea was made and she sat down again, her thoughts roamed to BJ once more. The longer time went on, the more excited she became but she was also frustrated at the not knowing. It was easier when he was on the ranch because she knew where he was, but now he could be anywhere. There was no way to contact him and it made her feel helpless.

Then, as sometimes happens with lonely people, Alice's thoughts turned dark. BJ had said in his last letter that his release date was 15 October, but he had mentioned nothing about when he would set off for home. What if he had decided that he wasn't coming back? He might like it out there too much to leave. It could even be that he'd met someone, a girl, and they planned to marry.

Alice slammed her empty cup on the table, again remonstrating with herself. *Alice, you need to do something to fill your time!*

On a whim, she went to the sideboard drawer and pulled out some paper and a pencil. Dropping into her chair, she began to consider new ideas for the bakery. Before she knew it, Alice was sketching out tall cakes, short ones, christening and wedding ones with flowers, and only when she yawned did she realise she was tired to the bone. Looking at her designs, she smiled. That would do for one night. Securing the house, Alice then went to bed, feeling better than she had in a while.

After taking her drawings to Ellen in Russell Street the next morning, Alice returned to open the bakery. She saw Doris standing by, ready to begin work selling the cakes and buns the bakers had provided over the previous couple of hours. Within minutes, a queue had formed, quite separate to the one next door, and Doris was in her element. Almond cake, lemon tart, deep-fried pastries called Cruellers, rock cakes, all were flying out of the door and by the end of the day Doris was exhausted. The staff had thoroughly cleaned the kitchen before going home; Doris made sure all was safe then she locked up and went to see Alice with the day's takings.

'You *have* been busy!' Alice said when she saw the money.

With a nod, Doris answered, 'There's enough done to fill the shelves when we open tomorrow. The girls have worked wonders today, they only stopped for a bite of lunch.'

'Marvellous, thank you, Doris. Now, how is Joan feeling?'

They chatted a while about Doris's tearful conversation with her daughter then Doris stood to leave. 'Today's bumper trade might have been because the shop only just opened,' she said, nodding to the bag of money, 'but if it ain't and we're that busy every day...'

'I know, we'll need more staff,' Alice finished the sentence.

With her legs aching, Doris treated herself to a cab, despite it not being a long walk to her home.

Indoors at last, Doris dropped gratefully into her armchair and in a matter of minutes she was fast asleep.

Sophie cooked their evening meal, not wanting to disturb her mother until it was time to eat. Sitting at the table, Sophie asked, 'Work's not too much for you, is it, Mom?'

'No, darlin', it was my first day. I'll soon get used to it so don't you be worryin' about me. You need to take care of yourself and those babbies,' Doris said, pointing with her knife.

The family settled down to chat over their food, everyone relating how their day had been.

Mary and Phoebe washed the dishes and Joan and Doris picked up their knitting. Sophie's babies would need lots of hats, cardigans and pretty blankets as well as christening shawls.

The evening passed quietly, the household relaxing by the fire until it was time to go to bed. As Doris climbed the stairs, she thanked God for her wonderful family.

39

The rocky headland of the Cape of Good Hope was in sight and the captain issued orders to downhaul the mainsail. 'Gentlemen,' he said, 'we will be stopping here to take on board fresh water, fruit and vegetables. Then we'll be off again before the seas get too choppy.' With a smile, he wandered away to yell more orders to the sailors dashing around the deck.

'Choppy?' Colin asked. 'What does—?'

'It means what he said,' John intervened. 'This is where the Atlantic and the Indian oceans meet, causing *choppy* waters. Now, if I remember correctly, it rains a lot at this time of year too.'

'Bloody hell,' Colin moaned, making the others laugh.

'Another little interesting fact is it's known as the "Graveyard of ships",' John informed them.

'Would somebody please gag that man!' Colin said, his grin belying his words.

Leaning over the rail, they watched the ship slip easily into her mooring, as sailors threw ropes to men standing on the dock. Already the cold wind was picking up and they shivered as they glanced around. Other tall ships were coming and going and the shouts of the crew echoed across the water. Once the *Lady Juliana* was tied fast, the gangplank was lowered. The crew ran niftily down to retrieve barrels of water which they rolled into the hold. Boxes of food followed and the cook took this time to prepare a hot meal for everyone. Fire on board was the biggest hazard for ships so only when they were moored were they allowed to light a brazier to cook over, although this rule was often broken. The aroma of sizzling meat wafted on the breeze and bellies began to rumble in anticipation. The passengers watched as an argument broke out on the dock, with men yelling at each other before it was settled with a flying fist. A hearty meal of beef, potatoes, vegetables and gravy was served, much to everyone's enjoyment. Then they resumed their stance at the rail, eager to be on their way.

In no time at all, they were replenished and ready to set sail once more. The ropes were dragged on deck again and the ship rocked gently as she was pushed away from the dock by sailors with strong long poles. Then she slowly manoeuvred her way back out to sea as the sails were hoisted and snapped loudly as the wind filled them.

It wasn't long before John's words proved correct and it began to rain. BJ and his friends scrambled below to their cabins, leaving the tars to their work. They felt the ship lurching as the wind picked up and churned the sea. The lashing rain kept the passengers below deck for days as the wind took up and filled the sails. The ship fairly flew across the water, gaining precious time, much to the captain's delight. Then at last the rain turned to drizzle and BJ braved the weather in the need for fresh air. He also wanted to know if there was any land he could spy. For weeks all they had seen was sea and sky and BJ's spirits dipped when he realised there was still no let-up. How far from home were they, and how much longer were they to stay on this ship?

'You all right, sir?' a sailor asked as he stepped past BJ, who was standing by the rail one morning.

'Yes, thanks. I was wondering how much longer...?'

The sailor smiled. 'Another couple of weeks and you should see England.'

BJ grinned. 'That *is* good to hear.' Turning from the rail, he hurried below to share the news.

'We've made good time,' John said. 'I thought it would take a lot longer but there again I believe these clippers are the fastest ships.'

'Liverpool, here we come!' James said enthusiastically.

'Then we'll be on the last leg, a train journey to our temporary home.' BJ patted his friend's back.

'I'm going on deck every day, no matter what the weather; I'm not missing that first sight of land,' George added.

'It would be a bugger if we arrive in the middle of the night, though, eh?' Colin teased.

George frowned, clearly not having thought of this possibility, and the others smiled. 'In that case, I'm gonna sleep in my clothes so I can be up first.'

'Not a good idea, mate, otherwise you'll look like a tramp.' Colin knew he was pushing his luck but he couldn't help himself.

'At least I'll get there. As for you – who knows?' George retaliated with a grin.

The camaraderie amongst the friends had grown even stronger during their voyage and cemented itself into an unbreakable bond. They had been through a lot over the last seven years, both alone and together, and BJ knew there were still trials to come. They had to settle again in their birth country, and although they were very wealthy men, BJ knew eventually boredom would set in if they didn't fill their days with work.

With each passing day, BJ's excitement grew. He stood on deck for hours at a time, his eyes straining as he scanned the horizon. Then, early one afternoon, a shout came from the crow's nest. 'Land ho!'

BJ followed the sailor's line of sight, searching desperately for whatever it was the tar had seen.

'There! See that dark line?' James said.

Shielding their eyes from the weak sunshine, the friends finally spied what James was pointing out.

'Gentlemen – England.' The captain had come to join them as the ship barrelled along. Each of them shook his hand, their smiles wide, then they turned back to watch England emerge. They were wrapped up warmly against the late winter weather, which they felt keenly after the temperatures of Australia.

The ship ate up the miles as she raced towards her destination, and BJ could hardly contain himself as the land loomed bigger. The sails were trimmed and the *Lady Juliana* slowed as she approached and passed the southern tip of Great Britain. It seemed they were barely moving after the speeds reached on the open sea. Eventually the tall ship inched her way into her mooring at Liverpool; the dock hands securing her ropes thrown down to them. The gangplank was lowered but the friends didn't see it, they were below, hurriedly packing their bags. These were hauled up on deck by the crew and carried onto Victoria docks while BJ and his pals said their goodbyes to all those who had brought them home safely.

The short walk down the gangplank took them onto dry land at last, where they stood a while next to their luggage, trying to find their land-legs.

'Thank God!' Colin gasped, hardly able to believe they had survived not only their penal sentence but the journey back too.

'Look at all these people!' John was aghast at the folk ambling about looking for work, as well as those doing jobs.

'Hello, dearie, fancy a good time before you go on your way?'

John turned to face a middle-aged woman dressed poorly, the red spots of rouge on her cheeks denoting her profession.

'I hardly think so, darling,' John said, much to the amusement of the others. The woman blew out her cheeks, knowing exactly why the man had refused her. A smile then spread across her face as John gave her a shilling.

'You're a soft touch, John,' BJ said as the woman wandered away.

'She wasn't my type,' John replied, making them all laugh yet again.

'Cab, mister?' a young man called out and John grinned, saying, 'Now that one...!'

BJ shook his head at his friend as they watched their bags being loaded then they climbed aboard.

BJ called out, 'The railway station, please.'

A short time later, while their bags were being unloaded, BJ went to the ticket office. 'I'd like five tickets, please.'

The ticket officer asked, 'Where to, sir?'

Then BJ said the words he had practised so often in his mind. 'Wednesbury, please.'

40

Although BJ was at last on British soil, Alice was completely unaware of that fact. BJ was always on her mind, but she had been extremely busy over the last weeks with the new shop and making sure Doris was coping. All four of Alice's bakeries were doing incredibly well, not only with bread and pastries, but also with wedding and christening cakes. She met regularly with Grayson who, as her accountant, assured her that she had a very healthy bank balance.

With Sophie very near her time to give birth, Alice had employed another baker so Sophie could be at home resting. She knew that as a new mother of twins, Sophie would not be returning to work, and Alice was pleased that her replacement had settled in well.

At the end of the work day, Alice sat by her fire with a cup of tea. This was her quiet time when her thoughts turned to BJ and where he might be. Watching the flames in the hearth took her back to when she used to build a fire on the heath. She wondered if their shelter was still there; maybe she would go and have a look one of these days. She recalled the freezing winters when she and BJ scavenged in the market trying to find enough to eat. Even now, there were youngsters doing the same thing, and whenever she was out and about she would give them a few pennies to help them.

Alice recalled the last time she saw BJ when he was in Stafford prison. They were so young then, only children, and now they had grown into adults. They had been apart for over seven years and Alice thought she could probably pass BJ in the street and not know him. He would not recognise her either, she was sure. From a thin child she had developed into a very attractive young woman, who had fought hard to build up her own business. She was well respected in the man's world in which she lived because she worked like a demon and would not be trodden on by anyone. Her reputation for being kind preceded her and the local populace loved her. Alice also remembered those who had helped her when she was younger, like the ladies on the market stalls, and she often took them a box of cakes to share.

Now, as she relaxed after a busy day, her feet propped on a stool, she realised just how lucky she was. What would make life complete for her would be if BJ would come back safe and sound.

After a bite to eat, Alice went to bed early, feeling exhausted. She had been asleep for only a few hours when a loud banging on her door woke her. Grabbing a dressing gown, she made her way carefully downstairs in the dark. Pausing only to light the gas lamp, she opened the door and was surprised to see Phoebe.

'Our Sophie is in labour. She's gone to the hospital!'

'Is she all right?' Alice asked, worried for her friend because even in these modern times women still died in childbirth.

'Yes, but the doctor said she'd be better to have her babies there. Mom and Jake are with her.'

'Come in and have some tea.'

'No, ta, I'll get back in case I'm needed. I'll let you know when we have any more news.'

'Thanks for letting me know, Phoebe.' Alice watched the girl turn and climb back into the waiting cab, thankful Phoebe hadn't decided to walk so late at night.

Alice re-locked the door, doused the gas lamp and returned to her bed. Unable to sleep now, she tossed and turned and finally, exasperated, she got up and went down to the kitchen. Feeding the range, she enjoyed its warmth as she set the kettle to boil. Leaving the range doors open, she sat with her cocoa, praying all would go well and that Sophie would deliver her babies safely.

In the early hours, there was more loud knocking and Alice rushed to open the door where Doris stood, tears rolling down her face.

'Doris! Come in.' Alice ushered the sobbing woman into the kitchen.

'Alice, I'm a grandma!' Doris managed.

'Oh, congratulations! I was so worried when I saw you crying. Is all well?'

Doris nodded. 'Sophie's tired, of course, and Jake is with her, much to the hospital sister's annoyance, but he wouldn't leave her.'

'The babies?' Alice asked as she made more cocoa for them both.

'A boy and a girl. Oh, Alice, they'm so beautiful!'

'Is it any wonder? With Sophie as their mother, how could they not be?'

Doris's grin was wide. 'They'm only little, six pounds each, but what lungs they have on them!'

Alice laughed as she sat at the table opposite Doris. 'Do they have names yet or is it too soon?'

'Paul and Esther,' Doris announced proudly.

'How lovely! Goodness, it will be different in your house when she brings them home.'

'Noisy an' all. Phoebe said she wasn't joking when she said she might move in with you!'

'She'd be most welcome, I'd enjoy the company,' Alice admitted.

'Feeling lonely, are you?' Doris asked.

'Sometimes.'

'You need to get out of this place and have some fun.'

'It's not easy when you're on your own,' Alice said a little sadly.

'I know, bab, but you can't spend your life stuck in here.'

'It might change when BJ gets back.'

Doris nodded. 'Ooh, Alice, I still can't believe I'm a grandmother!'

'Think of all the years you have to spoil those babes,' Alice said.

The two good friends talked until the light of day crept through the window, prompting Doris to say, 'Bloody hell, look at the time! I'd best get off home. I need forty winks before I open the shop.'

'I'll do it; the girls can manage so you take the day off and go to see your grandchildren.'

'Thanks, Alice.' With a hug, Doris left.

Alice yawned, but she didn't dare sleep now otherwise nothing would get done.

* * *

Unbeknown to Alice, across town BJ and his friends had arrived and booked into a hotel for the night. The travelling and excitement had left them all feeling tired to the bone and they each slept soundly on their first night on dry land and in a proper bed.

Over breakfast the next morning they discussed their plans.

'I'm going straight to see my daughter if she's still at the same address,' George said.

'Colin and I thought we'd take John around to see if he remembers anything,' James added.

'I'm off to the bakery to see Alice. I suggest we book our rooms for a week at least. That way we have a base to come back to,' BJ said.

Within the hour, they went their separate ways.

BJ walked through the market where he bought a huge bunch of flowers from the florist's shop. He smiled at people who stared at him, knowing because of his very dark skin, they thought him a foreigner. Reaching Union Street, he sauntered towards the corner where he saw queues of women lined up. Should he push through to the front or wait his turn, joining the end of the line?

He decided he couldn't wait so, going to the doorway, he asked, 'Does Alice Green live here?'

Spotting the flowers in his hand, the woman nodded before yelling, 'Mek room, wenches, there's a chap 'ere to see Alice!'

BJ grinned and inclined his head as the women moved aside. 'I'm here to see Alice Green,' he said.

Sylvia stared then mouthed, 'BJ?' He nodded and brought a finger to his lips, asking for secrecy. Then he asked the women waiting if they would shield him from sight. Happy to be part of the conspiracy, they crowded together in front of him.

'Alice,' Sylvia called as she stepped through to the back room, 'someone to see you.'

'Can it wait?' Alice's voice sailed into the shop, which was silent now as everyone waited with bated breath to see what would happen.

'No! Alice, I'm busy out here!' Sylvia smiled, as did the customers, who felt privileged to be part of whatever surprise was going on.

Alice, covered in flour, was wiping her hands on her apron as she came through to the shop. She looked around but she didn't see the man hiding behind a group of women. Rounding the counter, she asked, 'Who is it that wants to see me?'

Then the women parted, revealing a very handsome, tanned young man.

'Hello, Alice,' he said.

41

Alice's mouth fell open. 'It can't be...'

BJ grinned and nodded. 'Bertram Jordan at your service.'

'BJ? Oh, my... BJ!' Alice ran to her friend and threw her arms around him. He in turn picked her up and swung her around, the customers bursting into spontaneous applause as the two friends hugged tightly.

Holding his hand, Alice dragged him through to the back room as her tears threatened, leaving behind customers buzzing with excited comments and conversation.

'I can't believe it!' Alice gasped finally.

'Well, it's true. These are for you.' BJ handed over the flowers.

'Thank you. I wasn't sure when you would be home. Why didn't you let me know?'

'Alice, I was aboard ship for months,' he said with a smile.

'Oh, yes, of course. Sorry. Tea – I'll make...'

'Alice, sit down. We have all the time in the world to catch up.' Alice exhaled noisily, making BJ laugh. 'Look at you, all grown up and very beautiful,' he said quietly.

'You too – well – handsome, oh dear, I'm all over the place!'

Alice was about to sit when BJ caught her up in his arms again. 'I can't tell you how much I've missed you.'

Alice melted into him and whispered, 'Me too.' They stayed in each other's arms for a long time, enjoying their reunion, and satisfying themselves this wasn't a dream.

Eventually Alice pulled away. 'Welcome home, BJ.'

'Thanks. I wouldn't mind that tea now.'

Alice laughed and as BJ took a seat she went to the kitchen. Bringing back a tray complete with cake, Alice set it on the table. 'I can't get over how different you look.'

'You too,' he said, giving her a dazzling smile.

Alice's heart fluttered and she suddenly felt very shy. Pouring the drink, she said, 'I have so much to tell you.'

'And I, you.'

Looking up abruptly, she asked, 'Where did your accent go?' BJ shrugged as he bit into his slice of cake. 'You're a gentleman now.'

Swallowing, he informed her with a cheeky grin, 'And a very rich man.'

'Oh, BJ, I'm so pleased for you!'

They spent the rest of the day catching up, laughing sometimes and crying at others as each related their lives since they had last seen each other.

It was late in the afternoon when Sylvia finally came through. 'I've locked up, Alice.' After being formally introduced to BJ, she went on, 'I guessed from your suntan that it must be you. It's very nice to meet you at last; we've heard so much about you.'

'I'll bet none of it was good,' BJ said with a little laugh.

'I couldn't possibly say, but I know Alice has been looking

forward to seeing you. Well, I'm off, I'll see you tomorrow,' Sylvia said.

'Thank you, Sylvia,' Alice acknowledged.

An hour or so later, BJ stood. 'I should be getting back...'

'You don't have to.' Alice had waited so very long to see him she was loth to let him go.

'I promised to meet the others at the hotel. Besides, I will not compromise your reputation by outstaying my welcome.'

'Thank you for your consideration, but please say you'll come back tomorrow. We still have so much to tell each other.'

'I will be here early as long as it won't take you from your work.'

'BJ, I've worked hard for over seven years, so I think I deserve a couple of days off.'

'Until the morning then,' BJ said as he made for the door. Then he turned and hugged Alice until she could barely breathe.

Waving him off, Alice returned to her fireside where she gave way to her emotions. Crying torrents of relieved tears, she thanked God for bringing her friend back to her safe and well.

As the evening wore on, she relived their reunion over and over again in her mind, still unable to quite believe it. Too excited to eat, Alice went upstairs to choose something to wear for BJ's visit the next day. Making her decision of a navy-blue wool suit, she then returned to the kitchen to polish her boots. Once she was finished, she made herself a hot drink. It was late when she finally went to bed, even knowing sleep would evade her. Watching the moonbeams stretching their long fingers into her room chasing away the shadows, Alice smiled. The misery of being parted from BJ was behind her now, and they could both begin to look forward in their lives. BJ had told her about his wealth earned from the gold hunting so he would not need to seek work from necessity. She thought, however, he would choose to go into business of some sort once he had settled into living in the Black Country once more.

She guessed she would meet his friends at some point as he would meet hers. Alice had decided she would take a few days off work to spend time with BJ; the girls could manage perfectly well without her. Alice had waited and waited for this day and she wasn't about to waste one minute; she would be by BJ's side as much as possible, for now, at least.

As promised, BJ arrived bright and early the following morning. Alice explained to the staff that she was leaving the business in their capable hands before she and BJ left the shop.

'Where are we going?' BJ asked.

'The heath. I've often wondered if our shelter is still there.'

'So have I.' BJ grinned and Alice saw again the cheeky face of the boy he once was.

They walked side by side, reminiscing about their time in the makeshift home. Both were surprised to see it was indeed still standing, although only just.

'I'm amazed,' Alice said.

'I knew it would be here. My wall has stood the test of time,' BJ replied.

'*Your* wall! I seem to recall helping to build it,' Alice said as she gave him a playful push.

BJ's laughter echoed across the expanse of land. 'Shall we visit the market next?'

Alice nodded. She was happier than she had ever been as she and BJ sauntered away.

42

Colin, James and John strolled around the town, wrapped up warmly. They were really feeling the cold after the stifling heat of Australia.

'I've been away for so long and yet nothing has changed,' John said, glancing around at the grimy buildings.

'Nor will it.' The voice came from a young man standing on the corner in the bread line.

John turned and as he glanced over he thought his heart had stopped. Twinkling brown eyes beneath a mop of shiny dark hair stared back at him, and he immediately knew this man was meant for him.

'There are too many men for too few jobs,' the man added with a smile that made John shiver as he strode over to them.

'It was ever the way,' John answered, eventually finding his tongue.

Colin and James stood idly watching the exchange, small smiles gracing their faces.

'What sort of work are you seeking?' John asked.

'Anything. I taught in a school until it closed because there were not enough funds to keep it open,' the man answered.

'I was a teacher once too. We were just going for tea, would you care to join us?' John asked.

'Thank you, I'd like that as long as it's all right with your friends.' The man looked to Colin and James, who nodded their agreement. 'My name is Christopher Marshall,' he went on, extending his hand.

'John Tobias,' came the reply as John stripped off his glove to shake the other man's hand. 'This is Colin Crockutt and James Alexander.'

As the four wandered away, those left in the bread line sighed. They had not heard the conversation and had assumed the lucky fellow had just been given a job.

Colin and James led the way, looking for a café or tea shop, John and Christopher bringing up the rear.

'How about here?' Colin asked, pointing to a building squashed between two others.

John nodded and they entered the café. Taking a table at the back, they sat and looked around. It was small but well laid out with white cloths on the tables, a single flower in a vase on each. A girl in a black dress covered by a white apron approached their table with a smile.

'Can I help you, gentlemen?' she asked.

'Tea and your finest cake for us all, please,' John said, automatically taking the lead.

The girl went to place the order in the kitchen and Colin whispered, 'She could help me – a lot!'

James gave him a nudge, casting a glance around at the other customers.

John and Christopher began a quiet conversation and Colin and James exchanged a grin.

The beverage arrived and they all enjoyed the refreshments as they chatted amiably. Once finished, Colin and James decided to leave and continue their walk around the town, saying they would meet John later.

John ordered another pot of tea; he and his new friend were getting along handsomely.

'Why did you leave teaching?' Christopher asked.

'I went to Australia.'

'My goodness! Well, that would explain the tan, but why? I mean, it's on the other side of the world!' Christopher was aghast.

'I was transported,' John answered honestly.

'I'm so sorry, I didn't mean to pry. It just took me by surprise.'

'No matter. Tell me about yourself; do you have a family?' John asked.

'Not any more, my parents died years ago and I was an only child.'

Glad the discussion had veered away from his time abroad, John nodded. 'Are you married, have children?'

'No.' The answer came a little more sharply than Christopher had meant. 'I will never marry or have children.'

'May I ask why, or is that too personal a question?' John probed.

Christopher looked John directly in the eye then answered quietly, 'If my guess is correct, and I'm fairly sure it is, then John Tobias, you know precisely why.'

John flushed. 'I do, Kit Marshall.'

'Kit, I like that.'

'So do I,' John whispered. 'Tell me, where do you live?'

'Wherever I can find a space to sleep,' Kit replied.

'We can't have that. As it happens, I'm looking for a house to buy – somewhere away from prying eyes.'

'I could help you look, Toby.'

'Excellent. I suggest we start immediately.' John paid the bill and they left the café on their quest. 'Toby, nice,' John muttered as they headed for the nearest estate agents.

John silently prayed he had finally found a life partner, but he knew they would have to be extremely careful to keep their relationship a secret, otherwise he could find himself in jail, especially as transportation to the colonies had now ceased.

As they walked, John said, 'I will have to tell the estate agent that you are... my butler, maybe?'

'That's all right with me. We don't want him poking his nose too far into our business now, do we?' Kit gave John a flirtatious glance and was pleased to see John blush furiously.

'This is all very sudden, Kit, don't you think?'

'Toby, men in our positions can hardly dally around. We have to grab what we can, when we can. I don't want to spend the rest of my life wishing or regretting. The moment I saw you I knew... and I think you did too.'

'I did, but we must take things slowly, otherwise we'll get caught and jailed.' John drew in a breath and went on, 'I'd like nothing more than to get to know you.'

'Slowly it is then.' Kit grinned.

* * *

As they wandered around the town, Colin and James quietly discussed John's luck at finding a friend so quickly and both hoped it would work out for him. After a while, they returned to the hotel for lunch, both wondering how BJ and Alice were getting along. After they had eaten, they ventured out again to find a decent pub for a glass of beer and their conversation once more returned to John.

'I hope he's careful,' James said.

'Me too, but I do worry it was all a bit quick,' Colin answered. He glanced around but they were the only two in the room; nevertheless, he kept his words to a whisper. 'I mean, he doesn't know that bloke from Adam.'

'I know, but I suppose they'll have plenty of time to get to know each other a bit more. I mean, it's not like they'll be living together any time soon, is it?' James replied, happy to see Colin concur with a nod.

Neither could know at that moment just how wrong they were.

* * *

Over in the marketplace, BJ smiled as he heard Alice say, 'I recall doing that,' as she nodded towards the ragamuffins scavenging the market stalls and ground.

'It seems a lifetime away,' BJ acknowledged.

'Hello, Alice!' a woman yelled.

'Hello, Mrs O'Connell. Do you remember BJ?' Alice asked as they walked to the fruit and vegetable stall.

'I do. Bloody hell, look at you! You ain't a skinny kid any more.'

'All thanks to you for keeping us alive with your kindness,' he replied.

'Gerraway with yer,' the woman said, handing them an apple each. 'For old time's sake,' she said with a little laugh.

Thanking her and with a wave, they moved on. 'Oh, I almost forgot, I have some things of yours at home,' Alice said suddenly.

'Then I think we should go and take a look.' BJ crooked his elbow and smiled as Alice threaded her arm through his. With a spring in their step, they walked briskly back to the bakery. Once indoors, they took off their coats and Alice built up the fire in the living room then said, 'Follow me.'

BJ obeyed and in the scullery he burst out laughing. 'My wheelbarrow!'

'The very one you stole from the boy in the market.'

Holding up his hands, he answered, 'Our need was greater.' His heart hammered as Alice laughed; the sound like a stream rolling over smooth stones.

Back in the living room, BJ sat next to the fire, still struggling to keep warm.

Excusing herself, Alice ran upstairs and returned a moment later. 'I kept this for you too.'

BJ looked at the object she passed to him. 'My penknife!'

'It was so important to us back then. It cut potatoes, rope and tarpaulin; I couldn't leave it behind.'

'Thank you, Alice.' BJ slipped the knife into his pocket. 'I'll get it sharpened.'

'Let's have some lunch then I'll take you to meet Doris and her family. You met Sylvia, one of Doris's daughters, last night.'

BJ nodded. 'I'll help with lunch. What are we having? Please don't say beef because it's all I've lived on for years.'

'Lucky you,' Alice said jokingly. 'How about faggots, peas and thick onion gravy?'

'Marvellous! I'm drooling already.'

Once again, after a gap of over seven years, BJ and Alice cooked a meal together, chatting as though they had never been apart.

43

Clem Read, who had taken the identity of a dead man, George, in order to return home, travelled to the last known address he had for his daughter.

Walking up the path, he hammered on the door, his nerves taut as he waited. A moment later it was opened by a woman.

'Sorry to bother you but I'm looking for my daughter, Ellie Read.'

'Oh,' the woman said, clearly feeling uncomfortable as she shuffled from foot to foot. 'Mr Read, I'm sorry but she passed away a year ago.'

George felt his legs buckle as the shock hit him like a pole axe and he grasped the door jamb to prevent him falling to the ground.

'Are you all right, can I get you anything?' The woman reached out to steady the big man.

'No, thanks. Do you know...?'

'Childbirth, I believe. The babe also passed. I can't tell you how sorry I am.'

'Thanks.' George turned and walked away, feeling his heart

breaking with every step. Climbing into the cab that had brought him, he called out, 'Back to the hotel.'

Safely hidden from the view of the public, George covered his face with his hands and cried until he could barely breathe. He had waited so long to see Ellie and now she was gone; he would never see her again. 'I'm sad I wasn't here for you, bab, rest easy until I come to you,' he whispered once he had dragged his emotions under control.

Back at the hotel they were staying at, George paid the cabbie and went indoors straight to the bar. Ordering a whisky, George was hell-bent on getting drunker than he had ever been in his life.

Colin and James heard the noise the moment they stepped into the hotel, and following it they found their friend singing and swaying. 'Bloody hell, what's happened now?' Colin muttered.

'I don't know but we need to get him to his bed before somebody fetches the coppers,' James replied.

Colin relieved George of his glass, saying, 'Come on, pal, enough's enough.'

'I want another drink,' George said but allowed Colin on one side and James on the other to lead him away.

Finally getting George to his room, they took off his jacket and shoes and laid him on the bed.

'She's dead – my Ellie. My little girl is gone!' George wailed.

Colin and James exchanged a concerned look before they pulled the eiderdown over their grieving friend. 'Aww, mate.' It was all Colin could manage as he watched the tears roll down George's face.

'Get some sleep, then we'll talk,' James said softly.

George nodded and rolled onto his side before passing out cold.

The two young men crept out to return to the hotel sitting room where they ordered coffee. Here they quietly discussed George's bereavement.

In the meantime, John and Kit were getting along like a house on fire. Despite only knowing each other a matter of hours, they were both of the opinion that their relationship would grow and endure. They both knew it was a big risk they would be taking by moving in together, but they also knew life was too short to waste a moment of it. It was clear they liked each other enormously but it was very early days. Once they were living in the same house, then would come the challenges. John had been alone, relationship-wise, for a very long time and would need to get to know his new partner, as indeed would Kit. John had explained he was not getting any younger and was more than willing to share his life with Kit. The younger man had reciprocated, saying he was looking forward to learning all about John. After all, if things didn't work out, they could hopefully part as friends.

Now, sitting in the estate agent's office, they saw the man was puzzled about why these two men were looking for a house together until John said, 'Kit here is my butler so I need somewhere with servants' quarters as well as a butler's pantry. It needs to suit both our needs.' Kit inclined his head, immediately falling into the ruse without missing a beat.

'Ah, of course,' the agent replied, instantly feeling more at ease. 'I'll have a look through the books and send a runner with a message tomorrow. Where will he find you, Mr Tobias?'

'The Anchor Hotel, which is expensive, so the sooner the better.'

'Very good, sir. Please be assured I will do my best for you.'

John and Kit left the office and returned to the hotel, where John paid for a room for his new friend. Then they joined Colin and James in the hotel's sitting room and bar where they learned of George's drunken misery.

* * *

Over in Church Street, BJ was being introduced to Alice's friends and colleagues over tea and biscuits. Then they moved on to Russell Street to meet with Ellen, Joyce, Phoebe and Mary. Eventually BJ met Doris in the newest bakery.

After the whirlwind tour, BJ was sitting now in Alice's living room, where he voiced his pride in what Alice had achieved in such a short amount of time.

'What are your plans now you're home?' Alice asked.

'I rather like the idea of buying a farm. I want to raise cattle,' BJ replied.

'You have plenty of experience, that's for sure.'

'I'll take a look around and see what's on offer. It may be that I will have to buy the land and start from scratch, that's if I can't find a going concern up for sale.'

The rest of the day was spent enjoying each other's company and sharing aspects of their lives whilst they had been apart. By the time BJ returned to the hotel, Alice felt exhausted, the excitement of their reunion having sapped her energy. The following day would be just as tiring as BJ was bringing his friends to meet her. Alice felt she had lived the last few days in a cyclone and would be glad to see her bed that night.

BJ found John, Colin and James in the bar along with Kit Marshall. After being introduced to John's new acquaintance formally he was told all about George having lost his daughter and attempting to drink himself into oblivion. He watched the new member of their coterie closely, looking for any signs that Kit was taking John for a ride. It was clear that John had money and BJ didn't want to see him bled dry by this newcomer. However, as the evening wore on, he had to admit the two seemed to be meant for each other, and he prayed it would all work out safely for them both.

44

When everyone had retired for the night, BJ knocked on John's bedroom door. Rather than enter the room and possibly be seen, which would cause gossip and maybe trouble, BJ and John spoke quietly in the corridor.

'I'm worried, John,' BJ began. 'I know it's none of my business but you've only known Kit for one day and you're already looking to move in together.'

'I understand and appreciate your concern. However, as you know, there are very few opportunities to find a partner for people like me.'

'I know, I'm just scared for you. If you're caught you could be transported again.'

'Not according to the newspapers, BJ. The *Hougoumont*, the last transportation ship, arrived in Australia in January this year.'

'Thank God for that, but you could still both go to jail. Please, John – take some time to get to know each other. That way you'll know if he's on the make.'

'What better way to do that than living together? Kit will be my butler and I promise you I will be careful.'

BJ nodded. There was nothing more he could do to protect his friend. 'That's all I can ask for. You should know also that I like Kit and I just want the best for you.'

'I hope you don't like him too much!' John said with a grin and a wink.

BJ laughed. 'No, and you'll know why tomorrow when you meet Alice. Goodnight, my friend.'

'Goodnight, BJ, and thank you for caring.'

* * *

The following morning, John did indeed understand BJ's words. Alice was breathtakingly beautiful even to his eyes, as well as kind and considerate. She made them all welcome and gave her condolences to George when told of his loss. Alice charmed her visitors, and before long all of them fell a little in love with her. In turn, they entertained her with tales of their time in Australia. Kit sat quietly listening but BJ noticed his eyes never left John. The young man was gazing adoringly at the older man and BJ was convinced then that he was in love with John. *When you find the right one, you know*, BJ thought as he subconsciously turned his eyes to Alice.

Providing coffee and a selection of cakes at mid-morning, Alice blushed prettily at the compliments she was given for her baking.

The conversation then moved to the future and the plans the friends were putting together to go into business, cattle farming.

'You will need a good accountant and I know just the man.

Grayson Atherton, Sylvia's husband, does my books and he is excellent as well as being a thoroughly nice person.'

'We'll bear him in mind but first we need to get up and running,' BJ responded.

Their conversation was interrupted by one of the shop girls who led a dirty ragamuffin through. 'Sorry, Alice, but this fella has a message for Mr Tobias.'

'Thank you,' Alice said as the girl disappeared back into the shop.

'I went round to the 'otel but you wasn't there,' the boy said.

'Weren't there,' John corrected without thinking, making everyone smile.

'Whatever. I asked around and a woman said she'd seen some gents coming in 'ere so...'

'Thank you for your efforts. Now, your message?' John asked patiently.

'Oh, ar, I nearly forgot. The estate agent fella sez for you to visit 'im agen.'

'Many thanks, young man.' John dipped a hand into his pocket and drew out a sixpence which he gave to the boy.

'Ooh, ta, mister!'

Alice stood to show the youngster out. Her guests heard her say, 'Please put together a box of cakes and a bag of bread for our runner here.'

'Blimey! Ta, Alice!'

Alice smiled and returned to her visitors.

'I'm amazed the runner system is still in force,' BJ said.

'It's bigger than ever now. These children usually live together in an abandoned building and share everything they earn from running messages. Their network has spread all over the town so you can normally find one with a whistle or a shout,' Alice explained.

Getting to his feet, John said, 'I suppose we should answer the summons.'

'Why don't you all go? If anyone could find you a farm, I would think it would be the estate agent,' Alice suggested.

'That's an excellent idea. Will you come along with us?' BJ asked.

'No, but thank you. I really should be getting back to work. The girls are under a lot of pressure and I haven't been any help since your return.'

Alice saw her guests out and waved them off before rushing back to the kitchen. She had a lot of time to make up.

The men walked through the town to see what the agent could offer. John and Kit were told they had two properties to view and the estate agent offered to accompany them. John, however, requested they go alone, assuring the agent that as a gentleman he could be trusted to return the keys before the end of the day. So with keys in hand they set off, leaving BJ and the others behind to explain their needs.

The first house they looked at was not at all what John wanted but the second suited him admirably. On the edge of town, it sat in its own grounds, shielded from the road by high hedges. With four bedrooms, one of which John suggested could be made into a bathroom, it also had two top rooms originally used by the maids. Downstairs had a living room, a sitting room which looked out onto the gardens, a kitchen and scullery. The privy block was at the back, as was the standpipe. Light and airy, John immediately fell in love with it. 'What do you think?' he asked.

'I really can't say as I'm not paying,' Kit replied.

'Give me your opinion.'

Kit smiled. 'Personally, I love it!'

'Then let's go and buy it!' John said enthusiastically. As he turned to leave, Kit grabbed his arm and swung him round, pulling him into an embrace. John thought he'd died and gone to heaven as, in the privacy of what was about to become their new home, John and Kit shared a tender kiss which left John floating on air.

On their return to the estate agent's office, they learned BJ, George, Colin and James had gone off to look at a farm. John signed the documents for the house, the agent assuring him he could collect the keys once the transfer of money had been completed. John and Kit then went to the bank. Kit waited in the foyer while John entered the manager's office, where he opened an account to deposit his money. The manager gasped as John unwrapped his money belt and slapped it on the desk. It was the manager who began to count the notes, licking his finger as he flicked through the piles. When he had finished, the manager said he would happily provide the estate agent with a banker's draft for the house and would let John know when all the necessary arrangements had been completed.

BJ and his friends had taken a cab to the farm and were pleasantly surprised at its size. The elderly farmer, Mr Shuker, showed them around. 'I'm ready to retire and my kids have no interest in farming. I'd love to be able to give them some funds to set up businesses of their own.' The farmhouse was huge, easily able to accommodate the four of them, and large barns stood nearby. There were four huge fields attached to the property, one of which held a few cows.

'Them's all that's left,' Shuker explained, nodding at the cattle. 'I've been selling 'em off because I struggle to see to 'em now.'

'I take it then that you are looking for a quick sale?' BJ asked.

'I am, lad. I'll go and brew up while you fellas talk it over.' The old man hobbled away after naming his price, groaning about his arthritic hips and knees.

BJ looked at the others in turn and was thrilled when each nodded. 'Well, what do you think, are we all in agreement?' he asked.

'Yes,' Colin said.

'I'm in,' George concurred.

'It's a sound investment,' James agreed.

Joining Mr Shuker in the house, they each shook on the deal, the farmer delighted he could at last take life easy. 'The deeds are with the estate agent, lads.'

'I'll arrange for the bank to pay you,' BJ assured him.

'Bostin!'

'Where will you go?' George asked.

'I've got me a little cottage in the country which is just waiting for me to move in.'

'All right, Mr Shuker, we'll get back to the estate agents and sign the documents. With luck you should have your money in the next week or so as we intend to pay cash.'

With a look of surprise, the farmer gasped, 'Bloody hell! Cash, is it? Marvellous!' He was not about to ask these young gentlemen how they had come by so much money, he was just glad to be rid of the place.

Clapping his hands together, Farmer Shuker danced a little jig then groaned loudly as he rubbed his hip. 'Too bloody old for all that nonsense now,' he said with a grin.

BJ and his friends left to do the necessary paperwork which the agent would take to Mr Shuker to also sign. As they left the office, they excitedly began to discuss how the farm was to be run.

45

By the end of a fortnight, Mr Shuker had gone off to his cottage; BJ, Colin, James and George had moved into the farmhouse; and John and Kit were settling into their new home, although they still maintained they would take their relationship slowly and not rush into something they could come to regret.

Alice was delighted for them all and was not surprised how quickly things could be finalised, which she knew from her own experiences of buying property. Although she had suggested Grayson as an accountant for the farm, BJ explained that John would take over these duties as he didn't work with cattle. John was happy with his friends' choice of the farm and to celebrate he and Kit went clothes shopping, while ever practical BJ and George attended an auction to buy some horses. While they were there, they inspected the cattle for sale.

James took a cab to the Servants' Registry to request a cleaner and a cook. He explained that as there were four men living on and working the farm, it would not be appropriate to have female servants living in so therefore the cook should come every day and the cleaner twice a week.

Whilst all this was going on, Alice continued to work hard producing bread, buns, pastries, cakes and tarts; all of her bakeries were still extremely busy and the wedding cake side had really taken off.

The weather had steadily improved now that March had arrived and in the heat of the bakery kitchen Alice propped the doors open for a welcome through breeze.

One morning, as she opened up the shop, she was surprised to see Doris waiting. 'You're here early, Doris,' she said.

'I thought I'd come and tell you – our Phoebe is getting wed!' Doris gushed.

'Oh, Doris, that is such good news! Come in and tell me all about it.'

Over tea, Alice listened intently. 'Samson proposed last night and Phoebe said yes. They plan to get wed in late autumn and no – she ain't pregnant.'

'Goodness, that gives us six or seven months to plan and make her cake, plenty of time,' Alice said.

'She knows which one she wants so I'll nip round to see Ellen and Joyce tonight and pay for it. I hope they can fit it in because I know how busy they are.'

'They will get it done, have no fear, and no payment is necessary, it will be my gift to them,' Alice assured her.

'Thanks, Alice. Right, I'll get myself next door but afore I go, tell BJ and his pals they will be invited to the wedding. I expect Phoebe will tell Ellen today when she arrives for work, but I'll go anyway.'

'Thank you, I will let BJ know when I see him.'

Doris left Alice humming a little tune as she stacked the shelves ready for the day's business. She was so pleased for Phoebe and thought Mary would probably be next, when she met the right man, that is. Her thoughts turned to Joan and everything she had gone through, being jilted then losing her baby, and Alice felt in her heart that Doris was right, Joan would most likely stay single.

Her hands hovered in mid-air as she considered, *and what about me; will I ever marry, or am I also destined to live alone for the rest of my life?* With a shake of her head, she marshalled her thoughts back to the task in hand.

As the morning wore on, the heat in the kitchen was almost unbearable and Alice made sure everyone drank plenty of fluids and took a break in the cool of the scullery where she'd placed a couple of chairs. She dreaded to think what mid-summer would be like if it was this hot so early in the season.

By the end of the day, everyone was exhausted and Alice provided a jug of lemonade from the cold shelf where the butter was kept. Then, when her staff had left, Alice put her feet up, ready to enjoy a good rest.

The weather broke a couple of days later with a storm. Dark clouds shut out the light, then forks of brilliant white lightning split them asunder. Loud claps of thunder overhead sounded before turning into a rolling rumble. Heavy raindrops splatted onto the hot cobblestones of the road, raising little plumes of steam as people hurried to find shelter. Slowly the storm moved away, leaving a heavy mugginess in its wake; eventually the air cooled and folk breathed easier.

* * *

Over on the farm BJ had, as promised, written to Mac in Australia to let him know they had arrived home safely. He told him all about his reunion with Alice, that John had found a friend, and that between them all they had bought a farm. He knew it would take months for his letter to be delivered and the same again to receive a reply, so all he could do now was wait.

Shuker's farm was renamed as Home Farm, jointly owned by BJ, John, Colin, James and George and each decision was discussed by them all before being made, and before long the fields were filled with cows.

One fine evening, they were surprised by a visit from Alice, who arrived by cab. BJ paid the cabbie before leading Alice indoors, where he made tea. Alice had brought fresh bread and a selection of cakes as well as a letter addressed to BJ. 'This came this morning,' she said as she passed over the envelope.

BJ smiled as he saw it was from Australia. 'I expect it's from Mac. He won't have received mine as yet so he'll not know the address here on the farm,' BJ said.

Opening the envelope, BJ read the correspondence, the colour draining from his face.

'BJ?' Alice was very concerned when she saw his hands begin to shake.

BJ handed her the paper, then he began to cry.

Alice was horrified to see her friend so distressed. She scanned the writing then said quietly, 'It's from Pete Worthington, the chief drover. He says Mac has passed away.'

Suddenly the men in the farmhouse living room all burst into tears, and Alice was at a loss as to what to do. She sat watching these burly men sobbing unashamedly. Leaving them to their grief, she went to the kitchen to make a fresh pot of tea. It was all she could do not to cry herself when she returned, where she saw the friends standing in a tight circle, arms around each other and heads bent together.

Slowly they let go and retook their seats. 'God rest his soul,' John whispered, the others nodding their agreement.

'What will happen to the ranch now?' Colin asked.

'I have no idea,' BJ replied. However, it wouldn't be too much longer before he would find out.

46

A little while later, BJ walked Alice to the roadway, where he whistled for a cab.

'If I can do anything...' Alice said.

'Thanks, Alice, but there's nothing any of us can do from here.'

Alice hugged her friend then boarded the cab that had responded to BJ's alert.

BJ waved her off before going back to the house where he and his pals talked of their Australian saviour for many hours. Finally, John left to go home, where Kit would be waiting for him, but the others continued their conversation long into the night, wondering what had caused Mac's death. They assumed that Pete would keep the ranch working until it could be decided what would happen next but BJ felt terrible his friend had died without them by his side. Being so very far away, all they were left to do was to wait and see.

Alice sat at home thinking about BJ's reaction to the sad news he'd received. She couldn't bear to see him so upset and her eyes misted over as she recalled how violently he had sobbed. She had guessed from his letters that BJ thought of Mac as a father figure, so naturally he would be bereft. Time would slowly heal the wound but BJ would always miss his good friend. She hoped she could help BJ, if only lending an ear when it was needed.

She knew precisely how he was feeling because she had felt the same when she had lost her beloved Green family in a fire at their bakery. Josie and Joshua Green had taken her in when BJ was deported, and it was Joshua who had taught her how to bake.

A sob escaped her lips as she thought of the jolly couple she had come to love like parents. Her grief had been acute, cutting through her heart like a knife, and now BJ was experiencing the same. She wondered if he was wishing he had stayed in Australia, even though in his letters he had always said he couldn't wait to come home. It would be very difficult for him missing Mac's funeral. Whatever happened, Alice would always be there for BJ to provide whatever comfort she could.

Alice didn't hear from BJ over the next week and she assumed he was doing his best to deal with his grief; she didn't visit, not wanting to intrude. The farm was also in its infancy so would be taking up a lot of his time. Nevertheless, she missed seeing him, despite being so busy herself. The bakery business was booming and they had loved coming up with the design for Phoebe's cake, which was well in hand. Doris was taking her daughter to buy her wedding gown soon and Alice had promised to provide bread and pastries on the wedding day as Doris would have enough to do.

The next day, Alice was in her regular meeting with Grayson and was surprised and gratified at just how well her business was doing. 'You have more than enough money in the bank to buy another shop if you feel so inclined,' he told her.

'Thank you, Grayson, but I think not. Not as yet anyway. I have enough; I have no time for anything else as it is.'

'That's a sensible decision. You need to get out and have a social life,' he said tentatively.

'I agree but it's ever so difficult as a woman alone.'

'I understand. Sorry, Alice, I shouldn't have said anything—'

'It's all right,' Alice cut across him, 'please don't worry about me, I'm fine.' Once Grayson had left, Alice returned to the kitchen. It was almost closing time but there were lots of customers still waiting to be served. Alice told her staff to go home early; she could manage by herself until she locked up for the evening.

Sharing a laugh or a word with each customer, Alice enjoyed being behind the counter again and when the last of the stragglers had gone, she locked the door. Seeing a few loaves and cakes which had not been sold, she turned back, unlocked the door and stepped outside. Glancing around, she couldn't see a runner, which was unusual. A cabbie called to her. 'Need some help, Alice?'

'I was looking for a runner,' she answered.

The cabbie stuck his fingers in his mouth and whistled loudly and a moment later a boy dressed in rags appeared as if from nowhere. The cabbie pointed to Alice and the lad raced across to her.

Alice asked the boy to follow her. Back in the bakery, she packed a loaf and a few cakes, asked the boy to run them across to the cabbie and then to come back. She then parcelled up the rest of the bread and cakes and took a sixpence from the till.

'Cabbie sez ta very much,' the boy panted as he came back into the shop.

'These are for you and your friends,' she said, handing him the package.

'Ooh, thanks!' Alice gave him the money and smiled when he clutched it tightly. 'This is my patch so if you need me just shout for Speedy.'

'Thank you, I'll remember,' Alice said as she saw him out. 'I close up at six o'clock so if you're about at that time, I may have some other things for you. It's better you have them rather than letting them go stale.'

'I'll be 'ere, ta, Alice.' With that the boy sped away.

No wonder they call him Speedy! Alice thought as she watched him go before re-locking the shop.

After a meal of cheese, bread and pickles, Alice relaxed in her living room, her mind back on BJ. Sitting bolt upright, she finally acknowledged what she'd known all along – her feelings for this man were more than friendship, they were love. A hand covered her mouth as she blushed furiously, feeling a little silly as she was quite alone. She wondered then if it was at all possible that BJ could feel the same. What would she do if he didn't, how would she cope if he found himself a wife? Alice caught her breath as a pain cut across her heart; clearly she would be devastated.

Don't think about it, Alice, because it will only bring you heartache.

47

The weeks passed quickly after BJ's homecoming and the summer was thankfully not as hot as the early signs had suggested. BJ and Alice met up regularly and slowly BJ appeared to be controlling his grief to the point that he was coping well. The farm was turning into a going concern and Colin, James and George were happy enough with the quiet life they had made for themselves. John, however, was very quiet and BJ became concerned enough that he brought it up one day when they were alone in the farmhouse kitchen.

'I'm worried about you, John, what's wrong?'

'This is going to sound ridiculous, but – I'm homesick.'

'I don't understand, you *are* home.'

'I mean for the ranch, BJ.'

'Oh, I see.' BJ was surprised but not shocked. John had, after all, been in Australia for many, many years and although he wanted to see England again, evidently he thought of Australia as home now. 'You could always go back if you really wanted to.'

'I know and to be honest I've been considering it.'

'Would Kit go with you?'

John nodded. 'We've discussed it and he said he would come with me.'

'There you go then. It might be better for you both because with the ranch being so isolated maybe you wouldn't have to hide your relationship quite so much.'

'What about my shares in the farm?' John asked.

'We could buy you out. Or you could leave things as they are and I could bank your profits for you.'

'There would be less disruption that way,' John agreed. 'It's not long since I bought the house though.'

'I could deal with selling it for you,' BJ offered.

'You're right, I think that's decided. I've been putting off making a decision but with your help things can be tied up here. I'll book our passages as soon as I can, although I'm not looking forward to the voyage.'

'John, do you think you'll go back to Mac's ranch?' When his friend nodded, BJ went on, 'You could take over the running of it. I'm sure Pete would be glad to get back to being a drover.'

'That's what I'm hoping, although it will depend on what it says in Mac's will.'

'Either way, I think everyone will be excited to see you again. For my part though, I will miss you terribly.'

'And I, you, but let's not talk about it any more in case I change my mind. Now I'm going to book two tickets on the next clipper to Australia before I bawl my eyes out!' John grabbed his jacket and fled the kitchen, leaving BJ with a sad smile on his face. Life would be very different with John gone but BJ was sanguine. He knew his friend would never be able to really settle in England again. He had accomplished what he set out to do, and now it was time for him to live out his days where he would be the happiest.

Colin and James were shocked at John's decision when they were told but George said, 'I had a feeling. It took him a long time to make up his mind to join us in the first place.'

'We'll need Grayson's services after all then to keep our books,' BJ said.

Nodding their agreement, Colin replied, 'Will you contact Grayson?'

'Yes. I'm visiting Alice later so I'll mention it and see if Grayson can come out to see us.'

After the day's work was done, BJ took a cab to the bakery where he explained to Alice about John's decision to leave and their subsequent need for an accountant. Alice said Sylvia would ask her husband to call on them at his earliest convenience. Underneath his business concerns and attempts to keep busy, Alice saw BJ's sadness at losing yet another friend, albeit to the other side of the world as opposed to death. In an endeavour to lighten his mood, she changed the subject. 'How's your cook working out?' BJ had told her about hiring a woman to come in and cook for the men.

'She's amazing. Phylis is an older lady and her family are grown up and married. She comes in every morning and sorts us out a lunch and a dinner which we just place in the range to heat.'

'That sounds ideal,' Alice said.

'It is, especially as she buys our bread and cakes from an exceptional baker in the town.' BJ grinned as Alice blushed. On an impulse, he suggested, 'Alice, let's go out somewhere, maybe the music hall.'

Alice was taken aback for a moment but then she nodded. 'Yes, that would be lovely. I haven't been out for far too long.'

'I'll collect you tomorrow evening and we'll go to dinner first then, shall we?' BJ said, warming to the idea.

'That sounds wonderful, I'm looking forward to it already.'

BJ gave her a hug before he went home, little realising that he was leaving Alice all of a flutter. Her heart hammered at being in his arms even for a minute. Now they were going out together; not *walking out* perhaps, this was just as friends, but Alice was excited nevertheless. She had never been to the music hall and she couldn't wait.

* * *

The following morning, Alice remembered to mention BJ's request to Sylvia for Grayson to visit Home Farm with a view to becoming their accountant. Then she told her friend about her upcoming evening out.

'It's about time,' Sylvia called over her shoulder as she went to fill the shelves before the day's trading began.

'My sentiments exactly,' Alice whispered. As the day wore on, Alice became more and more excited, and as soon as the shop door was locked, she heated some water for a strip wash. There was not enough time to fill the tin bath so a good wash down would have to do. There was a knock came and Alice sighed – why couldn't people shop earlier? However, as she answered the door, she smiled to see it was Speedy. 'I'm sorry, I forgot you might pop by. I was in a hurry as I'm going out later.'

'That's okay, sorry to interrupt you,' Speedy replied.

Alice bagged up bread, Queen cakes and pastries and then also gave the boy a Victoria sponge.

'Thanks, Alice. You'm the best baker ever and me and the gang love your stuff.'

'Well, thank you, young sir. See you tomorrow.' As Alice began to see the lad out, she was surprised when he turned to face her.

'If you'm goin' out for the evening, me and the lads will keep an eye on the bakery for you 'til you come back.'

'Thank you, Speedy, I'm very grateful.' Watching him go, Alice locked up once more.

'Now, wash and dress. Do my hair, oh, and I'll need some money...' Alice muttered as she returned to the kitchen.

After a lot of fussing, Alice was ready and waiting long before BJ arrived and she was delighted when he gave her a bouquet of flowers.

'How lovely! Thank you, BJ.' Putting them into a vase of water immediately before they wilted, she then picked up her bag.

As they left the shop, a call echoed across the street. 'Have a lovely time, Alice!' Looking around, she saw Speedy and his friends sitting on a garden wall eating the cakes she had given them. She waved and smiled when they all grinned back.

'There's a nice restaurant near the theatre, I believe,' BJ said to the driver as they boarded his waiting cab.

'I know it, sir,' the cabbie replied with a tip of his hat.

Once they were on their way, BJ said, 'You look beautiful, Alice.'

'Thank you.' Alice's blush was lost in the shadows but she feared the increased beat of her heart could be heard.

'You have always been beautiful to me, even when you were covered in coal dust after scrambling over the pit banks.'

'Goodness, I'd forgotten about that,' Alice said as her cheeks burned. 'What a time that was.'

'Indeed, hard but great. We had such fun. By the way, can you still pick pockets?'

'I don't know but I doubt it. I haven't needed to for such a long time.'

'You can show me when we get back from the music hall,' BJ said, throwing down the challenge.

'All right. We'll have a competition to see who can still do it.'

BJ laughed, the deep timbre of his voice making Alice's heart hammer again.

Alice thought she couldn't be any happier than she was at that moment, not knowing fate would intervene and prove her wrong.

_____

48

After they'd enjoyed a roast chicken dinner along with a bottle of wine, BJ escorted Alice to the music hall. The street was crowded with people waiting to enter through the double doors lit by lights at either side. A busker stood playing his drum attached to his chest with a harmonica on a stand at the top. Cymbals strapped to the inside of his knees clanged together as he then wandered up and down the street, hoping for a coin to drop into the little dish secured to the drum. Ladies in their fine gowns and feathered hats were accompanied by gentlemen wearing top hats and carrying walking canes. Further along the line were the not-so-fortunate people; the women in drab skirts and shawls, the men in old trousers and jackets and sporting flat caps. An older fellow began to tap dance to the rhythm of the drum and folk clapped encouragement. A shout went up when the theatre doors opened and the line of people began to move forward.

Finding their seats in a box overlooking the stage, Alice felt like the Queen. Her excitement grew as the orchestra tuned up and she peeped over to see into the pit where the musicians sat.

Then she looked around at the other boxes where people were settling into their seats. The walls of the theatre were dimly lit, only just revealing the tired look of the place. The red and gold decoration was desperately in need of restoration. The buzz of conversation sounded like a beehive and Alice again looked over into the cheaper seats when a man yelled, 'Missus, get that bloody monstrosity of an 'at off your head, otherwise I won't see a bloody thing!'

She couldn't help but giggle at the reply. 'You shut yer trap, 'Arry Stonehouse, otherwise you'll have no bloody eyes to see with 'cos I'll poke the buggers out!'

A hush descended as the gas lights went down in the theatre, leaving a row at the front of the stage burning brightly to light up the acts waiting their turn in the wings.

Alice and BJ laughed at the comics, joined in with the singers and were awed by acrobats and jugglers. She felt a little sad that the evening was almost over but in the cab home they discussed the performers they had seen.

BJ accepted Alice's invitation to join her in a cup of tea, but not before he whistled loudly. Having paid the cabbie, BJ saw Speedy come running. 'There you go, lad, in thanks for a good job.' BJ pulled out a florin and placed it in the boy's hand.

'Ooh, ta, mister!' Speedy turned to join his pals to show them what he'd been given, and BJ was pleased when they all shouted their thanks before melting into the dark night.

Alice made tea then she reminded him it was time for their competition. She found an old purse from a drawer which she tucked into her skirt pocket and, pretending to browse a stall in the market, she waited. She heard BJ stand close behind her and when she felt him touch her pocket she slammed her hand over his. They both dissolved into laughter before Alice took her turn. Slowly she dipped her fingers into BJ's pocket, and nudging him sharply she withdrew the purse, holding it up in victory.

BJ had felt every movement but had kept his mouth shut, allowing her a win out of chivalry. More laughter filled the room before they sat down companionably and talked of John's return to Australia.

'He must really miss it to want to go back so quickly,' Alice said.

'He does, I just didn't notice how downhearted he was with being so busy on the farm.'

'I'm so glad Kit is going with him. I hope they have a happy life together.'

'Me too. John deserves it,' BJ said.

'Do you miss it, BJ, Australia, I mean?'

'It was Mac I missed, he was so very good to me.'

Alice saw the sadness cross BJ's face in the light of the gas lamps and her heart ached for him.

'It's late, I should be getting home.' BJ stood to leave and Alice held his coat for him to slip on. She was about to retrieve his top hat when he took her in his arms. 'May I kiss you, Alice?'

Alice drew in a breath as she nodded and as their lips slowly came together she draped her arms around his shoulders. Coloured stars blinked behind her closed eyelids as she savoured the warm smoothness of his lips. Her heart was banging out of her chest and as BJ pulled away her eyes remained closed, prolonging the pure bliss. Then he kissed her again, hungrily this time, and fire ran through her blood as she returned it with as much fervour.

Eventually they parted, staring into each other's eyes.

'Alice, I've loved you from the first time I saw you,' he whispered. 'It was you who kept me sane when I was transported.

For more than seven years all I could think of was getting back to you.'

Dragging in a ragged breath, she murmured, 'I love you too, BJ.'

He thought he heard Mac's voice in his head saying, 'Never pass up the chance of a lifetime, BJ.' Gathering his courage in both hands, he said, 'Marry me, Alice.'

Throwing her arms around him once more, she said on a breath, 'Yes!'

Kissing her again, he then stepped back. 'You've made me the happiest man in the world, but I must go before I lose control of my senses.'

Alice blushed and with a smile she saw him out. Watching him call a cab and board, she waved him off and locked up securely. Standing with her back to the door, she laughed before skipping back to the living room. Dancing around until she was dizzy, she dropped into an armchair, quite out of breath.

Alice went to bed but didn't sleep a wink all night, she was far too excited. It took the long hours of darkness for Alice to finally believe that she was going to be wed to Bertram Jordan.

* * *

After hours of tossing and turning, Alice got up, dressed and went down to the kitchen where, after a hot drink, she began work.

Sylvia was surprised to see Alice hard at it when she arrived. 'What's going on, have you wet the bed?'

Alice grinned. 'I was too excited to sleep. BJ and I are going to be married!'

'Oh, Alice!' Sylvia wrapped her friend in a warm hug. 'I'm so pleased for you.'

'Thank you. He proposed last night.'

'You *have* to go and tell Mom as soon as she opens up next door!'

'I will,' Alice said and when she did Doris was thrilled for her young friend.

'When is the wedding going to be?'

'He only asked me last night, Doris,' Alice said with a laugh, 'but for me – the sooner the better!'

'You'll need somebody to give you away.'

'I know, I thought Grayson...?' Alice responded.

'Ar, good choice. Bridesmaids, cake, reception... it's all go! I know with helping Phoebe planning hers.'

'It's all too much to think about yet. I must get back. Would you spread the word for me?'

'O' course, bab, they'll be so pleased for you,' Doris replied, giving Alice a tight hug.

At mid-morning, BJ arrived to announce, 'I'm taking you to town to choose an engagement – and wedding – ring.'

'Surely just an engage—' Alice began.

'No, we're getting both because I want us to be married as soon as possible. Alice, I've waited so long for this, I don't want to waste another moment.'

As she saw again a glimpse of the boy he once was, she whispered, 'Me too.'

By teatime, Alice was showing off her diamond solitaire set between gold shoulders and BJ had left her at the bakery before he raced away to see the vicar. Once a date was arranged, he sped home to the farm, where he would have to choose a best man. His friends were delighted for him and BJ explained his dilemma.

'It should really be John,' Colin said.

'I agree,' James put in.

'So do I,' George added.

'I won't be here,' John replied, 'unless I was to change our tickets so we sail after the wedding.'

'Would you do that?' BJ asked.

'Of course I bloody would!' Everyone roared with laughter as it was so unusual to hear John swear.

'Thank you,' BJ said, giving his friend a hug. 'I'm seeing Alice later so I'll tell her the good news.'

In the bakery, Alice was saying much the same thing after asking Sylvia if her husband would take on the task of giving the bride away.

'I'm sure he'd be honoured, Alice,' Sylvia said. 'Now I think you should get to Birmingham tomorrow and buy a "frock", as Mom would say.'

'I think so too because I have a feeling that, if BJ has his way, by the time the month ends, I will be a married woman.'

49

Alice was right in her prediction.

'Three weeks!' Alice was aghast. 'There's such a lot to do in such a short amount of time.'

'We have a best man, Grayson, to walk you down the aisle, and your wedding ring – what more do we need?'

'That's typical of a man. We have to organise a gown for me and a suit for you; flowers, cake, reception...' Alice giggled as she realised she was repeating Doris's words of earlier.

'Alice, darling, it will all get done. Let's just enjoy our short engagement.'

'I still can't believe it. Who would have thought that when we met we would end up being man and wife?'

'I did. I always knew it,' BJ said.

'You were ever the positive thinker as I recall, like when you tried time after time to build that stone wall on our shelter out on the heath. Each time it crumbled you thought of another way to rebuild it.'

With a grin, he said, 'I was right though because it is still standing.'

'I'll go to buy a gown tomorrow and arrange for the girls to make us a cake,' Alice said, bringing their conversation back to the wedding once more. 'BJ, it would make sense for us to live here after we're married, but if you don't want to I'll understand.'

'It sounds perfect to me. It wouldn't be fair to drag you out to live on a farm with the other blokes. We'll have some privacy here and the aroma of baking bread is much more preferable to the stink of cows.'

They chattered on excitedly until Alice tried to stifle a yawn and BJ got to his feet. 'I can see how tired you are, my love, so I'll be on my way.'

After sharing more loving kisses, BJ finally let his fiancée go. 'Goodnight, darling.'

'Goodnight, sweetheart.'

After seeing him out and locking up, Alice went upstairs to bed. She was totally exhausted and fell asleep in a matter of moments with the taste of BJ still on her lips.

When, the next day, Alice told Doris the date of her wedding, Doris frowned. 'There's only a few days between yours and Phoebe's. It's gonna be chaos trying to get organised.'

'I was so excited I didn't realise,' Alice said. 'I'm on my way out to buy a gown but I can ask BJ to change our wedding date when I see him so Phoebe can have her day.'

While Alice set off into the town in search of the perfect gown, Doris yelled for Speedy and gave him a message for Phoebe at the Russell Street bakery, paying him with a three-penny bit. Half an hour later, he was back. 'Phoebe sez to leave it with her.'

Throughout the day, Doris wondered what her daughter had in mind. She would have to wait to find out later when everyone finished work.

* * *

Alice hopped on the train to Birmingham, having decided to visit the shop she had taken her friends to when shopping for Sophie's dress. Seeing the crowds at the station, she purchased a first-class ticket, and sat back on the plush blue velvet seat waiting to be served tea.

The journey was short and the train chugged slowly into New Street station before grinding to a halt. Stepping down, Alice walked briskly out onto the street where a line of cabs were waiting for a fare.

Hailing the first cabbie in the queue, Alice climbed aboard and called out her destination. The streets were packed with people ambling about, seemingly having nowhere to go. Women beggars stood on street corners holding out their tin cups and slyly pinching their little ones to make them cry in the hope the well-off would feel sorry for them and give them a coin.

Trams drew to a halt dropping off passengers, and carts manoeuvred around them carrying their wares to the market-place. Children in rags and bare feet scampered around the crowds of people standing gossiping, some catching a clip round the ear from an annoyed woman.

Gentlemen in their smart suits and bowler hats strode towards their places of work while others escorted their ladies for a walk in the park.

Dirty buildings stood crammed together for as far as the eye could see, and somewhere in the distance a church bell chimed.

Coming to a stop outside the shop, Alice asked the cabbie to wait; his response was a tip of his old battered top hat.

Alice took a moment to watch a busker who had a drum

strapped to his chest to which a harmonica was attached. Tied to the inside of his knees were cymbals and around his ankles tinkling bells. She dropped a coin in his tin cup, for which he thanked her. Then she went into the bridal shop, suddenly feeling excited again.

Explaining to the modiste what she was looking for, Alice was pleased to be offered two dresses to try on. In the changing room, Alice climbed into a white silk shift covered with the finest Nottingham lace. Checking her reflection in the mirror, Alice shook her head. Then she tried the next one. This dress had a tight satin bodice and long sleeves, the skirt lay flat at the front and gathered to sit nicely over a small bustle tied around her waist.

'Oh, yes, I like this one very much,' Alice said as she turned one way then the other to get the best views.

The saleswoman brought out a small teardrop-shaped hat covered to match the dress and pinned it to Alice's hair. 'Beautiful, Miss Green.'

Alice shot a surprised look at the modiste, who said, 'I remember you from when you came with your friends.'

I'm impressed, Alice thought. 'I'll take this one, please.'

'Do you need shoes as well, Miss Green?'

Alice nodded and, after trying on a number of styles, chose a pair of white side-button boots.

The sales assistant tied Alice's boxes with string and after she'd paid and thanked the woman, she left the shop to head to the station.

When she arrived home, Alice hung her dress in the wardrobe before changing into her working clothes. Skipping downstairs, she hurried into the kitchen and settled to her baking amid a lot of questions about her dress from the staff, none of which she chose to answer. 'You'll have to wait and see,' was all she would say.

That night, a short while after BJ had arrived, there was a loud knock on the door. Alice was surprised but delighted to see Phoebe and Samson standing there.

'How lovely to see you both, come in.'

'Mom told us about your wedding date and that you said you were prepared to change it,' Phoebe said and, seeing Alice nod, she went on. 'Well, we've been thinking... why not have a double wedding instead?'

Alice was surprised and she looked at BJ, who simply shrugged. Seeing Alice's look turn to exasperation, he said quickly, 'It makes perfect sense to me, but how do you feel about the idea, Alice?'

'Samson?' Alice asked and at his nod she went on, 'We would have to change our date with the vicar...'

'I'll see to that,' BJ said.

'Then I think it's a grand idea,' Alice said as she and Phoebe hugged and the men shook hands.

'Tea and cake to celebrate?' Alice asked.

'Yes, please!' BJ and Samson chorused, making their wives-to-be shake their heads with a laugh.

50

The following morning, BJ visited the vicar, who was pleased to comply with the request put to him, and runners were sent to Alice and Phoebe to let them know the good news.

At lunchtime, Sophie called in to see Alice, the twins fractious in their perambulator. Alice showed Sophie into the living room where Sophie lifted Paul and passed him to Alice, and cradled Esther herself.

'Sophie, I can't believe how much they've grown!' Alice gasped as she rocked the baby gently.

'I know, gluttons, the pair of them.' There was no smile to accompany her words and Alice instantly picked up on her friend's low mood.

'What's the matter, sweetheart?'

Suddenly Sophie burst into tears and Alice became alarmed. Paul had settled enough to be laid in the pram and Alice then wrapped an arm around her friend.

'I... can't... cope!' Sophie sobbed.

'Oh, Soph, have you told Jake or your mom?' Alice saw the

shake of the girl's head. 'Sit you down; I'll put the kettle on. Everything is always better with a good strong cuppa.'

Once the water was set to boil, Alice ran next door to fetch Doris, who dashed back to Alice's shop, leaving her assistant in charge. Seeing her daughter crying, Doris took Esther, which allowed Sophie to dry her eyes and blow her nose. Esther, now sleepy, was placed beside her brother in the oversized pram.

Alice made tea as she heard Doris say, 'Right, what's all this about?'

'I don't know what's wrong with me but I just want to cry all the time,' Sophie confessed.

'You've got a case of the baby blues,' Doris said knowledgeably. 'It will pass with time. Don't forget you have two little buggers to deal with so it's no wonder you'm tired to the bone.'

'Mom, I'm scared!' Sophie cried.

'Of what?' Doris asked.

'I don't feel...'

'You'm frightened you don't love 'em.' Doris knew she was right when Sophie nodded. 'Look, darlin', think about it. Firstly, your body is all upside down, it's not long given birth to two babbies. Now they'm here, it's trying to right itself again and the twins are taking up all of your time, night and day. You ain't getting any rest which is making you tetchy, and the babbies are picking up on it, making them fractious in turn.' Sophie and Alice listened intently as Doris continued, 'When anybody else picks 'em up, they settle because that person is calm.'

'I noticed that with our Joan, she's so good with them,' Sophie said.

Doris nodded. 'She's probably wishing they are hers after losing her own.'

'I never thought of that,' Sophie said sadly.

'Look, love, we help where we can but we don't want to take

over looking after your kiddies and you playing hell with us. The fact that we all work means it's left to you to manage on your own but maybe I should quit the shop and stay at home with you.' Turning to Alice, she added, 'I'm sorry but I think that might be for the best.'

'Doris, family comes first. I completely understand,' Alice said gently.

'No, Mom, you can't do that!' Sophie was shocked that her mother would consider leaving the job she loved just because she couldn't cope with her babies.

'Sweetheart, you can't go on like this,' Alice put in.

'I know but... our Joan said she would do the same.'

Doris and Alice exchanged a glance before Alice said, 'Actually, that could be good for both of you.' She saw Doris nod. 'I'll be sorry to lose Joan, but this could be the making of her as well as giving you some much-needed respite.'

'In that case, I think we should discuss it tonight. If Joan leaves work, you'll need to fill her place,' Doris said.

'Don't worry about that, but it will mean Joan isn't earning.' Suddenly a thought occurred to Alice. 'How would it be if Joan went down to part-time? That way she would still have a wage coming in, and the rest of the week she could help Sophie with the babies.'

'That sounds like a good solution,' Doris concurred.

Sophie slumped with relief and murmured, 'Thanks, Alice.'

'All right, as your mom said, talk about it with Joan and let me know what you decide. In the meantime, you stay here with me while the twins are sleeping. We'll have some more tea and you can advise me on how to be a good wife.' Alice was pleased to see the ghost of a smile cross Sophie's face.

'I'll get back to the shop then,' Doris said as she hugged her daughter before hurrying next door.

Alice and Sophie talked for an hour more until the sound of snuffling came from the pram. With a sigh, Sophie rose to leave. 'They'll want feeding so I'll get off home. Thank you, Alice.'

'You are welcome anytime.' Alice saw her friend out and hurried back to the kitchen, apologising to the staff for being gone so long. The rest of the day passed in a flurry of activity and Alice was glad to close up for the night, after sharing the leftovers with Speedy.

The next morning, Doris told Alice that Joan had agreed to work part-time and was relishing the thought of looking after her niece and nephew so she dashed out to the Servants' Registry with a request for a salesgirl to work two days a week at the Church Street bakery. Within the next few days, the post was filled, much to Alice's delight and relief.

The following weeks flew by and Alice's wedding day loomed ever nearer. Grayson was looking forward to the honour of giving her away and Alice and Doris were kept busy sorting out the food for the reception, which was due to be held at the Union Street premises as it was the largest.

Joan was extremely happy in her role as nanny to the twins, and Sophie managed to get plenty of rest, enabling her mind and body to heal.

One evening, BJ arrived to see his fiancée after a hard day on the farm. As he settled down for a cuppa, Alice presented him with another letter from Australia which had been sent to her address. Tearing it open, he gasped as he read it. 'It's a copy of Mac's will!'

Alice felt her stomach sink, instantly worrying that BJ might decide to go back to Australia. She wasn't reassured when she saw BJ's mouth fall open when he read the will.

'BJ?' Alice prodded.

He passed the papers to Alice and she read through them. 'He's left the ranch to you,' she said flatly.

BJ nodded. 'So it would seem.'

'What will you do?' Alice asked, dreading the answer.

'I'm going...' Alice gulped. '...to put John in as manager.' Alice sighed with pure relief. 'It makes sense as he's going back anyway.'

'He'll love it,' Alice said, trying to calm her hammering heart.

Seeing her look, BJ said, 'Sweetheart, were you thinking...?' She nodded and BJ immediately wrapped her in his arms. 'My love, I'll never leave you again, I swear.' He felt her relax as he sealed his oath with a tender kiss.

51

John was thrilled with BJ's idea of him taking on the role of managing the cattle ranch back in the country he had come to love. Kit had accompanied John to the farm and was pleased for his partner. Over the previous weeks and months, they had become closer than ever and all the friends could see they adored each other. 'BJ, would it be presumptuous of me to ask you for a job on the ranch when we arrive?'

'Not at all, Kit, there will be plenty of work to do out there so I'm sure John will find you something,' BJ replied.

'Thank you. I'd really like to work with horses if I can.'

John and BJ exchanged a look and John said, 'I didn't know you liked horses!'

Kit grinned. 'There's a lot you still don't know about me, Toby, and we have a lifetime to remedy that.'

BJ smiled at the pet name his friend had been given and he was happy to see him so much in love.

'Well, there are a lot of the smelly beasts on the property, but as BJ will tell you, I don't ride if I can possibly help it.'

BJ burst out laughing at the memory of John on his steed shrieking in fear, and when he told Kit the tale, he laughed too.

'Enough, you two,' John said with mock severity. 'Now then, is everything ready for your wedding?'

'Yes, by this time tomorrow I'll be a married man. Remind me, when do you both sail?'

'The day after,' John said.

'So soon?' BJ asked, a stab of sadness piercing his heart.

'You knew it was coming,' John said quietly, seeing BJ nod. 'I will need a letter of authority from you concerning my managing the ranch.'

BJ moved to the desk. 'I'll do it now so I don't forget.'

The friends spent that evening together, remembering and reminiscing over stories of their lives in Australia.

'Thank God there's no more transportation,' Kit said solemnly.

'True but there is still the threat of jail, so I don't have to warn you to be careful even out there in the sticks. There will always be one spiteful bugger who, trying to better himself, would dob you in to the constabulary.' BJ's words were greeted by nods from the others as they recalled the overseers who had brought them so much pain and anguish.

In the small hours, John and Kit finally made their way home and everyone else sought their beds. Tomorrow would be a long day, one they would celebrate with their close friend, BJ.

The next morning, after rising early, BJ was the first of the household into the kitchen, having smelled bacon and eggs cooking. Colin and James came in next and George followed shortly afterwards and Phylis presented each of them with a plate of food while BJ poured the tea. She then went to toast some bread and Colin fetched the jam.

In between delicious bites, they discussed the weddings, which were only a matter of hours away.

At mid-morning, John and Kit arrived, looking dapper in their new suits and top hats and once he was dressed in his best outfit, George whistled for a couple of cabs. Kit, Colin and James climbed into one; John and BJ took the other.

As they rolled away on the short journey to the church, John turned to his friend. 'I wish you and Alice all the very best.'

'I wish you and Kit the same,' BJ replied. 'I'm going to miss you, John, and your counsel.'

'I intend to write often and I expect a reply to each and every letter,' John said, trying to be stern.

BJ blew out his cheeks. 'I'm nervous.'

'I can only imagine but you'll be fine. Just remember, the wife is always right – even when she's wrong.'

The two friends roared with laughter and by the time they had grown serious again they had arrived at St Bart's church.

All their friends and guests were there, sitting patiently in the pews, BJ noticed, as he and John walked down to where Samson and his best man were standing at the end of the aisle. They all shook hands just as the vicar called out, 'All rise.'

'It's like being in court again,' BJ whispered.

'Shush!' John reprimanded him but with a smile.

The organ started up after the bellows were pumped to within an inch of their lives and Phoebe and Jake walked through the open doors followed by Alice and Grayson.

Both BJ and Samson sucked in a breath at the sight of their beautiful brides and as they came to rest at their places next to their men, Phoebe and Alice beamed with happiness.

The sound of the organ had woken the babies, one in Sophie's arms and the other in Joan's, so Sophie pulled two banana-shaped feeding bottles from her bag, each containing a little sugar water, which soothed the twins immediately.

With a nod, the vicar began the service. Two brides and two grooms said their 'I dos,' and in half an hour of happiness, Phoebe and Samson and BJ and Alice were wed. As each groom kissed his wife, loud applause broke out and continued until the couples had left the church.

The line of cabs stretching all the way down the street moved up one by one as the previous occupied one moved off with its cargo of excited wedding guests.

Back in Union Street, there was a mountain of food in the kitchen along with barrels of beer and bottles of gin. Doris and her family had worked hard preparing the buffet of sand-wiches, sausage rolls, pork pies, cheeses, pickles and salad, as well as trifles, cakes and biscuits.

The two wedding cakes sat on a table placed in the corner of the kitchen, Alice's in lemon and white and Phoebe's in peach and cream, both piped to perfection.

Mary, Doris, Ellen and Joyce began to remove the cloths protecting the food and Doris grinned when James brought a drink through, which he handed to Mary. *There'll be another wedding there before long if I'm not mistaken*, Doris thought. James and Mary had met on occasion when Alice and BJ had taken his friends to call on the Wilkins family. It was only now, however, that anyone noticed how close the two had become.

'You pair walkin' out then?' Doris asked, making James blush.

'I was going to ask your permission,' he mumbled.

'You have it, lad; just be kind to my girl.'

'I will,' James answered with a grin.

Doris stood in the doorway, surveying the scene. BJ and Alice were wed, as were Phoebe and Samson, and Sylvia and

Grayson. Sophie and Jake had their twins and Mary was now courting James. Her eyes moved to Joan, who was seeing to the babies, and she sighed. Would she ever marry and have a family of her own?

'Come on, Doris, get this down you!' BJ shoved a glass of gin in her hand and kissed her cheek, prompting shouts and whistles from the revellers.

It was time to get this party started!

52

Despite it being the early hours before the revellers left the festivities, the friends were ready and waiting to see John and Kit off the next morning.

John cried like a baby as each of his friends hugged him and it was all BJ could do not to sob himself. The train would take John and Kit to Liverpool where they would board a tall ship. There they would spend the night in dock before sailing on the morning tide.

The group waved until the train disappeared out of sight, then they slowly went back to resume work for the day.

Alice and BJ had no time to honeymoon as work in the bakeries and on the farm kept them far too busy, but they were happy just to be together.

Everyone was moving on with their lives, but Doris was still concerned about Joan as she told Alice one day after their work was finished. Sitting in Alice's living room, she said, 'I'm worried about her, Alice. On the outside she seems content enough spending all her time with the twins, but inside I think she's yearning for a family of her own.'

'Have you spoken to her about it?' Alice asked.

'Not really. Our Joan just ain't herself any more.'

'What can we do to help?'

'There ain't anythin' we can do. In my opinion she needs a man; one who will be true to her and look after her.'

'Oh, that's difficult, I mean if she doesn't go out, how is she to meet anyone?'

'That's my thinking an' all. I tell you, Alice, I'm scared she'll end up a lonely old woman.'

'She will meet somebody one day. Joan is very attractive and can be so full of fun...'

'*Can* be, but she ain't.' Doris sighed loudly.

'Try not to fret. I know that's easier said than done but worrying like this will make you ill,' Alice said.

When BJ walked in from his work on the farm, Doris realised how late it was and with hugs all round she left the newlyweds to their domestic bliss.

Alice told her husband all about Doris's concerns as she began to prepare their evening meal.

'We should take Joan to the music hall one night,' BJ suggested, 'at least it will get her out and give her a break from Sophie's twins.'

'That's a wonderful idea! I'll mention it to Doris.'

'We could ask Colin along too. He's seemed a bit lost since James has been courting Mary.'

'BJ, are you match-making?' Alice asked as she looked him in the eye.

'No, I wasn't, but now you come to mention it...'

Alice laughed. 'We mustn't interfere but we can take two lovely people for an evening out.'

'Agreed. I'll see what Colin says tomorrow, but for now, Mrs Jordan, I think you should give your husband a kiss.'

Alice giggled as he pulled her into his arms and kissed her. 'I have to cook...' she said between his pecks on her lips.

'I'm not hungry – not for food, anyway,' he whispered.

'BJ!' Alice exclaimed, giving a quick glance around, even though there was no one else there.

'What? We're married now so we can do whatever we want, whenever we want.'

'But our meal...' Alice's protests were ignored as BJ swept her off her feet and carried her upstairs.

* * *

It was agreed that Joan and Colin would both accompany Alice and BJ to the music hall, and when Saturday night arrived, so did Colin, looking very smart in his suit and top hat. His boots shone and he had taken a bath and had a close shave. Shortly afterwards, Joan made an appearance, dressed in a beautiful burgundy velvet skirt and jacket. Her dark hair was pinned up and she sported a small hat. She smiled when Colin said, 'Bloody hell, Joan, you scrub up nice!'

Alice and BJ exchanged a grin as they all set off just as the sun set and strolled to the restaurant, chatting as they went. On arrival, they were shown into the dining room where other diners nodded to Alice and Joan, some exchanging a few words.

Once they were finally seated, BJ ordered wine and they made their selections from the menu cards. As they knew each other fairly well already, the conversation between Colin and Joan flowed easily. BJ and Alice shot each other surreptitious glances and tried not to grin at how well things were going.

Inevitably talk came round to John and Kit's voyage and Colin began to relate his own experience of sailing on a clipper for months on end.

Alice noticed how intently Joan was listening and was thrilled to see her friend laugh as Colin and BJ told their tales.

'John must be mad going through all that again,' Colin said.

'What happened when you got to Australia?' Joan asked.

Quietly Colin explained about Joe Burton and the sheep farm; Joan was totally absorbed as he went on to tell her about being saved by Mac.

'I didn't know you had it so rough,' Joan said, patting Colin's hand.

Colin squeezed her hand as he whispered, 'You as well, but we've both come through our ordeals and are stronger for it.'

BJ and Alice sat silently as they saw the bond between their friends form then tighten.

'Well, I ain't ever likely to be getting myself a husband after what I've done,' Joan said, instantly slipping into a morose mood once more.

'I don't see why not,' Colin said. 'You'm a beauty, Joan.'

Suddenly Alice and BJ felt like they should be anywhere else but there. Joan blushed but Colin's words brought the smile to her face again.

'Any man should be honoured to take you as his wife.'

'Give over,' Joan laughed to hide her embarrassment.

'I mean it! In fact, Joan Wilkins, I'd be delighted if you'd walk out with *me*.'

Alice choked on her wine and BJ passed her his napkin and patted her back.

'Good grief, Colin, couldn't you have given us some notice of your intent?' BJ asked.

'No, 'cos I d'aint have any until now,' came the answer. Turning to Joan, he said, 'Well, what do you say, Joanie, could you put up with me?'

Joan nodded timidly and Colin clapped his hands.

Thinking the man was calling for service, the waiter rushed over. 'Sir?'

'Champagne, my friend, this lovely lady has just consented to be my sweetheart!' Colin's voice sailed across the dining room and spontaneous applause broke out on the other tables as smiles covered every face.

Leaning down to whisper in Colin's ear, the waiter said, 'Champagne is very expensive, sir.'

'In that case we'll have two bottles, as quick as you can, please.'

BJ and Colin shook hands as the waiter scurried off with a very concerned look on his face. Joan and Alice beamed with happiness.

Doris, wait until you hear this! Alice thought as the waiter popped the corks from the bottles.

* * *

Doris was still up when Joan came home. 'Hello, cocka, you d'aint walk home on yer own, did you?'

'No, Mom, Colin walked me.' Joan sat on the sofa and went on to excitedly relate everything that had happened in the restaurant.

'Well, I'll go to the foot of our stairs!' Doris gasped, hardly able to believe her ears. 'He don't waste time, does he?'

'It was a surprise to us all, so much so Alice choked on her wine,' Joan said with a giggle.

'How do you feel about it?' Doris asked.

'I like him, Mom. He's had a rough trot like I have, but he's down to earth and says it like it is.'

'Ar, but will he make you happy?'

'I'm thinking so. He makes me laugh and that's halfway

there as far as I'm concerned. He can be spontaneous as he showed tonight, but in the long run I believe he will be dependable.'

'Can you love him, though? If you'm courting then there has to be feelings between you.'

'Mom, can I tell you something?' Joan shuffled in her seat.

'O' course you can, lovey.'

'Well, Colin kissed me goodnight on the doorstep and my belly went all of a flutter. It was something I never felt with Philip Sanders.'

Doris bristled at the mention of the man who had run away, leaving her daughter pregnant. Then she said, 'That sounds like the beginnings of love to me.'

'Oh, Mom, do you really think so?'

'I do, sweetheart, and God knows you deserve it more than most. Besides, when did that rat, Sanders, ever buy you champagne?'

'Never, and Colin bought two bottles! Do you know how much it is?' Joan asked and seeing Doris shake her head she went on, 'Nor me, but I know it's expensive!' Joan laughed and hugged her mother before retiring to bed.

Doris stared into the fire and sent up a silent prayer. *God, please make it right for our Joan. Let Colin and her be happy because if this doesn't work out and she gets hurt again – you and I will be having words!*

53

As time went by and the weather turned, fires were kept lit day and night. The pall of smoke hanging over the town thickened and people pulled out their winter clothing. Stallholders on the market complained they had hardly seen a summer, as the cold bit their hands and feet.

Colin and Joan, Mary and James went everywhere together and clearly were very happy.

Early one morning, Doris banged on Alice's door and when it was opened she rushed inside. 'Ooh, Alice! We're having another double wedding!'

Alice closed the door and ushered Doris into the kitchen, where BJ was eating breakfast. 'Morning, Doris,' he said as he poured her a cup of tea.

'Hello, lovey. Did you hear? Our Mary and Joan are getting wed in a double ceremony!'

This time it was BJ who choked and Doris banged his back. Pushing her arm away, he said, 'Thanks, Doris, I'm all right. So, the lads have decided to marry at last. What fantastic news.'

'Ar. They'll need wedding cakes and the girls will need frocks – gowns,' Doris corrected herself.

'I'm so pleased for them all but where will they live?' Alice asked innocently.

Doris stopped short. 'I didn't think of that and I wonder if they have an' all. It would be chaos at mine, it's bad enough now.'

'There's the farmhouse, but two women plus a cook in the kitchen...' BJ left the sentence hanging as he blew out his cheeks.

'Oh, bugger! I'll have to talk to them about that.' Doris frowned as she sipped her tea.

'If they both live elsewhere it will leave the farmhouse with only George in it,' BJ said.

'What about getting a manager with a family in there if the others don't want it?' Alice asked.

'That could work, but I think we need to see what the betrothed couples want to do first. I'll mention it when I get to work.' BJ grabbed his coat, kissed his wife, blew a kiss to Doris and left.

'I never thought I'd see the day,' Doris mumbled, 'all my wenches married.'

'It's marvellous, Doris, I'm so happy for them. Have they chosen a date yet?'

'Nah, I would imagine the springtime.'

'That gives us plenty of time to make the preparations.'

'Right, I'd best get next door open, thanks for the tea.' Doris disappeared, leaving Alice smiling.

After much discussion on the farm, both Colin and James decided they would prefer, with their prospective wives, to find homes of their own, so BJ explained Alice's idea to employ an overseer, preferably one with a family who could move into the farmhouse, and they all agreed. Everyone was surprised and delighted when George announced that he and Phylis, the cook, were to be married and would also find a place of their own. It wasn't long before each couple began house-hunting, sharing their knowledge and comments about properties they had viewed. Thanks to Colin and James being so wealthy from their time gold digging on the ranch, they were able to buy their houses outright, so it wasn't long until the men moved into their new homes, their fiancées eager now for their weddings to take place.

The winter months drifted by, finally being pushed aside by spring. Everyone was excited as the date for Mary and Joan's weddings arrived. St Bart's church was packed with family and friends and the marriages went off without a hitch. Doris cried buckets of happy tears and really let her hair down at the reception.

A few days later, a letter came from John saying they had arrived safely and had been made very welcome on the ranch. He explained that Burton's old sheep station was now thriving as part of that ranch. Pete, the chief drover, sent his regards and congratulations on BJ's marriage and wrote that gold was still being found on the land Mac had purchased. BJ and Alice would never have to worry about money again.

Sitting by the fire one evening, Alice pulled out knitting needles and wool from the cupboard.

'I didn't know you could knit. I've never seen you do that before!' BJ exclaimed.

'I've never needed to before,' Alice replied as she retook her seat.

'Are you...?' BJ began.

'Yes, sweetheart, you are going to be a father.'

BJ leapt from his chair and fell on his knees before her, the widest grin Alice had ever seen on his face. Placing his hand on her stomach, he whispered, 'Thank you, darling.' Kissing her belly, he went on, 'Grow well, little one, Mommy and Daddy can't wait to meet you.'

'If it's a girl, I'd like to call her Josie, after Josie Green; she was so kind to me after you had gone.'

'Josie Jordan... I like it,' BJ tried out the name with a wide smile, 'and if it's a boy?'

'Mac.' It was all that was needed to be said as BJ's eyes misted over.

'Perfect. I love you, Mrs Jordan, with all my heart and soul.' BJ's lips met those of his wife, feeling the warmth spread over his body.

'I love you too, Mr Jordan,' Alice said. 'I have never been happier than I am at this moment.'

'I ay 'alf glad to 'ear it.' BJ slipped into the Black Country accent he had left behind long ago, and husband and wife laughed loudly, something they would do often throughout the long years they would spend together.

* * *

MORE FROM Lindsey Hutchinson

Another book from Lindsey Hutchinson, *The Bad Penny*, is available to order now here:

www.mybook.to/BadPennyBackAd

ABOUT THE AUTHOR

Lindsey Hutchinson is a bestselling saga author whose novels include *The Workhouse Children*. She was born and raised in Wednesbury, and was always destined to follow in the footsteps of her mother, the multi-million selling Meg Hutchinson.

Sign up to Lindsey Hutchinson's mailing list for news, competitions and updates on future books.

Follow Lindsey on social media:

facebook.com/Lindsey-Hutchinson-1781901985422852

x.com/LHutchAuthor

bookbub.com/authors/lindsey-hutchinson

ALSO BY LINDSEY HUTCHINSON

Sixpence Stories

Introducing Sixpence Stories!

Discover page-turning historical novels from your favourite authors, meet new friends and be transported back in time.

Join our book club
Facebook group

https://bit.ly/SixpenceGroup

Sign up to our
newsletter

https://bit.ly/SixpenceNews

Boldwood

Boldwood Books is an award-winning fiction publishing company seeking out the best stories from around the world.

Find out more at www.boldwoodbooks.com

Join our reader community for brilliant books, competitions and offers!

Follow us
@BoldwoodBooks
@TheBoldBookClub

Sign up to our weekly deals newsletter

https://bit.ly/BoldwoodBNewsletter